Praise for

THE MOURNING WAVE

"Greg Funderburk's *The Mourning Wave* will wash over you with its powerful mixture of tragedy and faith, of suffering and hope. This a new telling of Great Galveston Storm of 1900, a story whose characters affirm the belief that ultimately, love is stronger than death."

— **Thomas R. Cole**, author of *Old Man Country*

"As *The Mourning Wave* rushes ashore and captures us in an evocative struggle of grief and loss, Gregory Funderburk pulls us through its powerful wake into a journey that gradually reawakens life and recruits hope."

— **Shelly Henley Kelly**, Editor of *Through a Night of Horrors, Voices from the 1900 Galveston Storm*

"Years have passed since I read a book so carefully and searchingly. Funderburk's words and tragic story invite the reader into the true wilderness of a hurricane. Will, a young orphan, searches for life amidst death, courage amidst fear, faith amidst doubt and healing amidst loss, trauma and mourning. This novel engaged my spirit in tears, gentle laughter and healing. A profound read!"

— **Dr. Tim P. VanDuivendyk**, author of *The Unwanted Gift of Grief*

"*The Mourning Wave* is one of the very best novels ever written about the Great 1900 Storm that devastated the island city of Galveston. Intense, descriptive, and based on historical events, the beautifully written story follows three boys through the night of terror as they struggle to survive and then as they witness the horrific images of death and destruction left by the storm. Through this captivating novel, readers experience the suffering and then the resiliency of the islanders. Based on real people, the book is a monument to faith, love and resurrection."

— **Linda Macdonald**, historian, descendant of 1900
   Storm survivors, and Director of Communications for
   the Congregation of the Sisters of Charity of the
   Incarnate Word, Houston

"A work of devastating detail and empathy, Funderburk's account of the catastrophic storm and its aftermath, as seen through the eyes of a young orphaned boy, is a sublime achievement. He captures the entire spectacle— both the physical and human toll— with grace and humanity, yet doesn't hold back on the abject horror that the storm left in its wake. In fact, it's the chaotic specificity that makes it feel so authentic, placing us firmly in the middle of a world we couldn't possibly imagine in our worst nightmare."

— **Mark Stolaroff**, Film Producer, *DriverX, The Last Days of
   Capitalism, Pig*

"A unique travelogue that documents an orphan's journey through the destruction of the 1900 Storm and following days. Full of interesting insights into Galveston and its history."

— **Nathan Jones**, Curator of the Bryan Museum, Galveston,
   Texas

THE MOURNING WAVE
by Gregory Funderburk

Published by

 köehlerbooks™

210 60th Street
Virginia Beach, VA 23451
800−435−4811
www.koehlerbooks.com

THE MOURNING WAVE

A NOVEL *of the* GREAT STORM

Gregory Funderburk

VIRGINIA BEACH
CAPE CHARLES

For Weldon and Patricia

Blessed are those who mourn, for they shall receive comfort.

–Matthew 5:4

There is an alchemy in sorrow.

–Pearl S. Buck

1

HENRY

Saturday, September 8, 1900
Galveston, Texas

Even before dawn, the Gulf was roiling. By mid-morning, the city began to flood. Sister Elizabeth Ryan had bogged down quickly after leaving town. From the front of the wagon, she squinted ahead blindly into the rain, looking for the large golden cross atop the girls dormitory building. She kept thinking it must be just beyond her sight, but another whole hour passed before she made out the steep angle of the building's roof. Feeling a keen sense of relief, she realized she'd been at the edge of the wagon's bench and clenching her teeth for three hours.

Henry emerged from the blur of wind and water, trudging toward her through the saltwater. He was yelling something, but whatever it was, it didn't survive the din. She nodded her head in the affirmative, agreeable to anything as he took the horse's bridle, leading it with the wagon toward the entrance of the building. He helped her down into the water, pointing her toward the porch. Stalwart Henry.

"I'll unload!" he shouted. "Sister Camillus moved the boys over. Everyone's in there."

"Let the horse loose!" she shouted back. He said he would with an exaggerated nod.

Henry emptied the wagon of the supplies she'd brought from town and unhitched the horse. The water was nearing its belly now. Of the nine sisters, he knew this Irish one, Elizabeth, was the best with the horses and with the wagon. Even so, it was remarkable she'd made it back. Henry looked over at the boys dorm to the west. Empty, it looked small and vulnerable. He patted the horse on the neck, stepped back, and gave it a brisk swat on its hindquarters.

"Ho, now!" The sound came from his barrel chest.

The horse darted through the geyser-like sprays of the breakers, before turning from the sea for higher ground. Henry watched it disappear with a furious beauty into the blinding rain. He looked at the boys building again. It looked still smaller in the distance. Henry retrieved the white blouses and skirts blowing horizontally in the ripping wind from the nearby clothesline and stepped out of the floodwaters and onto the porch. Dropping the sopping laundry at the foot of the large ceramic crucifix just inside the entrance, he took up the axe and the blanket he'd left at the door. He handed the blanket to Sister Elizabeth.

"Why are you still here?" she asked.

"Why did you come back?" he replied.

"What needs to be done?"

"Go on up," he said, shouldering the axe. "I'll put the food away when I finish down here."

With the blanket over her shoulders, Elizabeth complied as Henry marked out intervals around the perimeter of the great room with his eyes. A dozen children gathered at the rails of the atrium balcony to watch him. He hated that they had to see this. Raising the blade, he brought it down with all the force stored in his large frame. The hard wood floor gave way to five well-struck blows and the sea quickly gurgled up. As water flooded the expansive floor, he moved to the next spot, then the next.

"What's he doing?" Albert Campbell asked Sister Elizabeth at the railing.

"The weight of the water will keep us in place," she told the boy.

"But there'll be holes all over the floor," Sister Raphael whispered to Sister Elizabeth. "The little ones may fall in tomorrow."

"Tomorrow will care for itself," said Sister Camillus from behind them.

Sister Camillus had taken charge of the orphanage only last month when the elderly Mother Joseph who had cared for the St. Mary's children here on the beach for the last quarter century had died. Like Elizabeth, Sister Camillus was from Dublin. Only thirty-one, she'd proven poised and decisive already in her short tenure.

"Mother Gabriel finally let me go," Elizabeth said to her. "Mr. Unger helped me load the wagon. It took me three hours. She said I was to give you this." She handed Sister Camillus a small silver crucifix. "It was Mother Joseph's. Mother Gabriel said it belonged here on the beach with us. It's been through all the storms."

"We must take them up," Sister Camillus said calmly holding the cross before her. Sister Raphael nodded and herded the children away from the rail, then upward to the third floor which was no more than a large attic, its ceiling the underlayment of the building's high roof.

"I'm afraid we may be out of floors before the night's gone," Elizabeth said to Sister Camillus after they left. "The Gulf and the bay tremble for one another."

"Sister Elizabeth, when Henry is finished, have him bring me all the clothesline from storage he can find." Elizabeth assented and descended the stairs to Henry.

"We must stay with the little ones," she told Henry, passing along the instruction, both of them knowing what Sister Camillus had in mind. Henry shook his head.

"Ma'am, that will be trouble."

"We shall pull the children to safety."

"Or be drowned together."

"We must stay with the little ones," Elizabeth repeated. Henry shook his head again and did as he was told.

2

SISTER CAMILLUS

At seven o'clock, the wind shifted. What followed was not a wave, but the sea itself. The dome of water building offshore released, swallowing not just the beach and the first two floors of the St. Mary's Orphan Asylum, but the whole island. On the third floor, though farther from the kelpy depths of the ocean, the children and the sisters found themselves closer to the storm above. A locomotive traversed the roof every few moments. When it did, the children, all wrapped up in blankets, ducked down instinctively. The room seemed to be choking.

Sister Camillus had been last to leave the second floor. The sea had flooded forward, bounding up from the first floor in a single instant, chasing her up the narrow stairwell to the third floor, where she paused in prayer, reset her expression, and joined the children and the other sisters. Looking out over them all, she resolved here to do what her predecessor, Mother Joseph, would have done. It was Mother Joseph who organized the building of both the hospital and the orphans' home in the city long ago. It was Mother Joseph who had insisted the Order move the orphanage west of the city away from the threat of disease following the catastrophic yellow fever epidemics over a quarter century before, and it was Mother Joseph's voice she now heard when she prayed. So, she would pray. Then she would do what was next. Then she would pray. Then do what was next until morning came, willing their survival by incantation and efficiency.

Walking the floor, Sister Camillus touched each child on the head, tucking blankets up underneath their feet, offering encouragement, until she reached a fourteen-year-old boy named Will Murney. Will, too earnest for his age, saw matters in an uncomplicated light and did not varnish his opinions.

"God ought to stop all this presently, ma'am," he said.

"Yes, Will. Listen to me now. Each sister shall have charge over nine children. You're to be with Sister Elizabeth. Count the children with her. Help her until morning, Will. Nine."

Will did the math. "Sister, there are ninety-three children and ten of you. It doesn't square."

"Sister Catherine, Sister Vincent, and I will have ten. You are the oldest with Sister Elizabeth. Make sure she has nine. All night, Will Murney. Nine." She looked at him as Mother Joseph would have.

"I will," he promised.

"You will," she confirmed, then continued on in the near darkness. When she saw one of the sisters place her hand to her mouth in fear, she urged calm. When she saw signs of despair, she scolded.

"Be not anxious, Sister," she said to Sister Finbar, who was only a few years older than some of those in the orphanage's care. "But resolute."

Sister Camillus, still holding the silver cross in her hands, continued around the room, encouraging the children, tucking in blankets and buttoning up coats, until she reached Henry, who held several loops of clothesline at his waist like a lasso. He shook his head, reasserting the objections he'd made to Sister Elizabeth earlier, but extended the braided rope to her. She took it, thanking him. Henry, staunch and reliable, had refused to go home when she had told him to return to his family at noon, yet she knew he lacked the faith in the miraculous on which she understood their fate now depended. It made his decision to stay all the more impressive.

"Keep this, Henry," she said, giving him Mother Gabriel's cross. "For me. Keep it."

"Yes ma'am," he said and put it his pocket.

Stalwart Henry.

3

THE CHILDREN
OF ST. MARY'S

Henry measured out the clothesline for Sister Camillus, holding it taut for her to cut with his sharpest knife. He said nothing to her now, knowing we are not always responsible for our last acts. Her fingers faltered as she sliced through the cord with his blade. With the line, she then moved around the dark room apportioning an equal length to each sister to tether their children to them.

Will was counting Sister Elizabeth's children when he saw that Clement Beardshy, a small boy with deer-like eyes, had wandered off with his friend, Charlie Sharkey. Charlie held a glass bowl full of water to his chest. Inside it, his two goldfish, Miguel and Athena, darted about, circling one another anxiously.

"Come on back to Sister Elizabeth, Clement?"

"I got the willies," he replied. "We're cold."

Will rubbed Clement's arms and wrapped him up tighter, then did the same for Charlie.

"Which one's which, Charlie? Is that Athena?" Will asked, pointing at one of the fish.

Charlie shook his head. "Miguel," he said. "I think. It's dark."

"Clement, come on back. You're with Sister Elizabeth. Charlie's with Sister Catherine."

"Do we have to sleep up here in the attic?" Clement asked. "It's a little witchy up here."

"We'll see, Clement. Maybe the storm'll spend itself. I'll get you another blanket."

Sister Camillus had evenly distributed the children by age, the oldest being eighteen, and younger children, the youngest being two years old, with each sister. When Will returned with Clement, Sister Elizabeth was struggling with two toddlers, Elmer Miller and Ida Powell—one at each shoulder. When she tried to lower them to the floor, they locked their legs around her snugly, tenaciously. Each time the thunder clapped, Elmer wailed into her ear while the little wide-eyed Ida whispered into the other, "Mama, Mama, Mama."

After depositing Clement with the others, Will joined Sister Elizabeth near the door to the stairwell leading back down to the second floor. "Want me to take Elmer?" he asked.

"I don't think he'll have it. Just help me with the others, Will." Before he could turn, water began to trickle up and over the threshold. The trickle quickly became a spilling flow. Both of them backed away, reconsolidating their little tribe as salty water sloshed toys and dolls forward. Some letter blocks collected at their feet. Each sister, seeing this separately, gently pushed their children more densely to the middle of the third floor, forming into a single mass.

When Sister Elizabeth had attached eight children together, she motioned to Will. He shook his head. Nearby, Frank Madera, at the end of Sister Genevieve's line, watched this exchange and quietly loosened the knot around his own waist.

Most of the lanterns had now been extinguished, leaving only three. They cast three small, yellow circles of light above the children and the sisters in the center of the room. Their penumbra, a thin hovering glow, persisted even as the house continued to groan again beneath their feet.

Sister Elizabeth, still holding Elmer and Ida, gathered the rest of her group closer to her with Will's help. The storm was now locking in on them singularly, a dragon inside a whirlwind. Will lifted two hands, showing nine fingers to Elizabeth. Her nod back heartened him. She had the toddlers at her hips now. Will thought coming to the Almighty with evidence of their pressing need like this might spur rescue, but so far tonight, silence was God's only voice. Instead, now near seven o'clock, another low grinding noise rumbled up the building's beams. It sounded like a large herd of horses chewing oats, until a loud crack sounded, echoing throughout the space. The building then rose up off its foundation, pitching forward and began to roll at the whim of the venomous sea.

4

THE QUEEN OF
THE WAVES

Sister Felicitus's lips formed a prayer in her native German as the building began to rock back and forth. Sister Raphael held her children tight. Sister Elizabeth moved around the edge of her group, trying to conceal the restlessness natural to those at risk awaiting still greater crisis. It took profound resolve simply to receive the heightened awareness the approach of death brings. Sister Vincent's children began to sing a French hymn she had taught them long before. Her father, a French fisherman, had taught it to her when she was young, explaining how French sailors had sung it when seeking Divine protection from storms.

Queen of the Waves look forth across the ocean,
From north to south, from east to stormy west,
See how the waters with tumultuous motion,
Rise up and foam without pause or rest.

The other sisters took up a protective formation around the boys and girls as more began to sing, countering their terror with chorus.

But fear we not, tho' storm clouds round us gather,
Thou are our Mother and the little Child,
Is the All Merciful, our Loving Brother,
God of the Sea and the tempest wild.

Clement Beardshy had overcome the willies, but his face expressed a pitiful outrage as he sang. His normal look, an innocent, almost oblivious one, a shepherd boy in a Bible painting, had become wolfish, his teeth bared.

Help, then sweet Queen, in our exceeding danger,
By thy seven griefs, in pity, Lady, save.
Think of the Babe that slept within the manger,
And help us now, dear Lady of the Wave.

Elizabeth leaned closer to Will and whispered into his ear. "Remember these children, Will. Every one." She removed her rosary beads and placed them over his head and around his neck. The house tipped under them at a reckless angle.

"Are we to die?" he asked blinking rapidly.

Her response was soft, but penetrated the crash of the storm. "You are not. You are strong. Remember all who perish. Even me." She touched her rosary beads around his neck. "Be a servant to the least. It is the path on which God is found." She began to weep, but swallowed, brushed her tears away, and smiled at him. He was never even close to forming a response.

Over her shoulder, through the dark, Will saw Sister Felicitas, a child in her arms. Henry stood behind her with his hands against the building's western wall. He seemed to be holding it up on his own. In ten thousand indelible ways, Will's heart was imprinted with the knowledge that no matter how large the universe, he would never think of any woman or man as small ever again.

> *Up to thy shrine, we look and see the glimmer,*
> *Thy votive lamp sheds down on us afar.*
> *Light of our eyes, oh, let it ne'er grow dimmer,*
> *Till in the sky, we hail the morning star.*

As thunder boomed down on them, Will moved to Clement, checked the clothesline, and mussed his hair. He was next to the Simpson brothers. John was only four and his brother, Charlie was eight. John pulled on the line between them. Charlie pulled back.

"Will," they said without fear. "Sister Felicitus says we look like mountain climbers."

5

ALBERT CAMPBELL

Will watched and listened as Sister Elizabeth spoke to each of the children tied to her. Something had come over her. She had taken on the manner of a kind priest speaking to the dying, giving last rights. He had seen Father Kirwin administer the last rites once to a sick child. Like Father Kirwin had done, Sister Elizabeth was not using simply liturgical words. She was speaking to each child in a way they would understand. Sister Elizabeth knew each of their stories. What had brought them here. She spoke in a calm and steady voice despite all that was happening around them. She spoke as if she'd seen heaven.

"Don't be trapped by what your eyes tell you," she told Katy Faulkie. "There is much more than this." Katy nodded back to the sister in a way that conveyed trust. The girl took a few deep breaths and began to check her rope and that of the little boy in front of her, then the smaller girl behind her. Sister Elizabeth moved on to the next child and the next. She moved angelically, each child hearing in his or her perfect tongue. Coming to Clement, Elizabeth spoke closely into his ear, her whisper calming his wild eyes and restoring his normal demeanor. He looked like the familiar Clement again as he shook his head seriously, but agreeably. Albert Campbell sat nearby with his little sister, Maggie. He was offering her small pieces of hard candy. For every one that she put in her mouth, she'd take another from him and put it in the pocket of her smock. Maggie's eyes, usually sparkling jewels, were dull agates. She was shivering in rapid fits. He tried to keep her warm, wrapping the blanket more tightly around her every few moments.

"It's alright, Maggie," Albert said, rocking her gently in his lap, responding to her when she spoke. Maggie had asked what the Queen of the Waves looked like. "She has a beautiful dress and a necklace with emeralds," he replied. "A crown of jade and silver's around her sweet head. Her voice is a chime. She's the prettiest woman in all the realms of glory. She cares for us all the while."

He grasped his sister tightly as Sister Elizabeth bent down to hug her. "You are beloved," Elizabeth said to Maggie. "Dear girl, what do angels always tell us?"

She looked perplexed and turned to her brother for the answer.

"They say, 'Fear not,' right Maggie?" Albert said.

Maggie kissed Sister Elizabeth before she pulled away. Elizabeth brushed Albert's face with her hand and looked into his blue, lightning-lit eyes, as if she was seeing his future. "It sometimes falls to us to give meaning to the meaningless. Don't flinch from this. In this act is where the true meaning arises."

"Yes, Sister," Albert said earnestly. "I know."

Sister Elizabeth then sat down and tightened the cord around her. She took in the quality of all present in the spare light. Sister Evangelist stood in the center of the room, tending the remaining lantern, gathering her nine close to her. Sister Vincent led the final chorus. She sang in her native French, the children in English.

Then joyful hearts shall kneel around thy altar,
And grateful psalms re-echo down the nave.
Never our faith in thy sweet power can falter,
Mother of God, Our Lady of the Wave.

The air was thick with a dense current. It was difficult even to take a deep breath. The building was shedding vital parts of itself into the storm on the crest of each successive wave. It wouldn't divide though without protest. Reverberating deeply in a low, bass register, another low grinding followed. The faces of the women were grave, but those of the children remained serene, like St. Stephen before he was stoned.

6

SISTER ELIZABETH

Sister Elizabeth thought she had absorbed all the fear that death could carry. She had felt her faith and devotion strengthen her as she was speaking to the children, but it now ebbed. The floor wrenched under her. "I'm not ready," she said quietly to herself. Her arms extended around her little family as the structure pivoted slowly, like a tooth tearing from its roots. An old chest of drawers began to slide slowly across the floor. Part of the house seemed to be moving one way, the other in another direction. The torque began to pop the walls like firecrackers. Water spewed from the openings, spitting cold streams of rain at the children on the edges. Large gaping wounds coursed open along the moldings. The building leaned backwards, shuddered, then righted itself again, but the exercise left them all rattled.

Sister Elizabeth pulled her children closer. She felt in her throat the primitive sense of being trapped. Cedar shingles sheared off above them, ripping away in sheets, as if a mechanical machine or destructive giant was doing the work. The walls shuddered. Another high-caliber crack sounded. The south wall peeled back, revealing a dark and open sea. Everyone reached for something that might hold them. Wind and wave seemed to be one. Some of the children began to disappear into the void. Elizabeth reached out her arms, tightening them around the shoulders of the children closest to her, leaning into them. Her hands reached, fumbling for others at the limits of her grasp in a series of quick maneuvers, the kind one makes around the neck of a bolting horse. She tried to keep all of them close, under her control.

Stay calm. Move quickly, she thought. Shorten the reins. Brace a steady hand on the horse's neck. Hold one rein low and tight. Grab the mane. Raise the other rein up to the shoulder. And pray.

The house, corpse-like with rigidity, rumbled again as it tugged forward. Then an avalanche of noise fell upon them. The wind hit them as if generated from an array of artillery. There was a strange and curving nature to its sound. It started low, like a hand siren, increasing fiercely in pitch, accelerating like a battle scream. Gusts whipped up with stunning focus. The threat of detonation surrounded her. The roar muffled the piercing cries of children. The lightning flashes and crashes of thunder fell one on top of the other. Elizabeth gathered and pulled her children into a tight corner that offered protection against the worst of the wind, but the rising water was now threatening to swallow them. In the powder flashes of lightning she could see the other groups fall away in nines and tens, tumbling into yawing cavities.

The roof caved down onto Sister Vincent's children. It took Elizabeth's breath. She pulled at the clothesline around her waist, bringing her children back into her tightening corner, instinctively trying to count them. They were being hunted. The wind shifted and rain rushed now directly against them, as the water rose again and grew more violent. Lightning sheets lit the sky in a swift sequence of days and nights. The building twisted. Maybe they were still upright. It was hard to tell. Between the strikes and sheets, there was now no light at all, only motion. Cold water rushed into her children's faces in torrents. They knocked her down. Limbs and torsos flashed by in the curls of waves. She reached for those attached to her, but they rotated away, and she spun around with them. More vanished, folding into the churning water. Flying timber shot by. Shingles and framing rolled away. The remaining floor rippled. The locomotive careened overhead again. Three quarters of the crashed in roof folded back and disappeared into the locust-colored heavens. The remaining structure thrust upward with all its helpless passengers, each one now sensing the coming fall, the one from their most harrowing nightmares.

7

WILL MURNEY

A few of the older boys had freed themselves from the clothesline and were climbing upwards, their silhouettes lit by a climactic sheet of lightning in the asymmetric sky. When the roof fell away, they disappeared into the dark. Will reached for the smaller ones around him. The next sheet of lightning enabled him to see only that there were more he couldn't reach. He thought he saw Henry, holding a child in each arm, as the building collapsed. Will tumbled and slid along a fragment of framing, then was under water. Breaking the surface, he was surrounded by wreckage, but there was no inside anymore, everything was breaking up.

The rain stung. Will was without means to contend with the velocities of the wind and rain. No one was around him anymore. In the midst of lumber and crumbling walls, he felt the rising sensation of the sea, then spiraled down at the speed of an explosion in the utter darkness. He took the sort of quick breath linked with going deep underwater and hit the surface again with the brutality he assigned to fatalities.

The cold water fueled the immediate pumping of his arms and legs. The second he broke the surface, the sea fell over him again, stealing back the breath he'd stolen. He found the surface somehow again, his neck taking a knife each time he inhaled. His hearing had shut down. In the next lightning flash, he thought he saw something, maybe a distant section of framing. Near it, he also saw what looked like the tops of trees. The framing, almost like a raft, seemed to be scudding down the back side of a black wave. Each succeeding wave brought Will closer to whatever it was.

The storm thundered around him, pushing him toward the object which he now saw was not a remnant from the building, but something stuck in a motte of submerged trees. In the valley of a wave, he grabbed at a tree trunk, but missed, managing only to hold firm to some bare branches. His hands bled as the branches dug into them. The wind and rain continued to overwhelm him. He felt like he was being filled with wet cotton. Up and down he was flayed against the bare tree branches but continued to hold on. After a few minutes, Will found he could make small adjustments to his body between the gusts, recalibrating where his strength was focused. He breathed in short painful bursts and his ribcage hurt. Concussions of thunder filled the air and his eardrums were bursting. Planks, walls, and cedar shingles slashed through marbled waves around him like sharks, then disappeared. Everything had a clarity here: everything wished to kill him.

On one of the objects, a chunk of roof, he thought he glimpsed another boy, but if it was a boy, he looked more like a helpless insect balancing atop a broken toy in a violent river. Maybe someone else had survived. He felt the urge to help the boy, but the elements were hard set against the notion. Will continued to hang on, reacting to his diminishing strength with small, but innovative calibrations of his grip. Clinging to the tree branches, he rode the storm over the next few minutes with concentration. He saw his survival would be a question of agility and intensity. His time in the water advanced his understanding of its motion. Will began to see ratios and relationships in how the waves broke. He counted them as they came and went. He found an aptitude for comprehending both sides of their equations. Within the quick slices of time he could look around, he saw a metal bolt in the structure he was holding onto, then another and another. He was on the deck of what was left of a boat.

8

FRANK MADERA

Frank Madera whispered the name of Jesus quickly over and over again into the long wooden beam on which his life depended. It was a chunk of roof from what had been the highest point of the building. Spinning timber cut through the air and sea around him, missing him barely in mathematically impossible ways. He had survived the collapse of the building by holding firm to the pitch of roof on which a golden cross, the symbol of hope on which the orphanage's mission was based, was affixed. Bent at a heretical angle, the cross seemed to have lost its salvific properties and the roof itself was becoming nothing more than just a loose congress of sticks. Holding on, Frank felt like a spider on a piano string during a lively concert. Unless this beam was fortified with an unknown alloy, it'd soon splinter in his hands. He scanned the waves. He didn't know what he was looking for. Children and the sisters aboard an elaborate rescue vessel, a big ship with life preservers and warm blankets, he supposed. This was wishful thinking, a waste of the concentration he'd need to stay above the waterline.

During a sheet of lightning, he thought he saw the tops of trees. Perhaps it was only his mind seizing on hope, but he deserved some hope. He was entitled to some hope. The possibility fortified him as he looked over the waves again. There was human movement in the next crack of lightning. A shadow in the flare near the tree tops some fifty feet away. Another boy perhaps. A boy crawling hand over hand in the rain, clambering up something caught in the branches.

When a waterlogged mattress whirled by, Frank thought of transferring himself to the mattress, but questioned how he would achieve the transition. In his hesitation, the mattress flipped over and submerged. Jagged boards broke the water like dorsal fins where it had been as if it had been consumed. The rain stung him like ball-bearing shot. He spit out saltwater and moved his legs to stay on the roof, but the sea tore at him, attacking him like the jaws of a beast.

There were trees ahead. And they were close. Too close. His section of the roof was thrown against the sharp claws of their bare branches and he reached out for them. These must be the salt cedars behind the orphanage. He couldn't calculate what this meant other than conclude the whole earth must be covered with water. He thought of Noah, but then white water punched him in the stomach. His back wrenched badly, and he felt serrated branches ratchet across his face. He could hear nothing but a dull roar. He scrambled and reached for anything to hold him in place, his numb hands hunting friction. The chaos of the storm seemed to shake an angry finger at him for presuming he had found sanctuary and the branches slipped through his grasp.

The next wave lifted him upwards, free like a circus acrobat. He twisted, reaching for a non-existent trapeze. Speed and force denied him, throwing him down into the maelstrom below again. It did what maelstroms do. It swallowed him up, keeping him beneath the water for what he knew was too long. Then the water rushed at him again, but in the other direction. He pulsed upward and his nose and mouth barely broke the water.

He thought he heard someone shout. The wind took the sound and flung it away, but the possibility that he wasn't alone renewed him. He urged himself toward the voice, but there wasn't enough oxygen in the air. It was like breathing through a bucket of water. Frank felt he was going under again, when something grabbed him by the midsection, tackling him hard, like in a football game on the beach. Pulled into the quill-like branches, he reached out and touched inexplicably, a pole. There were iron bolts through the wood and nail heads. Another wave rushed over him hard, but it didn't crash. It just ran by as the wind tore at his clothes. The storm's fury diminished slightly, and Frank gathered himself around the pole as tightly as he could. It was the broken mast of a boat. He was in a boat, or at least the wreckage of a boat, lodged fast at an angle within the branches of a clump of submerged trees. He looked up as more lightning lit the sky.

There was a second mast forward and above him rising out of the branches. The stern of the boat was in the air above the treetops. The bow behind him was below the water. A large wave rolled over him, but the broken vessel held. He grabbed at the branches and released the mast, making for the second mast in the branches, higher up out of the water. The water rose around him again, but its motion pushed him upward and along advantageously. He felt like a spider crawling along its web as he reached the second mast. The water receded once more, and he inched himself now along through the branches and down the second mast toward the slanted deck of the boat. Though damaged and pelted with rain, it was out of the water. Grabbing at the higher tree branches and rigging, wood, whatever his hands could find, he moved upward and aftward along the angled deck, until he managed to find purchase close to the highest point of the marooned ship.

Just then thunder boomed down and Frank ducked instinctively. A blue bolt of lightning cracked the sky nearby, giving off a sizzling electric scent. He looked up again into the shimmering sky to see, perched a few feet above him near the stern, another boy.

"How'd you get here?" Will shouted down to him.

Frank had never been happier to see anyone.

9

THE EYE
OF THE STORM

Unsynchronized with the more distant thunderclaps, the lightning popped and peppered above them like a series of almost continuous flashes. The work of the storm seemed now higher in the heavens. Rippling, hidden like an enormous blue-green lantern behind the rolling clouds, it illuminated the sea periodically like a tin roof in an angled sun. The rain let up, moving now in sheets rather than a single blinding curtain.

Will and Frank could now assess their situation better. The boat was a small double-mast schooner, wedged at a twenty-five to thirty-degree downward angle, its bow under the water, its stern held in place amidst a group of sturdy salt cedars. The boat was maybe thirty feet long, but it was hard to tell in the dark with so much of it underwater. Maybe ten to fifteen feet of it remained above the rolling waves jammed securely in the trees. There seemed to be three separate trees, each of marginally different heights. The boat was caught three quarters up to their tops and seemed to be fixed where it was for now. It was hard to see where the rigging stopped and the branches began, and hard to find a secure perch on the broken and angled deck, but this was their provisional home for now. Will wondered if the boat were to slip out of its peculiarly arbor-locked position, it would right itself and float or sink. He hadn't the information to assess the variables and could do nothing about it anyway, so instead he aimed to prepare to ride out the other side of the storm with Frank here.

"Is it over, Will?"

"No. There'll be more."

"Is it safer in the water hanging onto the ropes and branches or above the water up here on deck holding onto something. It's awful slanted. We could get blown away up here if the winds come back."

"Depends if you'd rather drown or be carried away by the squalls. Probably somewhere in between. Let's look."

Frank followed Will, crab-like, as they moved deeper into the spiny web of quills and wet, weathered ropes, back toward the water, holding on to the branches around them. They had advanced about as deeply as they could go, when they heard another voice.

"Save Maggie," it said. "Save Maggie."

Will pulled at obstinate branches in front of him in a frantic digging motion, pushing his face into the space he'd made, feeling his way toward the sound until he sensed more than saw the small battered face of another boy in the water, his head and shoulders amidst the dark branches.

Will turned back up to Frank behind him and shouted.

"It's Albert Campbell!"

"How is he?"

"Sore distressed."

Will moved in closer. He felt Albert's head. It was bleeding. His lips were moving, forming the only words he now knew.

"Save Maggie," he repeated. Then he reached down into the water around his waist and raised his hand up offering to Will the ragged end of a length of clothesline.

10

SHELTER FROM THE STORMY BLAST

It took some coercion to convince Albert to come up above the waterline and through a layer of the branches. He thrashed against Will's attempts to lift him up, but when Albert saw Frank, his face took on a pensive quality, then calmed except for his lips, which continued to move, mumbling, ". . . and deliver us from evil. For thine is the kingdom, the power, and the glory, forever and ever."

When he met their gaze again, Albert's countenance took on a more certain look, though it remained at odds with his circumstances. Frank, in an attempt at solidarity, glanced up through the black lace of dense branches and into the heavens, where he assumed God still presided, and seconded Albert's supplication with a bruised benediction.

"Amen," he said.

This expression struck Albert as most effective and he climbed up past Will and then Frank, upwards onto the deck to survey the black sea and broken sky. He looked down at Frank, at Will, then at the strange merger of boat and tree in which they had somehow found themselves deposited together.

"Our shelter from the stormy blast," he concluded. "Are we safe? Is it over?" he asked Will.

"No," Will said. "We're in the middle of it. The eye. We'll have to ride out the other side."

The wind whistled cleanly above them. Out of the water was almost as cold as in the water, but they each found a spot on the rough, wet deck, within a latticework of spiny branches where they could rest for a minute without slipping. They were small, wet creatures in a meager nest.

"I need to tell you both something. Something you ought to know," Albert said. He looked around as if this was to be treated confidentially. "I can't swim. Can't swim a lick. I don't know how I got this far. Campbells, we don't swim."

"I've seen you swim," Frank said.

"No. I don't," Albert concluded. "I can stretch my legs pretty far though." Albert exhaled as if he'd been holding his breath for some time. "Will," he finally said. "You got an awful knot on your head."

"I was about to say the same thing to you."

Albert pulled his bloody sleeve over his hand, reaching out to the older boy and dabbed at Will's forehead. It started to bleed.

"Sorry," Albert said as blood ran into Will's eyes. He breathed deeply again, looking around as if he'd forgotten something. "Have you seen Maggie?"

Neither Will nor Frank managed a response.

"She can't swim either. Not a stroke." He sighed hard, deeply. "Campbells can't swim," he added again, crestfallen, wiping the blood from Will's face with his sleeve.

Frank moved up a few feet, digging, grabbing something tangled in the density of the branches.

"Get some sleep, Albert," Will said.

"No. I need to be awake. Maybe a rescue ship will come by," he said. "I don't want to miss it."

"Albert, we're on a ship," Frank said, holding up a battered ring buoy with letters on it. "I don't know about it being a rescue one though."

In faded black stencil was written, "John S. Ames."

11

JOHN S. AMES

Will spotted the floating house before Frank. Bobbing toward them on the surface like a fugitive cork, it was soon upon them, washing by almost leisurely in the relatively quiet currents of the eye of the storm. A strange, whistling wind pushed it along slowly. The rain had ceased, but the night sky still flashed in an almost constant jaundiced yellow high above in the distance. Will spotted the movement first, a woman perhaps, at a window. Frank remained poised next to him, grasping the side of the boat, his knuckles white, his eyes locked on her, as well. Albert had fallen asleep lower down in the branches.

She gazed back at them from the window frame, then suddenly disappeared. She returned; her wet, black hair wrapped around her pale face. She held a baby out the window to them. They stared at one another until the house drifted beyond their sight, but the boys remained frozen.

"Think that was a ghost?" Frank asked in a whisper.

"Don't know," Will said, just as quietly. Their phantom-like breath mixed in the midnight chill. "Doesn't matter, Frank, we have work to do."

As the storm wall approached, Will began to prepare them. He woke Albert and bandaged his head with a strip of his shirt. They were both relieved Albert had not seen the woman with the baby. It may have unhinged him. Frank, apart from the indignity of having lost his britches, was generally battered about the neck and arms. Will had suffered a number of lacerations and bruises, and his head and chest hurt acutely. But in addition to the shock and grief over his sister, the gash and swelling above Albert's brow indicated he had received a serious blow to the head. The deep cut had mostly stopped bleeding, but he looked as pale as the ghostly woman. He was groggy, coming in and out of consciousness, thinking he was speaking to Henry about poor Maggie. Will, using the clothesline around Albert's waist and the schooner's rigging, secured him to the deck using some secure blocking he'd found on the port side. He reeved the ropes through, though it took a while in the dark. Frank was tethered loosely to the second mast with considerable slack. Will elected to stay free for now but held onto one of the ropes in case a large wave was encountered. He'd tie himself down with his friends as the eyewall approached.

As the winds started again, the trees held firm to the earth below and to the John S. Ames above, but the sky turned a sickly green. Dr. Cline of the weather bureau, whose boots Will shined at the Tremont Hotel on Saturday mornings, called this the dirty side. The lightning sheets now flared in olive hues across the edges of the sky. To look to the horizon was like looking through tinted glass. Severe clouds whipped toward them now at considerable speed, and with the increased whistle of the wind, the rain soon began to fall again upon them. A few moments later, it picked up again, and soon returned like a waterfall. The phosphorescent green flickering from the electricity in the sky now fell away, replaced by a razor cold sharpness in the night air. Will began silently counting the waves again as the wind continued to shift. Branches and boat began to rise and fall in the same rhythmic pitches as before, but the motion was in the opposite direction. It became frigid again by gusts.

"We're getting a haircut here," Will told Frank. "We've got to get down."

The choice was to descend lower and risk drowning or stay here and get blown away. The branches, having been bent violently in one direction for several hours, were reacting badly now to being violently curved back the other way. More of the limbs protecting them vanished with each blow.

"Will, my arms and legs won't cater to me," Albert said.

"Brace your heart. Nerve your limbs, and let's go down."

Albert closed his eyes tightly. "I might fall in. I can't feel anything."

"We've got to get lower, Albert. Come on," Frank encouraged.

"Alright, but I have to do something first," Albert said, remembering how Mother Joseph formerly calmed the mighty Gulf winds when they rose up out on the beach. Albert stood up, and with the same defiance, conviction, and technique he'd seen the Mother Superior use against the ocean gales from the orphanage's balcony, began to rebuke the heavens.

"Old Boreas!" he yelled out holding a long, loose branch aloft like a tiny Moses with staff. "Lay low, Old Man."

"Frank, I'm going to undo him. Keep him down," Will called out. "Or he's gonna blow away!"

Frank pulled Albert to him, even as the smaller boy continued to shake the stick at Old Boreas up above. Below them, the water sloshed back and forth violently, as if sea monsters were thrashing just under the surface. Tree branches raked over Will's numb face as he moved downward. He swiftly tied Albert to the lower section of the mast with the clothesline as the rain plummeted down harder upon them. Albert was cooperative, having exhausted himself in his futile engagement with Old Boreas. He bent forward toward Frank and said something into his ear. Frank agreed and patted him on the chest.

"What'd he say, Frank?" Will asked, as the wind increased.

"He says Old Boreas ain't listening tonight."

Will adjusted the bandage on the younger boy's head. "Just hang on, Albert," Will said.

They began to pitch, hanging in defiance of gravity, then crash down beneath the water. In the next rise, Will re-tied Frank to the mast making sure he was secure, then tied himself down. They rotated, shuffled back and forth, and elevated up and down, swiveling like riders on a misconceived boardwalk attraction. Yet water flowed in and out of the canopy of branches in rough harmony with the storm's own rhythmic methods, producing a tenable, if temporary refuge for the castaways.

They were holding their ground.

12

OLD BOREAS RELENTS

An hour later, the leaves on the branches had been thinned out considerably, leaving only long leaf-less spines in the water, but the rain was letting up. They rested in their resilient jumble of twigs and boards, rocking back and forth on the percolating sea. Every so often, a big wave would break over them, filling their noses and mouths with saltwater, but they managed through a series of cooperative exercises with one another to emerge again and again each time. Will could now gauge the arrival and size of each ensuing wave using his honed instincts and a full night of experience. He'd gone to school. Albert agreed to remain tethered to the mast, but Will gave Frank some additional slack so that he could move around, then untied himself completely as Old Boreas finally and mercifully relented.

When a thin board about the size of the surface of a small table floated into their lair, Will peeled it back from the dark water and propped it up at their backs, distributing the remaining wind and rain across its surface. Moving closer to one another into a single mass behind the sheltering board in the remaining branches added to their modest comfort. The wood, like a parapet, gave their voices a more resonant quality than they had earlier. Or maybe this is just what they sounded like now.

"I wonder where this came from," Albert asked about the board. Will considered the question. Maybe it came from their school on Rosenberg Street, or Unger's Market. Maybe it had come from Pearson Mercantile, from Lucas Terrace, or from the home of Grace Ketchum, the police chief's daughter.

"Grace," he thought. Will's veins coursed sluggishly, his mind slowing. Everyone he knew in the city might be gone. He felt his brain misfiring as he grappled with this emergent idea. His concept of a future was as fumbling as the work of his bleeding hands and numbing fingers as they worked the knots in the clothesline that kept his friends close.

"Are you alright, Will?" Frank asked.

"Yeah." His voice did sound different—older, sadder.

"Will," Albert spoke up.

"I know," Will said. He had noticed it too a few minutes before. There were voices in the air, personal, and much aggrieved.

"I hear hollerin' out there. Do you hear that?"

13

THE HOLLERIN'
OF THE DEAD

There were no words, just a deep wailing, like animals stuck in traps. Caught between the hope that some sort of help might emerge from the sounds and the hope that they would just go away, it seemed most likely that the noises came from unseen folks far worse off than even they were.

"Is that people, or not?" Frank asked.

No one said anything. Albert covered his ears, fearful of what the sounds might be. He soon voiced his theory.

"It's the hollerin' of the dead," he whispered edgily. "The hollerin' of the dead. We ought to plug our ears."

"It's not the hollerin' of the dead, Albert," Will said. "There's no such thing."

"It's most queer though," Frank allowed, seeing that Will had hurt Albert's feelings. "Sounds like a sad dog."

"Sad dog," Albert repeated. "Or the hollerin' of the dead," he said more quietly.

Will and Frank craned their necks to listen. Albert pulled his hands down from his ears and let himself hear for a moment, then his eyes suddenly widened.

"Maybe it's the other ones," he said. "The sisters. Our people."

"Don't think so," Will said.

Then, closer, the weeping sounds began to take shape, forming into forlorn words.

"Help me."

"Please, Savior."

Albert plugged his ears again as a disembodied woman's voice cried out that she was bleeding. All of the voices prickled Will's skin, but the woman's made him shake all over. If he had thought there'd be comfort in knowing there were other survivors somewhere, it was not here.

"Do you see anything?" Frank asked. The voices had already begun to fade into the night.

"No. I think it's far away now."

"How long 'til morning, Will?"

"Probably three or four hours."

"I'm dreadful cold, Frank," Albert said, bringing his hands down.

"Me too, Albert. At least you've got trousers."

Far off or not, the voices still carried to them vaguely, but the words had largely faded, falling into the sounds of the sea itself, leaving only occasional distant calls for help, which none of them were sure they heard or not.

"Hollerin' of the dead," Albert said, renewing his contention.

As the eerie voices faded, the boys focused their attention on a light some distance away, rolling toward them along the surface of the water. They briefly considered the plausibility of rescue, but then heard a crackling sound as it came closer. Albert put his hands over his eyes this time. Will pulled his hands down, but

Albert put them up again.

"The fires of hell," he asserted. "Hades' flames. You shouldn't look."

"Albert, it's nothing."

A burning board hissed by, the waves lapping at its edges.

"Don't worry," Frank said. "Look, Albert."

As the fire rolled away, new noises formed and vanished somewhere in the low clouds. Thinly constituted, they haunted just the same. Sporadic splashes sounded around them, as well. Every once in a while, it sounded as if heavy objects were being dropped into the ocean from a great height. All of this unnerved Albert further.

"Grindy-lows," he said.

"What?" Frank asked.

"They come for children in the cold water," Albert explained. His mother had warned him about them long ago.

"You mean vodyanoys," Frank said casually, remembering the stories his Slavic aunt, Lida, had told.

"Quiet," Will said. "Let me think."

The boys didn't speak for the next ten minutes, but even Will had to admit there were tricks in the air. The chilling thuds and splashes seemed to be getting closer.

"Grindy-lows." Albert whispered.

"Shh," Will responded.

Albert pulled Frank closer. The noises began to fade, leaving only the sound of water lapping rhythmically against the John S. Ames and the remnants of the trees. Finally, Albert spoke up quietly.

"There's an awful lot of goblin-visitin' goin' on out here. Between the hollerin' of the dead, the flames of Hades, and the grindy-lows," he said. "I'm plum tuckered out."

14

TOMORROW ALREADY

"I'd sure like some trousers," Frank said finally.

"I can understand that," Albert said.

Albert looked at Frank, shivering, then back into the sea.

"I'm still fierce cold, Will," Albert said through chattering teeth.

"I know, Albert," he said.

"Do you feel that?" Will asked.

"What?" Albert asked.

"The water's pushing against us," Frank responded.

"I think the water's going back in the Gulf. It's pushing against the hull," Will said. What had been a nudge became a current and the trees began to bend. "Find something to hold onto," Will instructed. "We could come loose."

"Will, is the John S. Ames going to sink?" Albert asked, panicking. "Campbells can't swim. Untie me!"

"We'll be alright, Albert," Frank said, trying to calm him. "We'll keep you up. You're not going to drown. I've got you."

"I need some more slack at least."

"Just stay put, Albert. We'll be alright," he said, but sounded unconvincing as he retied Albert more loosely using the rigging at hand.

The tide leaned against the raised stern harder each passing minute. Will edged out over the side to see what was occurring beneath them. It was impossible to see, but he could feel it and hear it. He had no idea what condition the forward part of the ship was in, or even if there was one beneath the waves. Frank gave Albert the stenciled life ring and Albert slipped it over his head. This relaxed him marginally.

It was now clear they were slipping from the clutches of the salt cedars. With sounds of heavy friction, the boat's hull scraped against the trees, until the aft section, the boy's refuge, fell, hitting the water with a heavy pop, deflecting off the water and listing to starboard. The branches raked astern, carrying Frank with them and nearly off the back, but the rigging attached the second mast held, as did the knot around his waist. Will held Albert with one hand. With his other, he held on to the side of the boat. Though listing badly, the vessel remained afloat. Frank stumbled back down to them.

"I almost took a bath," he said, as a cracking sound was heard.

The forward mast broke free, but then the schooner righted itself, its bow rising up a few degrees as the tide, now rushing harder, began to push them south, presumably out to sea at a moderate pace for several minutes. Soon though, buffeted by opposing waves, they began to lose momentum and slowed. The stern of the boat now sat stable, though very low in the water. Waves lapped over the bow, but the craft had found a sort of equilibrium, bobbing in the slowly rocking water.

"Is that it?" Frank asked.

"We must be halfway to South America by now," Albert said.

"Albert, we can't be that far out," Will said. "We were stuck in the trees before. Near home."

"Look up there," Frank said, pointing.

The moon appeared for an instant between the racing clouds. This seemed to buoy Albert, but then the rain started up again, first rippling in snake-like trails over the water, then, the skies opened again, pouring down upon them as it had done before. Frank grunted and tried to stand up but fell back down. Exhausted, angry, he found his balance and raised his hands above his head like an orchestra conductor.

"It's past midnight," he yelled belligerently. "It's Sunday!"

Will scooted toward Albert, rubbing the boy's arms and shoulders. His shivering slowed as they watched Frank yell at the sky. Upright, but unsteady on the inclined deck, Frank continued his angry diatribe directed at the clouds. "No more!" he yelled. "It's tomorrow, already."

Albert adjusted his bandage and looked up at Frank.

"Old Boreas," Albert said to Will. "He still ain't listening."

"Let him go on," Will said to Albert.

Frank's voice carried over the water, gliding over the waves.

The rain finally lessened to a drizzle, then stopped altogether. Frank remained silent for a moment, surprised.

"Damn right," he said, and fell back down with his friends, his work done.

Albert glanced at Will and shifted his weight. He looked at Frank, impressed. Will smiled. Another half hour passed with Frank mumbling to himself, Albert shivering, and Will checking on how low the boat was sitting in the water.

Albert fell asleep first, then Frank. Sleep wouldn't come to Will because he knew what his friends didn't: slowly, but surely, the John S. Ames was sinking.

15

ARGONAUTS

The horizon still admitted no suggestion of dawn when Albert nudged Frank awake. They were rolling in heavier, undulating swells, or maybe it just felt that way because they were so low in the water. There seemed to be something apologetic in the movement of the water now. The choppiness that had carried them out into the Gulf had smoothed out under them. Will, still awake, had watched Albert stir, then get up and lean over the side without saying anything.

"Frank."

"I'm cold, Albert" Frank said. "Just get some sleep."

"I am, only look down there, Frank. In the water."

"Go back to sleep," Frank said.

"Frank, I think there's people down there. There're lights down there."

Will remained still, but a slow shiver threaded his spine. Frank stood up now and moved to the side still tethered loosely, as he had been since before they broke loose from the trees.

"Look. Under the waves," Albert said curiously to Frank. "Are they angels?" A long peal of distant thunder rolled far away, perhaps inland, if there was still such a place. "There. Down there, see the orange, in the light," Albert said pointing. "See?"

"What do you make of that?" Frank asked. Albert's lips were blue, but he stopped trembling as he had been all night. "What is it?"

"A foretaste of glory divine."

Albert untied himself from the mast. Frank's knots were not as secure as Will's.

"Frank. It's our people down there. Under the waves and all around. It's getting brighter. Heavenly host."

Frank untied himself too. He joined Albert, looking over the edge.

"Oh my," Frank said, leaning farther over. He ran his hand across the surface of the water and laughed. "How can it be like that down there?"

"I don't know, but there's Sister Genevieve. Sister Raphael," Albert recited the names in a sort of melody. A warm smile spread across his face. "Peter Faulkie and the little girl with the lisp. Look, Sister Camillus. Frank, see 'em?"

"Frank," Will said with intensity, sitting up. "How'd Albert get loose. Tie him off."

"Will, come see this," Frank said. "There's the Boudreaux's. Eugene Grube and his little brother."

"Frank," Will said.

Will could tell, even from looking at his back, that Frank wasn't listening. The long poem Miss Thorne made them read in school last spring came into Will's mind. Odysseus on the wine-dark sea. Homer. He retrieved the loose clothesline and slipped it through one of Albert's belt loops then reeved it through a rusty fixture of the John S. Ames.

"Frank," Will said again, his voice high and tense. "Are you with me?"

Frank was not with him, but drawn by something Siren-like from under the waves.

"Fair flowers of paradise extend their fragrance ever sweet," Albert half sung. "The world is dressed in green and gold. The mansions, glorious. White shores. Yonder fair green country."

"Will, you have to see this," Frank said, leaning over still more, searching beneath the slowly rolling water. "Look at those lights. Michael and Anastasia Zarkerey. Her hair has gotten so long, Will."

"No."

"Why do we tarry?" Albert asked, convening with Frank on the wonder of it all, reciting names together in a common narrative.

"There's the train. Do you see the trolleys?" Frank asked Albert.

"Frank, stay in the boat," Will commanded. Frank's face was near the water.

"The trolleys," Albert repeated.

"Frank, don't," Will said.

"Sister Elizabeth's going into town," Albert said. "Will, the oleanders along Broadway, they're raining down along the trolley's curving path. Come look. Heavenly fields, daylight serene." Albert was now secure but had swung his legs over the side. He put his feet in the water. "It's morning, Will. Blissful. Blissful beyond compare."

Frank's face was so close to the surface now that seawater splashed in his eyes. Will continued working fast, but the clothesline, once run through a shackle on the rigging, wouldn't reach Frank.

"The girls," Frank said. "The girls are going to the gardens, Will. All the children are following. The sky is blue. Everyone's there."

"Home of my soul," Albert said edging farther out. "Home of my soul."

"The sky's not blue," Will said.

"Home of my soul," Frank repeated, seconding all of Albert's observations now. "Look at the Pagoda. The bath houses on the beach. The Murdoch too." Will wanted to look down in the water but didn't dare. He stared ahead, but this handicap hampered his subjugation of Frank. "There's really people down there, Will," Frank said firmly. "Can't you see them?"

Will was losing. He glanced out over Frank's shoulder and across the water, still refusing to look down. The ocean swelled with bulging waves and long slow ripples. The sharp edges with marbled tips had disappeared, replaced by a becalmed, almost glassy rolling finish.

Keeping one hand on Frank's shoulder, Will wrapped his other around Frank's waist securely. A few inches taller than Frank, he could see over him. He glanced down, his heart beating hard. He shuddered and looked away.

"It must be warm down there," Albert said.

"It must. It's the day the seasons change," Frank answered.

"Like cotton bathed in sunlight," Albert said.

Will wanted to join them. He resented his part. Safety. Warmth. Home. A sheltering fold. He didn't want to be against these things, but they were all fatal beliefs right now. Frank and Albert were lost in echoes.

"Look now, Albert," Frank said. "There they go."

"Back home, safely led," Albert agreed. "The sisters are tucking the children in, Will. Their clothes, starched with salt air, folded beside their beds."

"They're waiting for us," Frank said. Will tightened his grip on his friend. "They're calling us. They're falling asleep."

"Time is fleeting," Albert added. Then his eyes suddenly grew wide.

"Maggie."

16

WELL, SOMEWHERE

Will released Frank and moved between Albert and the water. Albert now recognized he'd been tied off and struggled to escape.

"My sister's down there!"

"I don't care."

Will grabbed him by the shoulders with both hands.

"Let me go," he pleaded. "Please just let me go. She's down there!"

Albert pushed Will with surprising strength and Will fell backwards over the side and into the water.

"We'll come back, Will," Frank said.

Albert was getting loose again. Will was underwater, incensed.

"Save Maggie," Albert said as he worked the complex knot Will had tied.

Will surfaced.

"Frank, stop him. He'll drown!" Will called out.

Frank would not obey. Instead, he helped Albert with the knot.

Albert leapt over Will and into the water.

Before going for Albert, Will looked back at Frank. The severity of his expression may have kept Frank in place had he been looking, but he wasn't. He was about to leap in too, but instead paused a fraction of a second to see what would happen to Albert.

Albert was sinking. Campbells, Frank recalled, can't swim. The boy descended surely, falling away, quickly disappearing into the depths.

Will hated to be under the water again. It was pitch black. His eyes stung and he had lost sight of Albert's body already. He dove deep and swung his long arms, but had to come up for air. Breaking the surface, he saw Frank again looking over the side, pointing to a spot in the water.

"Stay!" Will yelled.

Frank shook his head and Will went down again as deep as he could go through the inky water. As far as his lungs could take him, fifteen feet below the surface, he had to make a decision. He plowed lower and the back of his hand hit something. He clenched it, pulled it close, guessed which way was up and began kicking. Albert was dead weight. Will gulped. Seawater brined his stomach. He'd been told once that drowning was peaceful. This was the opposite. The water was like wet clay. Pushing forward, upward, he sensed no progress, but saw a ripple of murky color above and kicked with all the strength he had left. He emerged twenty feet from the boat, Frank dove in and was there straight away, taking Albert's body. Will's vision was fuzzy and darkening, closing at the edges.

Frank pulled Albert up and over the edge of the boat and onto the deck and went back for Will, still bobbing in the water. Frank pulled him up and loaded him in.

Albert's eyes were closed. He was blue; his limbs limp; his face comprehensive in its fixedness. Frank moved over to Albert, praying for his survival. He shook the smaller boy, slapped him, unsure of other means to revive him.

"What do I do?" Frank cried.

"Stick your finger down his throat," Will prescribed, gasping. "Turn him on his side."

Albert vomited great quantities of saltwater, convulsing back to life. Will was dripping, freezing. Frank was repeating Albert's name and that of Jesus.

"They said," Albert gulped, still coughing up the sea. "They said. . ."

Will moved to Frank, who was shaking, and took Albert from him, holding the younger boy closely. "Don't talk. Just rest. Just rest."

"Sorry," Frank said to both of them. "I'm so sorry."

Albert, leaning back into Will, looked up into the sky, wheezing. Thinning clouds sped by. Frank looked up too, seeing hopeful pinpoints above. He reached his hand over Will's shoulder and leaned his head in, connecting all three of them.

"Stars," Albert said in a high voice, hoarsely. Finding he couldn't raise his hand to point upwards, Albert lifted it barely and let it fall back. A pleasant look of melancholy possessed his face. "They said. They said we couldn't go. We couldn't go with them."

"No?"

"No. They said we have to stay."

Frank looked across the ocean, imagining, hoping for a hint of dawn, then looked down into the water. Whatever had been there before, the waves were now shadowed darkly. Lightless. "I guess we ran them off," he said.

"No," Albert said. "We just can't see them anymore. They're still there." He went into a coughing fit again before he could go on. "Well, somewhere. Maybe up there," he added, trying to lift his arm again up into the vastness above. "More real," he coughed some more. "More real than real."

Will patted Albert's head and reached for Frank.

"But wherever," Albert said, turning to Frank. "Maggie's going to be happy."

Frank looked down at him as Will cradled the younger boy against his loneliness.

"It's almost all outside there. She loves outside."

17

A QUESTION OF
GRACE OR CHANCE

Soon, Will could distinguish objects in the moon's distant reflection. The rain stopped completely. Albert had fallen asleep next to Frank, mumbling Maggie's name.

"Frank," Will asked. "What was that all about?" Frank looked at him cocking his head sideways like a dog hearing a sound no one else can. "The sisters. The Pagoda, the trolleys."

Frank looked over his shoulder at him. "You didn't see it?"

"I was the one who got hit on the head. Not you. There wasn't anything down there."

"Albert saw it too. How do you account for that?"

Will shrugged.

"Maybe it wasn't real like we think of real, but I saw it. We both did."

Will breathed in the cold air and exhaled like none of it mattered. He noticed he couldn't see his breath anymore as he had most of the night.

"Suit yourself," Will said.

The seawater moved them side to side in a lullaby motion. A spate of stars could be seen above.

Frank shook his head. Sometimes Will acted so sure of himself that Frank knew that he wasn't, but there was no point fighting about the miraculous that was evident, so he dropped it.

"I don't know if I can make it for another hour, Will. How do we know which way is in and which way is out? What are we going to do?"

Will looked back and exhaled. His resentments washed out into a respectful fondness that had something to do with Frank's expression of forbearance and the idea of grace the sisters always talked about.

"It's almost morning. Things will look different then. The sun will tell us," Will said. "If we were stuck in a grove of trees before, like I told Albert, we can't be far out." He moved his sore neck experimentally and looked at his friend anew. Frank's head and shoulders, his legs and feet, every part of his body was covered with young bruises and fresh cuts. Will imagined his own body looked the same. He knew he had a gash on his forehead and his eyes felt swollen. One of his legs had a good rip in it. He wanted to put his arms around Frank because they were both still shivering, but he knew that would hurt them both too much.

He envied Albert's ability to sleep, though he feared Albert had been concussed and that perhaps he should stay awake. Even so, Will hadn't the heart or energy to wake him. He decided instead to just watch him closely. He couldn't fix everything. The peculiar atmospherics that purported to be the stillness after the storm were oppressive and called a new weight into his chest. There was a sort of creeping panic in the air as they waited for the dawn. The thought of what came next began to burrow inside him like a threaded screw. He suspected that whatever this forming emotion was, it would be disclosed further to him in the daylight, and with greater severity. It might be unbearable, driving all the way through him. He also had to acknowledge that they hadn't survived yet. Something else could always happen. These cyclones could turn. These typhoons never put a cap on what was enough. They didn't obey rules. Storms could come back, but it seemed surprisingly easier for Will to think of this than the other. Albert had water demons and Frank, his evil Slavic fin-folk. Then there were the Sirens, or whatever they were that'd nearly drowned poor Albert. Will thought of Miss Thorne, and how that Homer fellow she was so fond of would put it: it was the Scylla on one hand and the Charybdis on the other. On one side, he and his friends had seemingly made it through the night. They remained in jeopardy, at least until dawn and most likely beyond that, but he also felt the fear of the prospect of tomorrow and of all the following tomorrows. Will was afraid of what it would feel like when the sun came up.

The black sea trundled heavily back and forth and up and down, and the clouds elided together as this slow-moving anxiety washed over him, showing him what his life might look like in the daylight. He'd have to remember. He'd have to second-guess. It would recede away maybe, but he suspected would always come back like a tide. He felt in his throat the perverse magnetism of needing to sort it all out. The coming emptiness was pressing in at him already. He reached up and covered his ears, Albert-like, to keep everything in. Or out. He didn't know which.

"What if the storm comes back?" Frank whispered. "What if we sink lower. Water's about to come over the side already."

"The storm won't come back. I've already thought of that. And I've been checking the boat every half hour. We ought to stay afloat till morning though it'll be close." Will was the oldest. He thought of Sister Elizabeth. "And you know what else?"

"What?"

"If not, we're still not giving up."

Frank nodded his head in agreement. Will wasn't sure if Frank really agreed or was just trying to agree, but his marginal support cleared Will's head just enough. "Here's what's going to happen. The sun's going to rise. Right over. . . there." Will continued as if he was sealing a contract, putting a deal to bed. "We're going to paddle ourselves in and the very first thing we're going to do, Frank, is get you some britches. Then, we're going to look and we're going to find who we can find. The sisters—I don't know. Henry—I don't know. We'll find who we can find, Frank. Then we'll go into town and tell everybody what happened."

Frank's shoulders moved forward slightly in a way which told Will his plan, though rudimentary, was now something they shared, and he nodded his assent.

"Find who we can find," he repeated.

"The island's that way," Will said, pointing, though he wasn't positive. "At dawn, we'll see just how far. It's going to be a clear day."

Will wasn't sure how they'd survived this far. Whether it was by grace or by chance. Maybe this was the only question there was. Maybe both could happen at the same time.

"How's Albert?" Will asked.

"Should we wake him up?"

Albert was breathing steadily and strong, without real labor.

"Let him sleep. You get some too," Will told him.

Frank, obedient, closed his eyes. Alone for a few minutes, Will felt his place in a vast body of water, on an enormous globe spinning, revolving in endless black chaos. Starlight bounced off the sea, blurred, and multiplied in the salty welling of his eyes, tears threatening to roll down his face. The ineffable light made him think of angels.

"Fear not," he said. It was what the sisters told the smaller children like Maggie angels always say. At the edge of the sea, the barest suggestion of light readied to appear, he was sure. His gaze fixed in both hope and fear at the horizon's line, his mind softly noting how the water and sky met. The night, the stars, the ocean. They all seemed to dissolve, or perhaps unify into the present moment in the most captivating way. The rhythm of his breath fell, or perhaps it was led into a closer sympathy with the flow of the remaining wind, his heartbeat with the tide. And as he rocked in these primordial waters, Will felt such a strange peace descend upon him that he closed his eyes and he too fell asleep.

18

FROM THE SEA

Sunday, September 9

He was awakened by a seabird. It looked down at him with an expression bearing many questions from the top of the surviving mast of the John S. Ames. Will squinted upwards into a lavender-gray sky, unsure where he was. The gull had unusual, curved, gray markings on its head, like question marks.

"Yeah. Me neither. Don't ask me. I don't know," Will said, touching his bruised head. He closed his eyes. When he opened them again, the bird alighted into the air. Hovering for a moment, it banked into the wind and soared away.

Will tried to think of what had happened all at once, but his thoughts were like a dark field of clouds. Rain, velocity, loss, angels. He thought of Sister Elizabeth and then the police chief's daughter, surprised that his mind would go to her so quickly. Grace. Will looked around for the shore.

The hazy outline of Fort Crockett was visible in the distance, awarding him his bearings. The boys had been pushed eastward. The John S. Ames was now more debris than vessel, seawater washing over the deck. It had been close. Will took a deep breath and tried to sort his thoughts out again. He reached around his neck. Sister Elizabeth's rosary beads were gone. His curses made him feel the loss more acutely. The gray sea continued to tumble and curl around the dying vessel.

He reached down into the ocean and splashed his face. Blinking the sting of saltwater away from his eyes, he remembered, though it all seemed so implausible. Trolleys and people beneath the water cast in orange light. Frank, still asleep beside him—tangled in clothesline, salt crusting his hair—had seen it. Albert, also asleep, his head badly gashed, had seen it.

Fully awake, Will now felt the weight in his chest again, the wages of survival. He felt the pain of his body too. A new ballast seemed dispersed throughout his torso and limbs. He ached inside, knowing this was the place from which he would have to start again.

The shoreline to the west where the orphanage's two dormitory buildings had stood was barren, barely recognizable in the gathering daylight. He crawled to Frank and untangled him.

"Much obliged," Frank said, slowly sitting up. He looked down at Albert, wincing at the cut above his eye, then over the water and inland. He saw where Will's eyes were locked. "Fort Crockett."

Albert stirred now too, leaned forward and looked toward the beach. Under the vibrant red cut, his left eye was swollen almost shut. "Is that the fort?" he asked.

The three boys watched the sunrise and haze burn off the Gulf of Mexico as the world revolved obliviously into full daylight.

"You're still bleeding, Albert," Frank said. "How do you feel?"

"Born to sorrow," Albert said quietly, touching the swell of his forehead, then reading the life preserver ring floating in the water nearby. "Who in tarnation is John S. Ames anyway?"

"He's the one who saved you from being drowned last night," Frank said.

"Some little schooner," Will said, pulling up a broken board, testing its buoyancy with his foot. "It was probably tied up somewhere and got loose. Got wedged here in the trees." He ran his tongue across his salty lips and motioned for Frank and Albert to get into the water. "Ready?"

They hated to be wet again, but they could see land now and were ready to endure it. Albert stretched nervously and reminded them about Campbells and swimming. Frank helped him to the side of their little raft, next to Will. Then, into the salt tide, they each lowered themselves.

"This stings," Albert said, touching his wound.

"Here we go," Frank said.

Against the pain and cold, movement toward shore was a tonic.

"Goodbye, John S. Ames, whoever you are," Albert said, as they began to kick in unison.

Though exhausted, the three boys churned the water with conviction. Seeing figures moving on the shore near the fort added a rhythm to their pace. A half dozen soldiers, who looked as if they had recently fought a battle and lost decisively, soon spotted them. Three of them waded into the tide and pulled Will, Frank, and Albert from the breaking waves as if they were miracles.

The bedraggled boys, cut and bruised, their clothing torn or missing, had but one shoe among the three of them. They had been in the sea almost twelve hours since the St. Mary's Orphan Asylum building had moved off of its foundations, floated out to sea, and, buffeted by the force of rotating winds and heavy rains, fallen into the ocean. Sister Elizabeth, Sister Camillus, and the other Sisters of Charity of the Incarnate Word, along with Henry Esquior, had done all that was possible to save the ninety-three children. Their failure, except for these three, was complete.

19

THE BEACH

"Can you walk?" a soldier asked.

"We haven't tried in some time," Frank replied.

Will felt heavy on land, but also as he should, again on the firm foundation of the terrestrial ball. Frank found his footing, too. Another soldier, one with a sympathetic bearing, helped Albert up, then raised him up and over his shoulders. Albert's little body looked as frail and thin as a wishbone. He stared back at the Gulf with a baffled look on his face.

Before moving, Will announced his intentions. "We feel obliged to insist you take us to St. Mary's Hospital and Infirmary in the city proper. We aim to tell Mother Gabriel we're alive."

No one responded.

"We're from the orphanage," he added, conferring further heft to his position.

"Expect they know what happened," the soldier carrying Albert said.

"They don't know the part about us," Will said, standing solid on the beach. The soldier barely shrugged. Frank looked at Will and then at the departing soldiers. He shrugged too and followed the soldiers. Will turned squarely west toward where the orphanage had stood. He saw a dozen, perhaps a score of dark bumps, dreadfully still, scattered on the beach in that direction. Other similarly dark objects were washing back and forth on the tide, some tangled in seaweed. Fearful of being alone, he relented and caught up to the soldiers.

"Same thing liked to happen to them in town," the soldier said, shifting Albert above him. "All the buildings are down."

As they walked, Will looked inland. There were pools of water in the low areas with dead animals in them. More bumps in the water. A third soldier, who moved skittishly, kept insisting that they not cast their eyes about—but he gave this instruction so frequently that his remarks became alarming on their own. Will tried to obey because the soldier was a soldier. But Will was fourteen, and he couldn't fully do it. The dark bumps on the beach, were, it turned out, everywhere. After realizing their pervasiveness along the shore, he redoubled his efforts to refrain from casting his eyes about.

Fettered by pain, their young bodies moved awkwardly along the shore. After a quarter mile, Frank said he had to stop, but the soldier carrying Albert told him to keep going. It was good advice. The clumsiness in their steps worked itself out over distance.

The wind spun a burning campfire upwards near the entrance of the fort. Occasionally, a cry of anguish was heard from far away between the sounds of the waves crashing. At every hard gust, the soldiers' eyes darted about. They deposited the boys with a bullet-headed officer who was tending the hissing flames with a branding iron.

"This is Teague," the sympathetic one told Will, setting Albert down. "Do what he says."

Teague didn't look up, but nudged at the edges of his fire with the iron.

"Where'd you boys come from?" he asked.

"From the sea," Albert told him.

"The orphanage," Frank said, elaborating. "It fell. Can I get some britches?"

Teague looked at Will, pointing with the iron at Albert. "What's wrong with him?"

"He's weary," Will explained.

"And a bit broke up," Frank said. "He lost his sister."

"Well," Teague announced as if this decided something. Then he stood up, motioning that they follow him inside.

20

THE CAPTAIN

The captain in charge was a slight, olive-skinned man, somber in disposition, his deportment full of crucial intangibles, surely descended from a long line of soldiers. He was standing over a table, studying a stack of papers with several men watching him by the light of a kerosene lamp. The shadows danced as he touched his cropped beard and gave a succinct order. Two soldiers quickly exited. Will was about to announce again that they must be taken to the hospital, but the captain's command of expression in dispatching the soldiers captivated him. The captain then looked up at Teague, as if to say, what's next?

"Captain Benson, sir, these boys say the storm carried them away from the orphanage."

"We weren't carried away," Frank corrected. "The whole orphan asylum was carried away. Then it fell into the sea. Have you found any more of us?"

The captain moved to Albert and took one knee in the darkness, motioning for Teague to bring the lamp so he could examine Albert's head. He answered Frank's question with a subtle shake of his head, "No." Will inferred from the finesse with which he did, that they were being shielded. The captain glanced at Will, confirming it without saying anything. He then looked into Albert's weary eyes.

"This boy," he said, shaking his head and pushing a steady stream of air through his teeth. There was forbearance in his face implying he loved mercy though his vocation was at odds with its practice. "This boy," he said again as he inspected the gash in the orange light. Will gathered quickly that the captain was one who saw terrible things rightly.

"Have you seen Maggie?" Albert asked him.

"Just who is Maggie, son?" the captain replied in a tender voice.

"She's my sister," Albert said. "She can't swim."

The captain put his hand on Albert's shoulder, then brought him closer in a tender embrace that surprised everyone present.

Will found himself instantly devoted. Frank mentioned aloud how he still considered trousers a chief imperative.

The captain turned and said something quietly to Teague, nodding to Frank. He pointed to their feet also. Teague saluted more crisply than it might have been imagined he was capable of up to now and stepped out. Captain Benson turned to Will, instinctively seeing he was the one to be addressed, knowing he was the one who would act. "You boys received a severe blow. This one needs more care than we can provide here."

21

LEAVING FORT CROCKETT

Teague told Frank to stand up straight. The soldier took the boy's measurements in a glance and began his business, removing a pair of regulation trousers from the shelf, then addressing them decisively with a Bowie knife. He occasionally looked up as if interested in some sort of exactitude.

"Try these."

"Thank you," Frank said to Teague, slipping them on, before turning to Albert. "Look, Albert, new britches."

"Congratulations," Albert said, weakly.

Frank smiled, almost overcome with emotion. "Thank you," he said again to Teague.

Will inspected Albert's head, imitating the precision the captain had exhibited, sure that Albert had been concussed, as Teague found the boys each a pair of old Army boots. The soldier stuffed old socks down in the toes to tailor them for size.

"You soldiers must be properly shod," he said, in inflections which matched those of the captain they had just left. Teague took more time and care than they'd expected to arrive at the proper fit for all three of them, but his sartorial aim was true in each case. Will, with his boots on, acknowledged to himself that he liked being thought of as a soldier by someone like Teague.

"Let's get him some air," Teague continued, motioning to Albert and grabbing more supplies off the shelf. "It's gamey in here. I'll rewrap his head outside. Your bean, son, got conked awful good."

With a canteen of water, a dark green canvas sack with a short sleeve of crackers, and three apples, they emerged outside where Teague swabbed Albert's forehead and prepared to administer an ointment along the deep laceration above his brow.

"Hold him down. This'll smart. It's angry stuff."

"You don't have to hold me down, sir," Albert said, and they didn't. Although Will and Frank were taken aback at the depth of the cut, Albert didn't move at all except for a small ball of muscle at the base of his jaw which appeared and disappeared intermittently as Teague worked. Teague wrapped the boy's head with a gauzy material and secured it. He handed the rest of the bandages and a small green jar of the angry antiseptic to Frank who put it in the oversized pockets of his new pants. "Change him out with that."

"How often?" Frank asked.

"As often as you ought," Teague answered. "Wait here a piece. This afternoon, I'll take you into town myself. We've no one to spare presently." With this, Teague retrieved the iron from near the fire and disappeared back into the barracks. Will walked to the entrance and looked into the dark, following him a few steps before coming back out.

He returned to Frank and Albert and re-tied Albert's boots as tightly as he could.

"Frank, I've got the gunny sack. You carry the canteen." Will helped Albert up. "We need to keep drinking every hour."

An hour later, when Teague told him the boys were gone, the captain sent no one after them. However, he did go outside and look to the east, relieved that during the earlier reconnoiter of the area, the soldiers had discovered the body of Sister Elizabeth Ryan before the boys could stumble upon her. The soldiers had identified her by a laundry tag in her undershirt. She was face down, her short auburn hair free, her body half-buried in the wet sand. When his men removed her remains, they found a length of clothesline tied around her waist. Pulling the line from the sand revealed a smaller body completely buried in the sand, then another, and then another— seven children in all. The last was a little girl, her pockets filled with hard candy, the clothesline which extended beyond her little body ripped raggedly at its end. One of the soldiers had announced right there that he had lost his faith.

"Lord God," the captain had said when he had been taken to the bodies. "Lord God."

He ordered the bodies buried where they lay. The soldiers, some moved to tears, constructed and placed a single wooden cross made of driftwood to mark the eight graves.

"Should we go after them, sir?" Teague asked the captain at the entrance to the barracks.

"No, son. We can't do anything for those boys. The older one with the sandy hair seems capable. He's intent on getting the little one to the sisters." The captain's eyes narrowed; his bearing unchanged. He turned to the soldier who had lost his faith and handed him written orders and instructed him to start for the mainland by horseback. The captain told him the bridges would be out, but to try to find a steamer to get across. His last order was for the soldier to be resourceful.

Before mounting up, the soldier read the message the captain had entrusted to him: 'I fear the city is destroyed beyond ability to recover. Loss of life and property appalling.—Benson.'

22

THE MILKMAN

If there had been a morbid curiosity to truly lay eyes on the first of the dead bodies, this ended immediately upon seeing them. A copse of salt cedars at Heard's Dike held at least a dozen gruesome bodies like a scaffold. The boys tried not to look, moving quickly across the beach, staring out to the glassy sea, which gleamed a pleasant and peaceful green, belying its recent murderous past.

"Look," Albert said pointing ahead. "A cross stuck in the sand."

"They're burying people where they find them," Will said, noticing that trailing from the shadow of the cross, there were seven smaller humps in the sand leading to a larger one.

Frank looked at Will. Will set his face back to town quickly.

"Come on, Albert, let's keep up," Frank said, following Will's lead, electing to leave the arising questions unanswered.

"Poor souls," Albert said innocently. "May you rest in peace."

Ahead, the tangled flat scrub and rippled brown sand gave

way to a landscape marked with pancaked houses and splintered storefronts as they reached the outskirts of town. The oyster shell streets crunched beneath their feet as they entered the city. The path ahead was dotted with overturned boats, scattered lumber, and dozens of wandering souls sifting out intimate debris from the heartbreaking sprawl. Ahead of all this lay only more of the same.

Albert finally spoke the first words that had crossed any of their lips in an hour.

"Why's it so quiet?"

Neither Frank nor Will answered. Just looking ahead overloaded the senses.

As they advanced toward the city, only the sound of shuffling refugees across broken boards and an occasional far off wail broke the hush, but even these sounds seemed quickly swallowed up.

"The milkman," Will announced a few minutes later. He pointed ahead to a man whose slow path was leading to an intersection with their own. "Mr. Holman. I see him at Unger's. At the grocery."

Mr. Holman moved at a mournful trudge toward them, then stopped squarely in front of them. They would experience this time and time again: survivors speaking of their bewilderment, presenting and preserving their stories with little or no introduction.

An affable bachelor, Mr. Holman was known by his customers to move quickly from house to house each morning. Those in his path were also accustomed to his slow and measured way of speaking when he paused along his route, as he often did. Mr. Holman's eyelids now trembled. He began speaking in an accelerated manner, clipping his words. The more deeply he moved into his tale, the more confused he became about what he should say next, but the gist was that his home had been carried off in the storm. The boys listened carefully at first, intent on conveying their deepest condolences, but he seemed hopelessly caught in a loop and the effect of this on his demeanor was unsettling, as it would be to anyone who knew how he ordinarily comported himself.

"I'm looking for it now," he explained briskly. "My home. It was carried off in the middle of the night. Carried off I don't know where. To the sea perhaps. Likely smashed to smithereens." He pointed left and right to the neighborhoods he had traversed already. "How did St. Mary's fare?" he asked.

Frank told him resolutely.

"Maybe they'll find more of you," he said in an uneven cadence. "I heard a story this morning of a little girl. A little girl they found asleep in a tree. Not a scratch on her."

Albert's eyes grew wide. He gripped his hands in a heart-shaped fist, but couldn't speak. From then on, he could think of little else, very certain the little girl in the tree would prove to be his sister.

"We were stuck in a tree too," Frank said, changing the subject in a sense. "Stuck up in a grove of trees. In a wrecked boat. All night. The John S. Ames."

"I climbed a tree myself," Mr. Holman said quickly attaching his story to this theme. "An old oak near my home prior to it being carried off. My house, I mean. Strong oak. I crawled and swam and clawed and floated. Finally made it back to my house. Or where it had been. But by that time, it had been carried off. To the sea perhaps. Likely smashed to smithereens."

Holman blinked hard.

"Have you seen her?" Albert asked.

"Who?" Mr. Holman asked.

"Maggie."

"We have to go," Will said. "Do you know if the hospital's still up, sir?"

"Which one?"

"St. Mary's."

"I don't know."

"Which ones do you know are up?"

"I don't know. Do you?" he asked them.

"No."

"My brother lives by the hospitals."

"I'm sorry Mr. Holman, that doesn't help me. We have to go," Will said.

"Now, where're you boys going again?"

"To the hospital," Will said. "St. Mary's," he added before Mr. Holman could ask.

"I don't know if it's up, but I can't stop you. My brother lives not far from there," Mr. Holman said, rubbing the back of his neck.

"Yes, sir," Will said.

"For now, I'm looking for my house. It's been carried off," said the milkman. He then moved along and away from the boys, speaking swiftly of the sea and of smithereens.

23

A FEARFUL LACK
OF CHILDREN

As they approached the edge of the city, they heard the pealing of the Ursuline convent bells. They seemed to ring out with a special clarity, as if they traveled the distance more freely than before. It was difficult to imagine there might be more destruction than they had already seen, but looking ahead, they realized that what they had so far experienced had been only a prelude. The resort pavilions, the bright-towered bathing houses, the Olympia, Murdoch's, the Pagoda, they no longer existed. It seemed impossible. They had stood so whimsically and proud, teeming with life every day and night of the past summer, even yesterday morning. Now the enormous structures had been crushed, pushed into a giant wedge of accumulated debris and driven inland into the city limits. Downtown, at Q Street, the collected wreckage had lurched to a stop under its own weight leaving a mountainous range of the storm's demolition running east to west through most of town.

"Have you seen the ridge yet?" a dazed survivor would ask them every quarter mile. The boys would shake their heads and answer stupidly.

"We're going to," they'd say.

Albert fell behind, as he had taken to inspecting the branches of each tree they passed, then a rocking horse moving back and forth in a steely whistling wind in the middle of a street intersection. He orbited the toy horse slowly, as if he were admiring it in a store and considering a purchase. It was as lonely a sight as Will, even in this sad series of circumstances, had yet seen.

"Frank, keep him moving back there," Will called. "Fetch him. We can't get separated. It's getting thick ahead."

More men and women were milling about the streets now, aimlessly turning back and forth as if looking for many things at once. Others climbed over collapsed buildings with bleeding heads and unknown purposes. A few grieved in solitude, but only those with the stoutest of temperaments were equipped to do so. The others who did, Will noticed, had already succumbed to delirium. It occurred to Will that perhaps he and his companions must look the same as everyone else. There was a distinct lack of alternatives.

Frank returned with Albert, catching up to Will. It was still morning as they drew closer to the heart of the city. Lost souls now proceeded in waves, most in rags, others with nothing but blankets to cover themselves. Many, with nothing to protect their feet, traversed the ruins with a tentativeness that made their movements seem extremely vulnerable.

Among a multitude now, Will inspected Frank and Albert in a different way, feeling both a profound sorrow and a complicated guilt. But more than anything else, he was thankful for their companionship. When he put his hand on Albert's shoulder, it brought a faint, sad stroke to his heart. He could see no circumstance in which he would ever want to be alone again, but was uncertain whether he could ever become close to anyone or anything again, either.

Will concluded he, too, had probably taken on the same glassy look as those around him. There was simply no means to contest it. He missed home. He missed the orphanage. His friends. The sisters. He missed everything. The nature of the day and the foreseeable future was settling in, intractably. He had many problems.

Will now also realized that he missed the girl desperately. It made little sense. He had reassembled a life without his parents at the orphanage long ago, adopting a stoic temperament out of necessity to manage his innermost feelings. His concern over a girl he really barely knew made a mockery of this, revealing the thinnest spot in his cobbled-together armor. Yet none of this, it turned out, was up to him. His heart went where it went. He felt what he felt, though it was all confusing. He knew it presumed too much to even consider her. He felt like a trespasser. He'd no rightful claim to feel this way about her and had more pressing concerns, like how to reach the hospital before dark. Pragmatically, he tried to put her out of his mind, but as he did, as he looked around, he noticed something far grimmer. He turned around and looked more closely. Behind him and ahead. There was a fearful lack of children in the city.

24

DUELL GOULD

In addition to the general havoc, the fact that they had walked two miles and not seen any children at all was so distressing as to cause a growing alarm in all three of them. This was slightly moderated when the boys encountered Duell Gould. Will put his hands on Duell's shoulders to make sure he was real. Duell was in the grade below Will at Rosenberg, and known as a fine baseball player. He had a chubby face and round eyes, but today both were set hard in an uncharacteristic way. His spiky hair laid down soberly against his round head. He was wearing nothing but a baseball cap and a long wheat-colored linen sack with the words, Dry Feed printed on it in black. Like the others, Duell began his narrative without prompting. His presence here, alone and on his own, was foreboding, given that Will knew he came from a large family.

"Mama was swept out to sea. Just whisked away," he said, making a shooting motion with his hand as he would to describe a baseball flying over the fence. "I saw her go, clinging to a window frame. Night of doom. My pa's out of town. Still is."

Albert asked Duell if he had seen Maggie.

"No, but I've only been ten blocks from where my house was. It tumbled away like an empty barrel, come the third watch. Just whisked away," he said again, making the same motion with his hand, but with his whole arm this time. "I got separated from my brothers and sisters. I just moved from one sinking thing to the other all night. Our house is gone. Sunken down into the hoary depths. There's just a hole in the ground over there now." Duell's jaw set combatively. "Where're y'all going?" he asked.

"Onward," said Albert. The way Albert said it persuaded Duell to join them, talking as he walked.

"I'm going that way too. Searching for my family. I heard my brother's about. Not sure of Mama. Not sure about Effie and Gertie. They're my sisters. Not sure at all." Duell sensed how the boys were looking down, reading how it said 'Dry Feed' on the sack he was wearing. "I was stark naked most of the night. Naked as a jaybird. I'm just now thawing out. I moseyed all over searchin' for some duds. Mine were toted off by the flood. Where'd you get those britches, Frank? They're original."

"Teague gave them to him," Albert said. "There's no orphanage anymore."

"Doesn't surprise me," Duell said. "I sat still all by myself under a cock-eyed roof praying, watching all manner of trouble float by."

Will thought of all the voices they had heard last night when the storm diminished. He thought of the woman with the raven hair in the window and her baby. He thought of the hollerin' of the dead.

"Doesn't surprise me about your orphan asylum," Duell continued.

"I suppose they'll have to build another orphanage presently," Frank said.

"Maybe," Duell said with skepticism. Will looked into Duell's eyes, studying them with purpose.

"It'd be a good idea, I expect, to start a band of children," Frank said. "It might save them the trouble of collecting all of us altogether later."

"Have you seen anyone else from school?" Will asked Duell.

"No," he said, launching into a chilling explanation. The more troubling his words became, the less emotion Duell could muster. By the time he reached the part about his brother and his sisters, there was not a trace of passion in him. "Around seven o'clock, the water rose up four feet in a single bound. It was all a mad scramble. My sisters, Eff and Gert, they stretched out for Mama. Me and my brother, Jack, we just tried to grab 'em and climb up. We were all in a frenzy. Like rats in a trap."

Duell's face went white, but he began to speak as if this had all happened to someone else, or in fact, a rat. He walked steadily as he spoke, and they followed him, stepping over dead chickens and cats. He concluded his horrific story without a quiver. "If you hadn't a second floor or weren't nearby someone who could lift you, or if you couldn't climb up yourself like me and like Jack, you went down into the water." He stopped and turned to them. "It was a simple matter of lack of stature."

Duell, with this declarative, ran a few feet ahead of them, then stopped and started walking again. "Night of doom," he said, as they watched him go.

25

THE RIDGE

They stood before the debris ridge in a row and tried to catch their breath. It was hard to say what was more arresting, the height of the mountain or the flattened city. It looked like the result of an explosion of impossible magnitude, as if an ancient bonfire had been stacked high, but had collapsed before its sacrifices could be made. Inside, there must be hundreds of homes, shops and stores, barns and sheds, churches and telegraph poles, railroad tracks and vehicles of every kind, all smashed to kindling, reduced to an unspeakable mash of splintered, tangled refuse. The city had turned in on itself, swallowed all the wood and a large fraction of the brick and mortar in its path, ground it, compressed it, and then condensed it. Most everything along the beachline was likely to be found inside this three-mile-long snaking mass, which, once assembled, had then sought to annihilate the rest of the city. There were surely scores of sodden human corpses inside lying among dead animals, crushed furniture, broken fences, machinery, and other awful artifacts of the storm. Rafters and joists jutted out from it like the quills of a giant porcupine. Higher up, there were gaping spaces into which all but the hardiest and most composed were afraid to look. In dreadful glimpses inside the yawning gaps and throughout the debris, limbs were postured hideously, like those fallen in the worst of war. It was astonishing.

The survivors here were not as stoic as those they had seen wandering before. A woman, her hair gathered loosely behind her head, had just been taken to the location of the body of her missing child—dead, maimed and imprisoned in a smaller wedge of debris. The poor woman tore at her clothes, free of reason, her utterances like a wild animal that had sustained a gunshot but could not die. Her lamentations provided no lessening of her grief. It was as frightening as anything the boys had seen. Mercifully, she fainted, and they watched as the woman was borne away.

"I want to leave here," Frank announced. "And go to the mainland."

"We're going to the hospital, Frank. The bridge is down anyway," Will responded. "Are you going to swim?"

"I can find a boat and sail across," he said, but even as he did, he began to quail at the notion of spending a minute more in a boat in the water. His head dropped, realizing there was another layer to his own despair. They were trapped on an island.

"Take a drink," Will said gently, pointing at the canteen Frank had been carrying. "We've got to keep going."

Albert began to cry.

26

JESSE TOOTHAKER

The boys had walked along the ridge for a quarter mile, when Will felt Frank pulling at the elbow of his shirt, then pointed ahead. Jesse Toothaker, the Rosenberg School's most feared bully, was striding directly toward them over beams and debris with purpose. Will had always managed to stay clear of Jesse, but he could sense Frank's apprehension. Jesse was moving straight toward them.

"Don't worry," Will said. "I'll handle it."

He couldn't imagine Jesse's belligerence could've survived the storm, but this didn't look good.

"Frank, Will," Jesse called out, now waving at them with animation. "You made it."

"Who's that?" Albert asked. "He's wiry."

Jesse embraced them hardily and, upon hearing their plans, congenially pointed out a crossable breach in the ridge about a mile down to the east, near the Ursuline Convent. It was, he said with solicitude, pitched at a friendlier incline for climbing and, he assured them, for then descending.

"I've been over. It can be broached with little peril as long as you don't think too much about what you're stepping over," he said.

"Is your house in there, Jesse?" Frank asked, still a little tentative with the boy even in his new iteration.

"My house? No. My house didn't go anywhere. It's all wet, but it's on the other side."

Jesse had become a creature with a different personality. He'd discovered a quiet subtlety inside himself. He was far different than the boy who used to run Frank down between classes. He'd projected through time and now looked more like one of the workers downtown or on the docks. He introduced himself to Albert and asked about and listened with genuine concern about the orphanage, expressing his deepest sympathies before telling them of his own experience.

"We took a licking in town. Maybe not like y'all out on the beach, but a licking all the same," he told the boys. "About midnight our neighbor's house picked up off its foundations, then sluiced by, caught in the torrent. Like I said, our house stayed put, though I wasn't sure how long it would before the Ritter Café or some other godforsaken runaway building might run us over. We had neighbors join us and a couple of cows. We moved the cattle out to the other room and did our best to assuage the sufferers and the livestock both until the water came in. Then my pa began to swear up and down in eighteen language, but mostly Hebrew. He told us all to come on up on the roof if we didn't want to drown. We lashed ourselves to the chimney and waited it out. Sometime after that, I spotted a little baby in the water. I let out some line from the chimney, crawled to the edge and fished the tot out. Pa then reeled me back in. The tot was cold and blue, like an icicle. Eyes kind of glazed over, like your friend, Albert's there. Mama commenced to warm it up giving it a drip of brandy every so often from her lips."

"Boy or a girl?" asked Albert.

"Boy. Just a mite. He came to after a spell to wail at us severely the rest of the evening and into morning. Just yowlin' away. Mama's with the little feller now. Where you boys going to?"

"The hospital," Will told him.

"Will, I don't think I can make it," Albert said.

"He can't make it," Jesse repeated needlessly.

"We're going to the hospital," Will said again. "All of us. Jesse, you can come too, but we're going. We can't stay on this side."

"Will, look at him," Frank said. "He's beat."

"True. He looks unwell," Jesse observed with considerable empathy.

"He's why we're going," Will pointed out. "He's concussed."

"I am?" Albert asked.

Albert sat down and Frank took out the green jar of the angry medication to change the younger boy's bandage, it suddenly occurring to him that he ought.

"That looks dire." Jesse said about Albert's cut. "Is he alright?"

"He will be, as soon as we get moving again. I'm trying to save him," Will said. "You coming with us?"

"Much obliged for the invitation, Will, but I've got to go home. Check on the tot. He's just a mite."

"Were you scared, Jesse?" Frank asked.

"Folks said there weren't any time to get scared, but Holy Prophet, scared ain't the word for it," the boy said. "And I didn't need any time."

"Me neither," Albert agreed.

"And it was something cold up there on the roof too, the wind blowing right at us. You boys ever been to the north pole."

"No," Frank said. Neither had Will or Albert, who shook their heads.

"Well, I haven't either, but it couldn't be any colder than it was up there."

This seemed an apt conclusion to all and Jesse, begging their pardon for leaving so suddenly, reminded them of the breach ahead and waved goodbye to all of them most affably.

Will watched him go as Albert and Frank conversed about Jesse's good nature. Will missed the old Jesse who was more himself, and Frank, still tending to Albert, seemed more content sitting and tending and talking than moving. Albert was slowing them down. Frank was scared and wanted off the island. If Will left them, he could probably reach the sisters and the hospital tonight and tell them of the fate of the others at the orphanage. None of it could wait.

"Stay here," he told Frank. "I'm gonna look around. Albert, just rest here."

Will shook his head, and fostering his deepening irritation, scouted ahead, moving toward the entrance of Garten Verein park where another group of survivors thronged in front of the twisted wrought iron gate. He then considered the distance he could traverse by himself and what would be required in his pace. He was certain he could make it to the hospital before dark if he just kept going, but as he passed the crowd at the gate, he heard the men and women standing there swapping stories. He couldn't hear all that they were saying, but the tales were colored with themes of deep courage and heavy loss, all of them delivered in low and somber tones.

Their stories were the same as his—the ones he wanted to tell the sisters when he reached St. Mary's. How Henry had furiously cut holes in the floor, moved furniture, and held up the walls as long as he could. How he'd held little children in his arms until he drowned. Henry was as sure as the stars. He wanted to tell them of how Sister Elizabeth had trusted him with her rosary. How Sister Camillus had done everything she could.

He wanted so impatiently to do something right, but what was right was right before him. Will couldn't leave Frank and Albert.

The dead forbade it.

27

THE FAIREST OF
TEN THOUSAND

The exotic, octagonal-shaped building that had stood, bright green and white, in the center of the Garten Verein was now roofless. It had famously been one of the city's leading social clubs. Will had been enrolled by the St. Mary's sisters in a class for manners and etiquette here last summer. The class had included dance lessons, which he both cursed and eagerly anticipated since they brought him, for brief periods, into close proximity with Grace Ketchum.

The police chief's daughter's eyes were set widely apart. There was a certain blooming nature to her skin—it glowed from the sun. The way she spoke to him, in hushed and measured tones, about where he should place his hand along the contour of her back as each dance began, left him in a position far beyond his capacity to respond. Yet, he also recalled how his nervousness on the ballroom floor immediately subsided when they began to move together. She drew something from him. New, but familiar. More discovered than invented. It concerned the plausibility of living in congruence with how he should. He wanted to somehow tell her she had this power, but couldn't. He felt that probably they were meant to share this and other secrets, but he couldn't quite speak them into being when he was with her. As they danced, Grace spoke to him, not only without condescension, but with ardent curiosity about what it was like living in the orphanage. She told him about books she was reading while coordinating their steps across the dance floor. It seemed she exerted no effort in doing so. It was like she was from a different world where everyone was effortlessly incredible. She intensified his consciousness, even as he seemed to lose it in her presence.

Standing at the center of the empty, roofless ballroom, he realized that his understanding of hope had become tied up in whether or not she was alive. He told himself he would find her soon or at least view her from afar to verify she graced the world still with the same light and beauty she had so easily shed upon it before. This, once settled, fueled him to rejoin Frank and Albert.

Will, fortified, retraced his steps back through the park, but when he returned to the place he'd left them, they were gone. Will felt his heart begin to race. His eyes darted quickly across the panorama. He repented for having thought of going on without them and dashed down the street and back to the gate before spotting them near the croquet grounds just inside the park. He exhaled and regained his balance, beginning to realize who was really saving whom in this little troop. They had taken up company with a gaunt man, hobbled by deep grief.

With visible pity, Frank and Albert were offering consolation to the man who was making low sounds that could be categorized as neither moaning nor sad singing, but somehow both. Will moved closer and began to make out his words.

" . . . fast falls the eventide," came the man's muffled dirge, expressed in a tragic voice. He was well over six feet, shattered, and holding empty frames in both of his very large hands.

"What's he saying?" Will asked Frank quietly, as Albert stepped closer and began to hum lowly along with the man. Finding a purposeful harmony, a song emerged. Albert had always had a fine singing voice.

"Swift to its close, ebbs out life's little day . . . "

When they finished, the tall man began to explain his circumstances as Will and Frank joined Albert.

"I was felled by a flying brick to the head. When I came to, my wife and children were forever gone. The tallest one wasn't as high as this." He rested one of the frames on a broken knob of the fence post at the end of the croquet grounds. "She was the fairest of ten thousand," he continued. "And my boy was just learning to talk. He'd jabbered my name for the first time. 'Papa' is what he said, just last week. 'Papa.' My soul's delight."

The man lifted the other picture frame, touching its corner to his forehead on which there was a large knot and a gash not unlike Albert's own. This gesture helped him regroup somehow. He swallowed two or three times in succession. "And my wife. My wife, she was such a tender, delicate thing. Lovely in all respects one could record. Always so easily frightened." The man moved to one knee, where the boys could see the lines in his face more clearly as he began to wave vaguely in the direction of the sea. "Now she's out there. All alone."

Albert put his little hand on the kneeling man's hulking shoulders. The man looked up to him, his face creased deeply, severely stained. He took a deep breath, finding solace in Albert's presence. He and Albert exchanged a few more quiet words, which neither Will nor Frank could make out, something about ascending. Whatever it was, it swept the sharp edge of anxiety from the man's brow. As he arose to his full and impressive height, the man repeated, "Safe on

Canaan's shore. Safe on Canaan's shore. Much obliged, son. Much obliged."

Looking to the sky with the empty frames still in his hands, he nodded his head to the heavens up and down subtly, then departed. Albert watched the man disappear, then casually walked over past his companions to the tennis courts. Frank followed. Will trailed behind, thinking back to another time, then forward to the unknown. The blurry distinction between false hope and blind faith dissolved within his mind. He quickly caught up to Albert.

"What'd you say to him?" Frank asked.

"Dangers fierce assail our paths," Albert shrugged. "And through days of toil our hearts will fail, but this earth holds no sorrow that heaven's ascension cannot cure. God is our stay. Our refuge. We find rest safe on Canaan's shore, settled there like little children at home. Bathed in warm light, fadeless and pure."

Frank and Will looked at Albert and then at each other. "Who told you that?" they asked.

"I think I made it up."

Frank inspected him.

"Or anyway, it's something I've always known," Albert added.

"You look better."

"Thank you," Albert said. "It's just when I try to control things in my mind, when I try to change them, I can't."

Will looked at him in depth. Albert, concussed, deep in mourning himself, had mined a new measure of resiliency from his exchange with this most sorrowful fellow. Who was saving whom, Will thought.

"We remember by thinking of love I think," Albert said, his heart flooding warmth all over his body, giving color and life to his face. "Of how she smiled when you gave her candy. That's all you can do. And I can do that. I can do that in heaps without even trying."

28

SERPENT MARKS

The storm, Will concluded, had a special fondness for removing tin roofs and depositing them shining in the streets under the noonday sun. It seemed the ambition of the violent winds to have left at least one battered section of tin at every intersection and the goal appeared to have been nearly attained. There were hundreds of wandering cisterns, as well.

The next block, the boys encountered a diminutive girl between Albert and Frank's age, whom none of them knew. She was vigorously attacking a large tree with a small axe.

"God," she said at each blow into the tree, calling out to a deity who, she later told them, had assigned to her this very task. She explained that she had spent the whole night in this tree and had been bitten by a number of sea snakes. The boys had seen dead snakes all about and this girl, though she seemed strong and unaffected by toxins, had revolting purple fang marks on her arms and legs.

"How come you're not dead?" they asked almost together.

"Can't say. God, I think," the young girl said, putting down her axe. Sweat covered her brow. "I'm just not."

Frank inspected the small sideways 'V' the girl had started in the side of the tree. Unless she had just taken up the chore, she had not made much progress. Given the implement, her size, and the girth of the tree, it would be some time before the tree succumbed. Nevertheless, she seemed capable of bringing it down.

"Why is it God wants you to cut down this tree?" Frank asked, forthrightly.

"As a souvenir. He said I could have it. I'm not from around here."

"What's your name, girl," Albert asked.

"Althea," she said defiantly.

"We're going to the hospital, Althea," Albert said. "Do you want to come with us? They can nurse your serpent bites."

"Can't you see I'm busy tribulatin' here," Althea said, as she shouldered the axe. "Shoo. Shoo now."

Albert, Frank, and Will nodded in assent and left Althea, her axe, and the tree. They walked in silence together for several moments.

"She has a long way to go," Frank observed.

"True," Albert said, "but I'd say that tree's like to be overmatched."

29

THE MAN AND THE COW AT THE URSULINE CONVENT

Near the breach in the ridge to which Jesse Toothaker had pointed them, they found the steps of what remained of the Ursuline Convent. A gray-haired man stood there with a black milking cow. He barely awaited their arrival before beginning to tell his story.

"I tried mightily to save my cows for the good of my family," the man announced to the boys as they stopped before him.

"Yes, sir," Frank said.

"At least you saved this one," Albert said.

"At least you saved your family," Frank said.

"Why, I did not save my family," the man said, his bones threatening to collapse inside his skin. "They've all drowned." He accepted their most sorrowful condolences before he continued. "I had planned to open my mouth and let the seawater pour into my lungs when the time came, but I couldn't. Now I am here without my family."

No one knew what to say next and the man eventually turned to advance down the street with his cow. The boys didn't know where he was going any more than he did.

As Will and Albert watched him go, Frank kicked a piece of rock from the Ursuline steps, then nudged it with his foot toward Albert. Albert kicked it to Will, who kicked it back to Frank. In this way, they proceeded to the area immediately adjacent to the breach in the ridge.

The pass in the ridge was swimming with activity, dotted with little campfires where people were cooking what they could find. They gathered in little knots around the little fires drawn by something primordial, something deep inside and not fully understood. Wounds were bandaged and tended here using liniments, balms, horse salves—anything they could find to dress their wounds. It had become an intersection of importance. A kind of base camp before climbing and going over. It was a place to take a breath before moving on. A place to share stories and food and to begin sorting things out.

Frank kicked their rock into the ridge as Albert looked at the eyes of those present. Will searched for the way through. A woman gave them each a ladle of beans she had concocted into an impressive stew with celery and potatoes. She had, with her own children, gathered tin cans for the purpose of serving her offering and had commenced now to feed as many survivors as she could here.

"Thank you, ma'am. We're half-starved, workin' on being wholly starved," Albert said. "I'm Albert. We're from the orphanage out yonder on the beach. The St. Mary's one."

"Have a little more then, Albert. I'm a cook. My husband's a builder." She pointed ahead where a man and two boys were constructing a lean-to out of the kindling on the ground into what Will would soon hear people calling storm lumber houses.

"You boys keep looking for folks helping one another. Fall in with them."

The boys layered their gratitude over one another in response before they moved on.

Ahead, people were stepping over the jagged broken planks and the sharp edges of tin roofs at the edge of the ridge to get to one another. What they all had in common was a shared astonishment that there was no localization of the damage. The annihilation was total.

What had been a bright and clear place only a handful of hours earlier was now, Will thought, something out of another one of the books Miss Thorne was keen on reading to them last year. Will could not recall the man's name, the writer of the sad and sometimes angry book. Will watched as they came in waves toward the ridge, most of them with nothing, maybe a blanket or an old suitcase. It was like a series of Biblical plagues had befallen them all at once. They all trudged ahead, shook their heads, shuffled their feet and shook their heads again.

There were all manner of tears among them, as well. The most welcomed being the ones that flowed when someone thought dead suddenly showed up. But there were the awful kind too. While hope could turn to joy here, hope could also be dashed for good just as rapidly. This sense of chance produced an instability on the ground, which was reflected in the physical imbalance people exhibited as they climbed upwards, then disappeared over the uppermost spine of the ridge to then descend to the other side.

As he approached the breach himself, Will recalled what he'd once read in a diary of an old Texas war veteran at the Galveston Mercantile Library downtown. When the soldier wrote of a single popular man dying in a small skirmish on the picket line, he described it in the most heart-wrenching of terms, with remarks of personal sorrow denoting considerable soul searching. However, when the soldier's whole battalion was mowed down at Sharpsburg, the words of memory the soldier penned were blunted. He described the events and their aftermath in a strictly numerical fashion. Whatever temperament created this phenomenon, a merciful numbness perhaps, Will concluded it made pressing on possible. Those trying to clear the ridge, those cooking, those gathering supplies, and those caring for the wounded here, were simply choosing industry over becoming maniacs, and it was in this movement and the gradual perception of its utility toward sanity that they remained so. It was good and merciful that pain did not congregate as people did, Will thought. Perhaps by God's design, pain could not be summed, but must be borne individually. Comfort though, he saw here, worked on a different calculus. Comfort could be gathered, its power multiplied, as it was being multiplied here.

As the boys entered the queue then climbed higher together, they nodded, thanking those who were working, receiving in response mere nods back. But these were the only transactions. No one spoke on the way up and no one slowed on the way down for fear their eyes might be pulled down into the maw and settle on a dead body inside the craggy pile.

Will, thinking of the soldier's diary again, resolved to fight this numbing impulse and to look down as he crossed over. He aimed at logging the details, but found in the end, he simply couldn't. Perhaps this interior dialogue was a common instinct among all those present, for everyone's behavior turned out the same. Surrendering, looking upwards as they all did, Will squinted into the brilliance of the cloudless sky. He set his eyes on a distant spot, finding if he kept his line of sight arching high, he could keep all the death away for just a moment as he crossed.

At the top, he took Albert's hand and pointed downtown, toward where at least some of the buildings still stood. The scene jogged his memory as they then each began to climb down, maintaining their gaze ahead, until they returned to solid ground, at which time it fully came to him.

Dante, Will remembered. The writer was Dante.

30

VELOCITY AND
SLATE ROOFS

Once over the ridge, Will's heart sank. The wind and water had been just as formidable and lethal here as it was closer to the beach. Only brick chimneys survived on many of the homes. Only parts of walls remained on most of the large commercial buildings. Most of the island's splendid churches were decimated. The wind velocity through the slate roofs had produced something very much like a spray of cannon shot against the interior of the city. There were endless neighborhoods full of partially demolished, crooked, and misshapen homes. In between every such structure that had barely survived, there was more kindling.

Albert, exhausted from the climb, the descent, the day and the night before, had to stop again upon reaching the ground. Will, agitated again, told Frank to stay with him while he surveyed ahead for a clear path forward.

"Don't move this time," Will instructed firmly.

Just a few blocks down, a stout man approached. He was one part frantic and one part controlled. These two equal parts inside the man were held suspended in fierce battle over the terrain of body and of mind. Will recognized him as a contractor who had worked at the Rosenberg School last spring at the head of a burly crew.

The contractor was moving with unusual animation from pile to pile, damaged house to damaged house, in an increasingly manic way, providing a brisk running commentary concerning each structure's failure, issuing verbal opinions furiously in the absence of his engineering stamp, presumably lost in the storm. He was waving his arms, pointing, as if his crew was nearby.

"Studding frames here," he stated, measuring things with his eyes. "Four by four, then sills, six by six. Plates, four by four, three and one-half feet high, lifting the floor four and a half feet above grade." He began to give instructions to his invisible crew.

"Double open fireplace chimney in the middle of the structure. A good backbone when built of good material and well executed." He moved from casualty to casualty deliberately, scribbling in a battered notebook he evidently kept for this purpose. Seeing Will, the man began to address him directly as if Will might have a commission to award.

"This house had several feet of water in it. Good wood, though. Oak. Double framed at each corner, shouldered into the sills at the top for support, you see." Blueprints were spinning in his head. "Pillars spiked into the cornice work. Ungirded though, it won't scour. Had the pillars been undergirded, perhaps the braces would've held," he said.

He then moved to the next block, continuing to eulogize the homes with a mixture of regret and reproach. Inspecting a series of three houses flattened against one another, more mathematical calculations ran through his head. The contractor then looked back and saw two men coming toward him. They had long white aprons over their clothes like the ones Will had seen the orderlies wear at the St. Mary's Infirmary downtown. Seeing the men approaching compelled the contractor to address all three houses as a unit.

"The strength of the breakers. The rapid rise of the overflow. It all pushed ashore under the force of strong winds from the southwest. It floated these homes off their foundations. Now triplets they are. Triplets in common ruin."

Will watched as the men closed in on the contractor. "Drowned in your own homes," he said in a sad benediction, effusive pity now breaking through in his voice. Then the contractor surrendered to the men peacefully. He extended his upward turned hands out toward them. They took him by the arms firmly, but also with compassion, even a degree of respect, moving him along the muddy streets and away. Will expected the nervous hospitals were doing a good business right now.

31

LIKE CORD WOOD

When Will returned to Frank and Albert, the sun was beginning to descend. He had seen the top of the roof of the Sealy Hospital. He generally deduced that at least in its essential particulars, it had withstood the storm. This boded well.

St. Mary's was close to Sealy and made of sturdy stuff, he told them, but just as these words had left his lips, a parade of wagons made the corner, ambling slowly toward them, rocking back and forth. Will tried to get Frank and Albert away from the street, but it was too late. Canvas tarps covered many of the wagon beds, but they were inadequate even where present. Men walked along the sides of each of the lumbering drays with large planks which were laid down in front or behind them as they slogged through the mud. Two other men moved obstacles out of the way in front of the clomping horses.

The driver stood straight up at the front clicking at the horses and shaking the reins. All around them, there were scents of death.

Arms and legs, hands and feet protruded from the tarps. The wagons without any coverings at all required the boys to look away. Though Will didn't count, without his permission, his mind estimated twenty to twenty-five corpses on each wagon, stacked like cord wood. Some of the bodies were turned to the sky, their faces unprotected. Others were facedown, their arms hanging over the side of the wagons loosely as they bumped along, swaying one way then the other. At first, all those along the pathway of the wagons instinctively froze. Those wearing hats removed them out of respect, standing motionless in lines parallel to the street. Then, one by one, realizing such gestures couldn't be meaningfully repeated and retain their effect, they stopped and went about their prior business. Albert was the last to gain this perspective.

"Let's go back," he said when the last of the wagons had passed, sitting down with his legs pulled up close to his chest, shivering, though the setting sun burned down upon all of them. The humidity of September had set back in as the storm's tail continued northwards.

"We can't go back, Albert. Where would we even go?" Will said. "I need to get you to the hospital. That's where we're going."

Frank inspected Albert's head. He had changed the bandage again while Will had been gone. Although the gauze had remained so far bloodless, after the grisly spectacle of the wagons, Frank believed Albert simply hadn't the capacity to see anything else today. He was done.

"We must stop, Will," Frank asserted.

"We can't. We don't want to be outside when it gets dark," Will countered.

"Where's that fort we were before?" Albert asked. "I liked that captain and those green apples they gave us."

"Albert, we can't go back to the blamed fort." Will said.

"Will, he's gone as far as he can," Frank insisted. "Albert's played out."

Will's feet sank more deeply in the mud. Being defied by both of them after he had kept them together all of last night and all of today ruptured something inside him. What was most disgraceful about what Will said next was that he hesitated and could have changed his mind, but he did not. "What about Maggie, Albert? She could be at the hospital."

"Will," Frank whispered intensely.

"What about Maggie? Think of Maggie."

Albert suddenly looked heavier, almost inert, weighted with the length of the day.

"Don't make me, Will," Albert said barely audible. "Please don't make me." Huge salty tears rolled down his face and the bandage reddened in a spot on his forehead. Frank shook his head. His eyes were wet now too. Frank sat down next to him and pulled Albert close against his shoulder.

"He's bleeding again."

Will stood over Frank and Albert and looked down on them. They both bowed their heads. He wanted this, their submission, but now that it was his, he recognized it failed to deliver. Instead, he felt the force of his betrayal so deeply that he dropped in a heap next to them and put his head into his hands and closed his eyes. Though he could not see, he felt Frank shake his head ruefully. Will's confused anger shifted further onto himself and he was unable to give his apology a voice.

Cursing, of course, was forbidden at the orphanage, and it wasn't a corruption which heretofore tempted Will much, but when the last of the wagons disappeared, Will felt the overwhelming desire to rain down brimstone at them and at the sky. He was breathing hard and started to stand up, but before he could, his temper was quelled by Albert's still, small voice.

"Just sit with me a while, Will."

Albert waited until Will had caught his breath, then in a gesture as memorable as it was unmerited, he put his hand onto Will's shoulder in the same manner he had done with all the others who had sought mercy this day at his hands.

32

THE BULNAVIC
SOLUTION

After a long period of silence, Albert insisted he could go on.
"Let us arise and be going," he said formally.
"What?" Frank said.
"We should go," he said, pointing out into the gloaming, more casually. "It's fixin' to get dark."

"No," Will said. "We've got to think of something else for tonight. Frank's right."

Frank, with this vote of confidence, stood up and walked in a circuit around them. "I think I have an idea." Their eyes followed Frank, as he made another circle. "How about my cousins?" Frank offered. "How about that, Albert?"

"Cousins?" Albert said, raising his head higher. "You have cousins?"

"A whole mess of cousins," he said. "Nearby, too."

"In the city?" Albert said, getting up. "Like family cousins?"

Will realized he should have thought of this as Albert voiced the obvious question.

"Why'd you live in the orphanage, Frank, and not with your cousins?"

"Here we go," said Will under his breath.

"Because they're the Bulnavics."

Will had forgotten about the Bulnavics partly because he had sworn to Frank never to mention them. "My father wouldn't want me living with the Bulnavics," Frank explained. "They're Bohemian. My mama's kin." Frank looked down the street in the direction of the wagons. He stamped his feet into a couple of puddles, then watched the late afternoon sun's reflection regather in the water under him. "I suppose one night would be alright."

"Seems reasonable," Will agreed cautiously.

"Will they take us in?" Albert asked.

"I don't see why not," Frank responded.

"If they'd take you in now, why not before? In life, I mean?" Albert seemed refueled by curiosity.

"I imagine they would've if I'd pressed them on it, but being Bulnavic and all." Frank said, trailing off.

"What's so bad about being a Bulnavic?"

"Albert," Will said, making a motion designed to cut off the inquiry.

"Nothing's so bad about being a Bulnavic. It's just I'm not one."

"Still," Albert argued forcefully.

As the sun fell, Frank began a lengthy narrative explaining to Albert that he was not a Bulnavic and would never be one. It had been some time, but Will had heard all this before.

"If this is the plan, could we get on with it," Will said. "Albert's right. It's getting dark."

"Sure," Frank said. "Come on."

As they advanced block by block, Albert interrupted the

meandering course of Frank's prejudicial explanation of his family tree with a series of pertinent questions and keen observations. Soon they stood in the falling light in front of a blue Victorian home which was, according to Frank, not where it ought to have been, but then again, wasn't where it could have been. That is to say, the Bulnavic's home had pivoted off its foundation and scooted largely undamaged, though slanted almost whimsically, into their neighbor's yard.

Frank set his feet square to the front porch and put his hands to his mouth to make a miniature megaphone and called out into the evening air. "Ahoj!"

"What'd you say?" Albert asked, as the woman they would come to know as Aunt Lida stepped through the tilted threshold of the broken door and onto the crooked silt-covered porch.

The woman looked at the boys dully for a moment. Then, just as her face began to take on a look of recognition, Frank launched himself toward her.

"Jak se máš, Frank?" she cried, taking him up in her arms in a difficult bliss. "Frank Madera."

Albert now scaled the porch and embraced Frank's aunt, as well. She hugged the two boys at once, though certainly she had not seen Frank for years and Albert not at all. Will felt his heart swell, heave, and burst all at once as she motioned for him to join them on the porch. "Oh, in pity's name," she kept saying, before finally ushering them in.

Inside, mud oozed along the curiously slanted floor. The furniture, covered in silt, had all slid to one side of the room, which itself was set at an unsuitable angle. "Upstairs, upstairs," she repeated.

The Bulnavic boys, Lukas and Janek, as well as Uncle Oldrich, descended halfway down the uneven stairs where they met Frank, Albert, and Will. They welcomed Frank like he was one of their own which indeed he now was. Upstairs, there were more breathless greetings with the Bulnavic girls, Darja, Hana, Iveta, and Janicka. They all kissed Albert several times on his broken head. There were also several cats whose needlessly complicated names are not recorded in any history. The Bulnavics had spent last night upstairs in the girls' large bedroom. The family, working together, had also managed to move a piano up the stairs and into the room during the storm. The girls' four ornate beds had been pushed each into the four corners and several crates which had been used as beds last night for the rest of them were stationed here and there. The piano remained in the center of the room. The girls continued to fight over Albert, petting him as if he were one of their kittens, as Frank, in response to Uncle Oldrich's questions, began to tell them all that the three boys had seen last night. As they listened, each of the Bulnavics alighted on a particular crate. It seemed they had each claimed one to their liking last night and felt compelled to remain loyal to it even in the storm's aftermath. As Frank told his story, Aunt Lida, as she required being called by each of them, announced she could not abide the dreadfulness of it all any longer.

"Goodness," she said. "This is dreadful. More dreadful than I can abide."

Descending halfway down the stairs, she stopped to listen to the rest of Frank's sad narrative, crying silently, almost uncontrollably.

"In pity's name," she whispered.

33

THE PRAYERS OF
LIDA BULNAVIC

As a benediction to Frank's sad story, at Uncle Oldrich's urging, Iveta played a sorrowful song on the piano. Janicka sang along quite capably. Afterwards, Will, Albert and Frank were called downstairs by Aunt Lida, where, by the light of a small kerosene lantern, they consumed an extraordinary number of cucumbers soaked in vinegar. Decamping from the kitchen, led upstairs by Lukas and Janek, they returned to the bedroom where Hana and Darja had prepared crates for them. The windows were open and a light breeze brought a mild relief from the sapping humidity. The boys each found themselves so sore and exhausted that they could barely express their gratitude before falling fast asleep.

Around midnight, Will shifted on his crate. Its creaking awakened him, but it took him a full minute to realize where he was. Adjacent to him, Albert's breath moved his chest up and down. Albert had been in no shape to travel even beyond the fort today. When Will had finally managed to formally apologize to him over the cucumbers, Albert had looked at him so earnestly and squeezed his hand so tightly, conveying forgiveness so completely, that, while this particular stain was removed from Will's conscience, its lessons were left powerfully intact within the intimacies of his soul. The transaction made him feel lighter, more elevated, and heavier, more responsible, at the same time—as true mercy does. Albert, he realized, was a diminutive miracle, whispering partial thoughts of God out into the world. Will looked over at him with a painful gratitude, still worried about Albert's wounded head, when he heard a whisper across the room.

"We are clothed in sackcloth, covered in ashes. Earth's joys grow dim," Aunt Lida said, softly, tenderly, praying over her children. "Soothe our loss though it shall remain etched, deep-written upon our hearts. Give us each courage for the coming day."

Will feigned sleep as she prayed first over the girls then her boys, sometimes falling into a lovely and mystical Czech. Aunt Lida then moved successively over Frank, then to Albert, before reaching Will.

"We are buoyant and prosperous also. Our beloved Frank and his poor friends delivered, resilient little Albert the Concussed, and lionhearted William."

She lifted one calloused hand, then placed her other softly to Will's forehead as she spoke. He heard his mother's voice in how she pronounced his name, Will-i-am. Her prayer—brief, sincere, and coupled with this gesture—was so unexpectedly sweet that he found himself unable to move, much less speak. When she moved away, Will was left at peace, realizing for the first time in two days that he'd been both still and without fear. He soon fell back to sleep under the spell of Aunt Lida's divine restoratives—though they did not last.

34

A DEVIL HAUNTED NIGHT

It was completely dark when Will awoke again. The power of Aunt Lida's recent fervencies, avid though they were, could not bid him back to sleep this time. Jittery and agitated, he found it impossible to lie still. As his eyes adjusted to the room, he saw Janicka and Darja curled up, sleeping motionless in twin beds, with a long table between them on which new clothes and boots had been laid out for the boys by the resourceful Aunt Lida.

Will examined the clothes which Aunt Lida had evidently chosen for him, as they seemed to be the largest of the three sets, and quietly dressed. Janicka's eyes opened as he rolled his socks on. She smiled at him affectionately, then nestled her head back into her pillow. Will looked around the room and settled his eyes. Detecting no further movement, he navigated his way through the labyrinth of crates, creeping downstairs in his socked feet, quietly carrying what must have been a pair of Lukas' boots in front of him. These still didn't fit, but were sized closer to his foot than the boots Teague had given him, even when augmented with their sock-filling.

He quietly lit the lantern on the kitchen table and opened the door slowly with no meaningful objection from its hinges. Stepping out onto the porch, the neighborhood was desolate. The sky offered no moon and there would be no electricity for many weeks. It was the darkest night he could remember. He alighted from the steps pensively, breathing in the narcotic of the city's exhaustion. In the street, he felt a blanketing pall and the decay of its citizenry's belief. The fears from the night before and the anxiety about what lay ahead had birthed something of exquisite dread in the sun's deep absence. His light barely penetrated the darkness.

At the intersection of the block adjacent to the Bulnavic's Victorian, there was a broken pipe organ with a wraith-like woman sitting atop it. He lifted the lantern but wished he hadn't. Her haunting eyes followed him, but she said nothing.

"Ahoj," Will offered, seeking to annul her disquieting effect on him.

She responded with something garbled that sounded like, "Give up."

Will doubled his gait.

He sensed masses in the shadows and devils haunting the dark. Spectral demons seemed at work in the bushes and around each corner. In each uneven breeze that blew, there were unseen suggestions of opposition, notes of risk and imagined whispers of conspiracy. He was also afraid the pipe organ woman might be following him.

"Goblin-visitin," Will whispered, keeping his eyes fixed straight ahead with resolution. His jaw locked and his teeth ground together as he moved quickly in the dark and through his fear. The images of evil ghouls stealing jewelry from corpses, pulling survivors into the wet ground, filled his head irresistibly as he advanced toward Grace's home.

Once a thing of austere beauty and relative opulence, he could see even before reaching her neighborhood that it would never be the same. He climbed over boards and through the mud as carefully as Lukas' boots would carry him, as the lantern's wire handle cut into the bends of his fingers. His feet began to sink more deeply into the soupy ground as he got closer. Birds called to each other from the ancient trees, announcing his unwanted presence. Soon, vast pools of black water all but stopped his progress. The ocean had swallowed this entire area and hadn't yet fully regurgitated it. Galveston had, for a time last night, disappeared altogether.

Staccato yelps and peculiar whistles continued to bounce off the hedges and the ground, but he continued forward, casting trepidation from his mind with the conviction that Grace might be close. Though he had no plan as to what he could accomplish here beyond the bare verification of her residence, he tried to probe farther through the muck and dread, until he stumbled into a sign, knocking it over and into the mud. He lifted it up but couldn't quite make it out. He blinked, brought the lantern over it, and endeavored to read it again. Will tripped and fell backward over uneven ground barely saving his light.

Looters, it advised, will be shot.

Fearing that even reading the words might be an offense, he scrambled away from the neighborhood's invisible sentinels, their twitchy fingers and their vengeful hearts looking down on his retreat from mossy trees. Retracing his steps, he quickly returned to the relative familiarity of Broadway, regaining his balance and catching his breath. Overcoming the panic in his throat, he managed to find a therapeutic rhythm in the repetition of his steps, but it was impossible to avoid the notion that leaving his crate had been a mistake.

35

A LIVELY FEAR

Will managed to disappear into his movement. He moved off of Broadway, to the north until, near the waterfront on that side of the island, he heard the clattering sound of industry. Men were working down on the wharf, offloading the wagons with the inadequate tarps.

Retrieving the bodies from the carts, they wheeled them along inside a covered shelter, where they set them down in long straight rows. The sounds were muffled and the kerosene lighting dim, but the men worked at a deliberate pace inside a cloud of quick lime, wearing bandanas to protect their lungs against the granularity of the air. Will crept closer, carried toward the work in a powerful current of surprising fascination and a lively fear. He'd heard today that some five hundred had perished and thought that impossible, but now understood this was a vast undercount. There were several rows of bodies stacked on shelves already. Powder hovered above.

The scope of the operation was as mesmerizing as it was appalling. It fixed his eyes until, at the far wall, an arm suddenly jerked upwards from a body.

Will covered his mouth as his legs yielded and he fell slowly to his knees in surrender. He put the lantern down and rubbed his hands. Rising slowly, he turned, moving south, away from the horror before stopping to rest. Laying his face flush against the sod, he scolded himself, envious of Janicka Bulnavic, safe in her bed.

36

AN EFFORT TO
THE MAINLAND

Will gulped deep breaths of humid night air until he righted himself. Thousands must have died. It was impossible, yet apparent. The world was out of joint. He couldn't see that this could ever be put right and the instinct to flee swept over him. He began to move quickly through the dark. He felt like something heavy was pressing down on his aching lungs. His breath wouldn't reach deep, forcing him to breathe faster, shallower at each step. The faster he moved, the more acute the pain. He slowed in response to it.

Before seeing the warehouse, he thought he'd given up hope too easily. Now he knew he wasn't scared enough. He lamented the fact he had let Albert's faith infect him. This criticism, directed at himself, carried a certain scorching quality. He'd been told once by a surly teacher that, given his orphaned condition and all, he ought not fall into excessive cheer about his prospects or really the future of anything in particular. While his temperament was not suited to such a dark outlook, maybe it was time to reconsider that perhaps there was no sunny side in this world. Maybe he'd been fooled by the sisters and their talk of hope and grace.

"Give up," he huffed. Running was no use. He couldn't see ahead, his chest hurt, and Lukas' boots were unreliable in uneven terrain. Also, he had no destination.

Will stopped and repeated the injunction of the pipe organ woman. Unconditional surrender felt like the prudential course now. Full retreat seemed the only judicious alternative. Like an exile's compelled belief in a pagan god, it seemed a matter of survival to renounce all hope.

He slowed his pace further to a walk, submitting to the many invectives of the night. He ought to lay down his arms. No measure of courage, heroism, or even endurance could counter what weighted the other side of the scale. He remained in motion only because he was afraid that if he rested here, he might harden and sink down into the ground.

In the stifling dark, on the far north side of the island, he approached a small mound on the ground. When he raised his lantern, it looked like another newly dug grave, but when he got closer, he saw it was a small overturned rowboat half-buried in debris next to a large pool of brackish water.

Lifting his light, he saw the pool led to an inlet, which he suspected led to the bay, which separated the island from the rest of Texas. Maybe Frank's instinct to leave the island was right. He set the lamp down, flipped the boat over, picked up a sheared off plank nearby, threw it in, and jumped in the little skiff, launching it into the languid water with the intention of going across. Using the board to row hard, he lit out for the promise of the mainland. He pointed the bow toward a series of remote lights at the opening of the channel, aiming at to go as far inland as geography allowed.

The repetitive motion helped him absorb what he'd seen, and the feel of his oar then struck a chord in his muscle's memory. He remembered the pleasure of holding a baseball bat. He wasn't as powerful as William Scott on the mound or as gifted as Bobby Palmer in the field, but Will, smart and scrappy, made consistent contact at the plate, and always fielded his position well.

In the rhythm of digging at the water and in the tension of his grip, he slowly recognized himself again. A sort of calming resignation covered his soul. Breathing heavily, but now in a rewarding way, sweating, comfortable, he just kept rowing, pushing out at least half a mile before he finally brought his paddle in. It dripped onto Lukas' boots and clothes. There was an equanimity he'd gathered in his exertions. He fell back, low in the boat, looking up high as he had done at the top of the ridge. It seemed like months since he'd climbed up to its crest, holding Albert's hand. The stars, deep-set in their faint scattering, distant lights along a dark wall, they looked like far away windows. In the vaulting darkness, he considered the possibility that the earth had perhaps just fallen away from the rest of the universe. Maybe it could come back. Hope and fear would always struggle with one another inside him, as it does with all who examine matters fully. There was everything terrible he'd seen that was real, but there was also so much more he earnestly felt, but that remained unseen. Like Grace and how she kept entering his heart unbidden. Albert's innocence. Frank's hardy good nature. Aunt Lida's hospitality. There was Sister Elizabeth's trust in him. Henry's sacrifice. Maybe the earth could fall back into order driven by these, its vast array of elusive invisibilities.

The mainland was no doubt safer, but it was not his home. Damn the pipe organ woman, he thought. If there was an answer to the question of whether hope was worth its salt, it could only be found here. It would be a betrayal to surrender now. He put his oar back in the water to rudder his craft around. No retreat.

As the arc of the wake of his turning vessel disappeared along the surface of the dark water, Will considered all these things and squared himself up to his future. But it was the memory of the police chief's daughter which again persisted in the pictures of his mind, her countenance lit by its own beauty.

37

SHEET MUSIC

Monday, September 10

Alavender-blue morning light had broken by the time Will arrived back at the Bulnavic house. Aunt Lida had started a small fire in a space she had cleared in the front yard. She sat on a piano bench cooking eggs.

"Dobré ráno, William," she said, patting the bench beside her. "You mustn't go out like that." Will sat down next to her. Aunt Lida was quite homely when she sat still, but her features became attractively dynamic when in motion, giving off a sense of great wisdom and appeal.

"Do you have any of those cucumbers left?"

"I'm afraid the days of vinegar and cucumbers are gone for a while, William. Help me with these eggs. We must eat them today." Will cracked a large egg over the ancient black iron skillet and shared the fire with her. It was a simple, but pleasing, exercise. A balmy breeze fluttered through the bare branches above them, bending their reach upward lazily, then downward.

"Now, who is Maggie?" she asked, handing Will the large wooden spoon she had been using to work the eggs.

"Albert's sister. She was lost. He talked about her in his sleep after I left, I guess."

"No," she said. "I had a dream about a precious little girl named Maggie. Keep the eggs moving. They'll stick." Will began to scramble with vigor as Aunt Lida added the last of the buttermilk. "I don't have any plates. I had the most beautiful china from far, far away," she said, pointing to the ground where a shard of it lay like a broken robin's egg. It was the exact color of the changing sky. She then stood up, motioned for Will to stand as well, and lifted the lid of the bench, removing some papers. In one deft motion, she spooned a portion of his breakfast from the sizzling skillet, placing the eggs on a thin sheaf of sheet music which would serve as Will's plate. As he ate, he read parts of the lyrics of a hymn that peeked out from his beautiful meal:

> *. . . sifting out the hearts of men . . .*
> *Oh, be swift, my soul, to answer . . .*
> *be jubilant my feet . . . In the beauty of the lilies . . .*
> *like the glory of the morning on the wave. . .*

Will couldn't read the rest, but the eggs were superb.

38

A FAREWELL ON THE TILTED PORCH

When they went inside, Albert couldn't be roused for a frightening length of time. He suddenly sat up, announced that he had a tremendous headache and mumbled something about Maggie. He also said he felt dizzy when he darted his eyes about. Even following Frank's recommendation that he not move or dart his eyes about, he seemed much worse. Will told Uncle Oldrich, who was examining Albert's head, that as soon as Albert had some sheet music eggs, they'd be obliged to depart for the hospital. Uncle Oldrich advised against it, but eventually agreed, indicating the boy had surely been concussed.

"I wish everyone would stop saying that," Albert said.

Frank ascended the stairs, after helping Iveta and Janicka serve the coffee his Aunt Lida had brewed for the whole neighborhood and took Will aside.

"I think I better stay here, Will."

Frank glanced at Darja and Hana feeding the cats on the crates.

"They need you here," Will agreed, nodding in a way that expressed his comprehension of this decision as well as his overwhelming fondness and respect for Frank. They'd known each other for five years, but now exchanged no other profound thoughts. Had Will understood that they would both live long lives, but never see each other again, perhaps he would have searched for a weightier goodbye, but neither of them knew this and nothing momentous came to mind anyway. Instead, they simply regarded each other for a brief instant among the crates and the cats and the cousins, in a way that was far more intimate than articulate. Frank then went to Albert, bent down to tie the younger boy's new boots up tightly and whispered something in his ear.

"Me too," Albert said. Then Frank told him something else and made a wide gesture around the room toward his charming cousins. Albert pulled back so that he could see Frank's expression and nodded. They embraced and Albert smiled contagiously.

"A family," Albert said. "Capital."

Downstairs, as they prepared to leave, Will took up the canvas gunny sack Teague had given them which Aunt Lida had now re-stocked with provisions for the day. All four girls hugged Albert and Will fiercely, insisting that they soon return.

"William," Aunt Lida said as they descended the crooked steps outside. "Will." The way she spoke his name and the way she had held him close to her in the mud near the fire made him feel as if he was losing something crucial. Uncle Oldrich shook Will's hand as he would an older man and the boys nodded, wishing them štěstí, or good luck and success. Will nodded back.

"Ahoj!" Will said to the girls. They smiled back. Hana waved the paw of the kitten she was holding at them.

"So long, then," Albert said to all of them, waving casually. "Bye, Frank."

Will took Albert's hand and they turned together, setting their faces toward what remained of the city.

"I liked those people," Albert said. "They have a knack for rescue."

39

A SERIES OF
INTERMENTS

Will kept the top of the Sealy Hospital in view, but no straight path there existed. Debris, as well as bloated carcasses of mules, cats, chickens, and a distressing number of snakes were everywhere. What made it worse was Albert's bleary-eyed insistence that each deceased creature they encountered deserved a proper burial. Though he maintained a strict policy against what Albert suggested, Will could barely keep the younger boy moving because of this hyper-developed sense of civility.

"We're not stopping," Will said firmly.

However, when they found themselves in front of a body of a man impaled on a wrought iron gate, they both stopped. To pause here seemed required. The body had taken on a gray-yellow hue unimaginable until now and the poor man's limbs were bent akimbo in a terribly unsettling way. His mouth and nostrils were dark purple. His scalp was ripped back halfway. All Will could do was shake his head at the notion that this had been a human being only a day or so ago. Albert, seemingly unaffected by the state of the body, acknowledged the remains couldn't be removed without a tall ladder, a small scaffold, or by some other method which he, as a boy untutored in the science of engineering, could not yet conceive. Will responded that whatever sort of man this was before them, he deserved much better, but that trying to address the predicament of removing his corpse for burial now was out of the question. This would have to be left to others.

"If we can't help him," Albert said, "then, Will, we ought to at least bury something smaller and easier to get to."

"Albert, I've got to get you to the hospital. I've been trying to save you going on a day and a half now. You need to cooperate."

Albert looked around for alternatives, not hearing Will.

"No," Will said, seeing where his eyes had alighted.

"Look at that poor dead dog."

Albert went to it and, despite Will's protests, picked up the pup's body and found a dry stone to lay him on. He carried the stone and the mutt away from the road, cleared some of the debris in front of an abandoned, half-destroyed house, and picked up a short plank from a pile of rubble and lumber. With it, he began to dig a hole. Though it was a shallow grave, it took almost a half hour because of the rudimentary nature of the tool, Will's decision to remain a spectator, and Albert's own compromised condition.

After laying the stone and the body in the hole, Albert covered the canine remains with the plank, and the available sedge and moss nearby which would at least keep the vultures away. He then took a deep breath and looked around again. The dog burial, rather than satiating this pastoral urge in Albert, enflamed it. It fulfilled something sweet, terrible, and addictive in him, and he redoubled his insistence on burying everything that had once walked upon the ground, flew in the sky, or swam in the ocean. Will hewed to the position that even choosing a single category of these was lunacy.

"You're not the undertaker of the animal kingdom," Will said, making an appeal to Albert's understanding. "We've got to keep moving."

Will presented to Albert all the practicalities against these interments cogently, but it was Albert's unshakeable view that maybe if he did this, the act might be reciprocated for Maggie wherever she was. This argument, though untenable, was also unassailable. Thus, for a time, Will gave a measure of berth to Albert's inclination, telling himself that Albert had received a terrific blow to the head, was a good and decent person, and had been placed under impossible circumstances. Eventually though, to scuttle Albert's new avocation, he resorted to physically pulling him along. Even so, every block or two, Albert would pull away with the intention of entombing a duck, a gull, or squirrel with extended liturgy and sacred rites. Will next tried hygienic arguments, but his clinical narratives too went unheeded as Albert escaped, bent upon burying a large cat in a shallow grave.

"Alright, Alright," Albert finally relented, as he finished writing out "C-A-T" in the dirt over the hump which marked the feline's last resting place. "Just one more. Then we can go on."

"Promise me."

"I promise, Will. One. You have to help me though."

"Fine, but I won't be party to burying any snakes or rats, Albert. We'll catch the plague for sure."

Albert quickly found another plank which more ideally resembled a shovel and moved across the street with it toward a large dead goat.

"And nothing that big," Will shouted. "We're not burying a dead goat. Pick something proper. We've got to go."

Then, just beyond the goat, both of them saw a solemn young man with short dark hair beside a low stone wall. He stood in abundant stillness, one hand on his waist, the other holding a short stick. He tapped it on his thigh in a rhythm only he could feel.

The body of a petite young woman dressed in a ragged yellow dress that had once no doubt been the color of the sun, rested at his feet.

40

LILA

As Albert stepped over the goat, the young man bent down and rearranged the torn, pale yellow clothing on the woman's body. She had a small gold ring on her finger. The man began to rock back and forth, slowly biting the nails of his fingers, as if something still hung in the balance. Albert looked down at the body, moving with a quiet caution toward the mourning man who was now focusing on his approach. He stood alone, along a desolate block on which the homes had been all but swept clean, only the low rock wall was left behind him. Two telegraph poles stood crooked against the blue sky farther behind the wall. The ground the man occupied was especially boggy. His shoes had sunk an inch or two into the mud.

Albert began to use his shovel to dig, but as fast as he did, the mud leeched right back. In a few minutes, he stopped to wipe his brow with his sleeve.

"Sorry, mister," Albert said with a formidable gentleness. "I can't even make a blamed hole."

"The ground," the man said. "The ground."

Will had never heard such genuine sadness in an exchange. Albert turned to Will, looking ruddy and more robust now despite his vain exertions. "You said I could do one more."

Will looked at the woman's body then the man and, seeing these circumstances presented a special case, moved forward and motioned for Albert to follow. The man watched them with a peculiar mix of interest and detachment as Will looked over the low stone wall behind him.

"There's a patch there fairly free of roots. Considerably less greasy ground," Will said. He looked at the man, then turned to Albert. "Find some big rocks," he added, jumping up then lowering himself down over the wall, beginning to toil as Albert collected stones with single-minded purpose. If it took a half an hour for one boy to dig a grave for a small dog, Will thought it would take two boys twice that long to do this, but it didn't. Apparently, there were no reliable ratios in the mechanics of such work.

"Can we bury your wife for you now, sir?" Will asked. Albert raised his hand subtly to slow Will down.

The man stopped rocking. "I've been searching for her all day and night. Found her here about an hour ago."

"We can help you," Will offered, speaking slower. The woman, Will could see, had been striking. She had a long trail of blonde hair framing her face and spilling down her dress.

"Do you want us to go?" Albert asked.

The man turned to Albert and now looked younger, more vulnerable. He mumbled something about vanity and pride, dropping his stick. "No," he said. "Please don't go, friends. Let me think on this a spell. What I must do." He walked to the stone wall with his hand on the back of his head as if he was struggling with a complex equation. After making the short pilgrimage, he returned to his place standing over the woman just as he had been when the boys arrived. Then he walked over to the wall again, picked up the stick again and returned to the woman's body, this time trembling. He couldn't find words for the longest time.

"Lila," he said unwillingly. "We were married yonder at the church just last week." He bent down and lifted her hand. The ring around her finger reflected sunlight and it compelled him to say something about the Fates.

"Yonder was my house. It was to be our home."

Albert moved closer as the man fell back into silence. "Do you reckon we ought to help her find some peace now?"

The man interrupted Albert, but with no answer. He could barely breathe. He put his hands back on his hips then touched the back of his neck again looking down on Lila. His breath would not come. He bent at the waist, as if looking for it on the ground, then rose again.

"Well, let's let her rest a bit more," Albert said to Will. Will nodded, staring at the young woman's miraculous face. Her eyes, angled slightly downwards and almond-shaped, were closed and her skin was like cold marble. She somehow remained incredibly beautiful in death though hauntingly so. Her face was untouched by the catastrophe which had stolen her life. Bluish veins ran the length of the inside of her arms, somehow persisting, conveying an inextinguishable sense of life inside her.

"I could do nothing to save her."

"I can't imagine you could," Albert said. Will agreed, nodding once more. The man was on his knees again, now trying to straighten her yellow dress and began repeating himself. He ran his long fingers through his own dark hair.

"It's not like this. It's not like this," he said to her. Will had seen children at the asylum become so frightened and anxious that something chemical would seep into their spines and even the most well-meaning consolation could not be absorbed, no matter what was done for them. Though the man remained still, his expression looked like one of those children. "Lila," he said softly, still on one knee closer to her. "Lila. Oh," he said.

Albert put his hand on the man's shoulder, just as he had done yesterday with the tall fellow with the frames near the tennis courts, and then last night with Will on the street, and again over the cucumbers. "We can give her a proper burial."

He was unable to speak.

"We can care for her, I mean."

They remained still for some time before the man finally spoke again. "I'm not myself. Much obliged, friends," he said. "My soul is most weary. I'm not myself."

Will nudged at Albert to start as the man apologized again about not being himself and tried to rise, but it was as if a weight had been lowered onto his shoulders and he quickly fell back to one knee. He took a deep breath and apologized again. "I fear there will be little that is proper about it. No offense," he said.

"None taken," Will said. "I'm afraid you're right. Are you ready?"

The man nodded his head affirmatively though everything else about him said no and Will ambled over the wall. The man and Albert then lifted her up. Her limbs were long, yet she was lighter than a cloud. Her wet clothes stuck to her frail body and Will sensed that these might be heavier than she was. Albert took her feet and the man held his beloved under her arms as they gave her to Will. Lila's head swung to one side when Will received her. As they delivered her over the stone wall, her long blonde hair trailed behind her along the stones. The man felt the power and the sorrow of this, and Albert steadied him with a few words now from the other side. They brought her fully over the wall without the grace her lovely beauty was owed, as the man, recognizing this injustice, made a series of melancholy, barely audible sounds expressing this terrible inequity. Then they laid her down as softly as they could in the broad, shallow spoon of a hole which Will had so industriously dug in the good ground. Will, swallowing, settled her body into the soil. At the same time, the man took off his shirt to wipe her face. He then kissed the dead woman with an arresting softness. Albert recited the twenty-third Psalm so naturally, so sincerely, that it seemed as if it had come to him as an original thought.

Both in this moment and in retrospect, it was difficult not to think that his recitation had something to do with what happened next, but an immaculate sunbeam fell upon Lila in the grave through the naked trees. As majestic as it was tragic, in the instant that it occurred, she was suddenly shown to them briefly as she was in life. The man, overwhelmed by this small miracle, was moved again to his knees. Lila's peach colored skin was illuminated by the light that radiated over her finely sculpted features brightly, even fiercely, and it mesmerized them all. This would be how the man would remember her for better or for worse. Will thought the man might next remove the wedding ring from her finger to keep it, but instead in a gesture of elegant simplicity and devotion, he removed his own ring and put it into her hand, closing it in her grasp, then laid her hand over her heart. Her body was so fragile in this light that it seemed to almost disappear into the earth. He then said a few words over her that concerned a balm in Gilead, which purportedly revived the sin-sick soul.

Then Albert said, "Amen."

The man exhaled in long breaths as if he was about to dive deep into the sea and brushed Lila's hair from her face. He laid his shirt softly over her immaculate face, then, taller, more squarely, not nearly healed, but touched, he rose. His suffering was of such dignity that its memory would remain with Will throughout his lifetime with the very clarity he had experienced it today.

"Go ahead," the man said, blinking hard. He put his hands on his hips at his back and watched for a moment as Will began to shovel dirt in place carefully around and then over the young woman with his hands. They then placed the rocks Albert had collected around the raised earth. Each rock was placed in a sacred way that seemed just right, then the man, like Moses at the burning bush, removed his shoes.

"This is holy ground," he said when the operation was complete. They all agreed. "Thank you," he added. "You are good friends."

"We bid your sorrows will one day cease," Albert said.

They shook hands and, carrying his shoes, the man began walking toward his antagonist, the sea. Will and Albert never learned his name.

41

AN INTERLUDE ABOUT
WILL'S HEART

Although Will had regretted ever mentioning his feelings for Grace to anyone, he had done so hesitantly to Frank in the spring, but only to prevent his heart from catching fire. He confided he'd tried three times to speak to her at school, but each episode was characterized by heightening levels of humiliation. Frank suggested it would be far less painful for Will to simply watch her from afar. Though conceptually he agreed, this strategy required a deportment Will was unable to maintain for any length of time. All year he had prayed for an opportunity that involved a more natural exchange, one in which he could casually exhibit what he considered his finer capacities, but he had begun to realize that such occasions arose so unreliably, that this was no strategy at all. The heady evenings at the Garten Verein had been memorable, but ephemeral. His concentration had been thrown off by her unexpected kindnesses and, not least of all, by that dark green dress. In addition, there were all the technical maneuverings required in the dance steps, the precise accuracy of which all seemed a matter of life and death to Miss Ruby Winifred of the Women's Auxiliary. Will was so physically and emotionally wound up under Miss Ruby's vigilant gaze and terse instruction as these moments unfolded, that he was unable to prove himself worthy of Grace on the dance floor— as he yearned to do. Nevertheless, these tense waltzes, quicksteps, and peculiar promenades were the impetus for his vow that he would eventually prevail, no matter what Frank said about the danger of mismatched pairs. Frank—and all others who operated in the realm of the right order of things—could see she was far out of reach for a St. Mary's orphan, and repeatedly warned Will of the cruel saga ahead if he persisted in these unreasonable pursuits. In response, Will acknowledged he had a blind spot in such matters, but said nothing could be done to reverse course at this point, anyway. What he didn't confess to Frank or anyone else was his sincere conviction, an expectation even, that someday they might be thrown together by chance into some riveting adventure. A kidnapping perhaps. One in which they would be forced to escape together. Or perhaps they would find themselves in church during a wedding and become accidentally—but quite legally—married. In any event, Will had lost his heart already and felt the freedom engendered in the outright nature of this relinquishment might somehow tip the odds heroically in his favor, despite the considerable mathematical improbabilities.

42

THE LOCKET

Moving down Broadway, the number signs on the streets were diminishing in a way that brought consolation to Will's heart and mind. When they reached 8th Street, they would turn north and move up Market Street. There might be a shorter and more direct route, but the clearing work, now underway in earnest, seemed focused on the larger thoroughfares. Will thought staying on the main streets, in the end, would limit the possibility of unexpected delay.

Now at 16th, less than a mile from the hospital and near Unger's Grocery where Sister Elizabeth had traded the morning of the storm, Albert spotted a small heart-shaped locket on the ground. It was among a sheaf of correspondence that had spilled out of a black tin box in the midst of more castaway lumber. Though such items of jewelry were common for young girls to wear, Albert, on account of its color and shape, contended this one must be Maggie's.

"Mind you, I never took special care in inspecting it," he confessed.

Will glanced at one of the letters from the tin box. 'My Darling Little Wife,' the note began with tender fondness in a decisive hand. Will put it back in the box, vaguely comforted by the sense that there were still unwritten rules in effect to direct him in such matters. To show a certain decorum and respect for what remained of the notion of privacy seemed the only way to counterbalance the appalling lack of gentility that would be required to forcefully begin to restore the city to its previous position. To maintain small civilities like this, Will realized, was a means of combat, really the only weapon at hand. In addition, there was the sign he'd seen last night, not to mention all the similar ones cropping up all over town.

"Maybe so, Albert," Will said, anxious about lingering over even modest jewelry on public grounds. It seemed an especially poor policy today. "But why don't we put the locket back in the box with the letters, Albert."

Albert opened his fist and Will took it from him.

"Will?"

Will placed it in the box, closing the lid and looked back at Albert.

"Yes, Albert."

"I'm going to have to miss her for a long time. I know it's not hers," he said. "I just wanted to hold it in my hand for a bit."

43

THE TEACHERS AT ROSENBERG SCHOOL

As the two boys passed Unger's Grocery, they were beckoned inside by the store owner.

"Nothing ever looked so good," Will said, as Mr. Unger handed him two large oranges. Aunt Lida's sheet music breakfast had worn off with all the exertions of the day.

"How is your family?" Will asked tentatively as he dug his fingernails through the thick orange peel. Mrs. Unger was usually about the store, aproned up, busy with her broom. He hadn't seen her. Mr. Unger wore an understated, but overwhelmed expression, which gave Will his answer. Unger couldn't or didn't speak further, as Will looked around the space. "Where's Birdy?" Will asked next, pausing in the excavation of the orange, his heart rising.

"She's in back," Unger said, still with suppressed agony in his voice. He tried to add something more but couldn't right away.

Birdy, Unger's eldest daughter, was a couple of years older than Will, but was always friendly with him in the halls at Rosenberg. She helped him with any complications that arose with his higher math when exams grew near and was Sister Elizabeth's staunchest advocate in the grocery business, setting aside the best produce for her each week before the sister came into town on Saturday mornings. When she knew Sister Elizabeth was short on funds, Birdy would fiddle mysteriously on the shop's weights and measures in the orphanage's favor, then throw in little treats for the smallest children. She'd also write Will's name on an orange or an apple. "This one's for Will Murney," she'd tell Sister Elizabeth. Birdy was always saving the day in this way or that. She always knew what to do. Will was awful fond of her.

"Birdy's tending after her little sisters back yonder," Unger finally said, having regained his composure. Will felt his own heart falling back down into place as Unger asked, with great sympathy, about him.

"Sister Elizabeth. The orphanage. Will, I'm terribly sorry, son," the kind grocer said, expressing the same measure of sadness at the conclusion of Will's woeful story as he had about his own loss. "I loaded the wagon for her Saturday morning in the rain. I urged her to stay," he added. "Told her she could stay with us here. I understand Mother Gabriel did, as well, at the infirmary."

"Sister Elizabeth," Will said, handing the peeled orange to Albert. "She's safe on Jordan's shores."

"Canaan's shores," Albert corrected, taking the orange. "Thank you."

"She was a pistol," Unger said as Addie Rogers joined them. Mrs. Rogers, a math teacher at Rosenberg, was holding a tin can from which she drank aromatic coffee in short, bird-like sips. A demanding teacher, Mrs. Rogers always required her students to show their work.

"Mrs. Rogers?" Will asked. "Have you heard any news of Miss Thorne?"

She brought a handkerchief to her mouth, trying to restrain her emotion. "Lucas Terrace fell. It's where poor Daisy lived."

A picture flashed through Will's mind: Miss Thorne standing tall at the front of the class, commanding the room with a means of leadership exclusive to the finest teachers, her reddish-golden hair congruent with her spirit, dressed impeccably as she always was. She lectured ardently on history, geography, and English in a soft, but vigorous voice, peppering her content with encouragement concerning elevation and hard work. She advocated that these subjects were vital to a full enjoyment and wholesome enrichment in life. With innate enthusiasm and utilizing the sort of interesting facts that made all her claims seem credible, she exuded the sort of charisma that made intelligence compelling. The photograph of her fiancé, Joe, which she kept on her broad and organized desk, was also a topic of constant conversation. She was to have been married this very week.

Will mourned her.

"Her stories," he said, remembering how her lessons were full of action and good ideas. As he finished his orange, Addie Rodgers put her hand on Will's shoulder. She meant to comfort him, but began weeping, herself. Unger quietly told Will and Albert that Addie had lost her husband, Ashby.

"Yes, he came to retrieve me," she said. "I had left the school to help my mother and couldn't get back." Unger sent Albert away for more oranges. "I packed some of Mother's valuables in a small trunk," she continued. "We started to leave, but the water was too high, so we returned to her apartment. Ashby found us. We went to look for higher ground, but we'd forgotten the trunk. Ashby went back for it. The building collapsed. It fell on top of him."

"I'm sorry," Will said, after pausing to try and think of something else. Mrs. Rogers' red eyes looked right through him.

"I still have my mother," she said. She seemed ready to shriek between every word. "I study myself," she added, winding the handkerchief around her hand so tightly that her fingertips turned white. "I know what has happened. My eyes are hot."

Will shook his head because he didn't know what else to do. He would always associate the scent of strong coffee and orange rinds with desolation, for what she next said was spoken in an indelible way. "The thought of taking my own life tempts me greatly," she said forthrightly. "I am undone."

44

THE SOMMERS

Outside the grocery store, Will and Albert encountered a pig. Without prejudice, it trotted up to every passer-by it spied along the road. When ignored, it would turn and skulk away down the path on which it came, only to soon find another person to approach.

"Don't pet the pig," Will said to Albert, too late. "We're not starting a farm."

Albert looked at Will flatly. He had barely spoken a word since they buried Lila, but after the brief lunch at Unger's felt more able.

"It's one thing not to bury a dead goat, Will," he said. "But it's something else entirely to ignore a live pig."

"Words to live by, Albert," Will said.

The pig followed the boys for several blocks until it was diverted by an old woman who kept repeating, "O my soul. O my soul." The pig remained with her, having changed allegiances for reasons known only to the pig.

Ahead, men continued to clear the streets. This was easy duty compared to those who had been assembled to serve within what people were now calling dead gangs. Within the organization of these little platoons, there were those assigned to scouring a neighborhood to find the bodies, and those charged with removing the bodies and collecting them in a central location within each neighborhood. A designee, typically one who lived in the particular community and had some familiarity with his neighbors would then make efforts at identification prior to the wagon's arrival. This person would scribble down on a note pad where each body was found and make inquiries if he didn't know the deceased. Often, he would part the lips and examine the mouth, making note of gold fillings or false teeth then attach the note with a pin to the victim's clothes, or if the corpse had no clothes, fold it, and place it between the toes, giving them a morbid squeeze before the body was removed. Typically, a single body would not be found exclusive of finding several others at the same time. Family members were most often found in the vicinity of one another and some family resemblance could be detected by the one who was engaged in the identification work. Will learned the bridge of the nose, in particular, was inspected for resemblances to reliably verify family connections. The designee would typically write something like this if he knew those whose remains were found:

Sommer, Ferdinand (SW Corner 59th & Avenue W)
Sommer, Mrs. Ferdinand
Sommer, daughter of Ferdinand (1)
Sommer, daughter of Ferdinand (2)
Sommer, daughter of Ferdinand (3)
Sommer, Joseph (son of Ferdinand, same residence)
Sommer, Mrs. Joseph
Sommer, child of Joseph

Or, should he not know, and could not identify those found:

Unknown man who took refuge in Francois house (1)
Unknown woman who took refuge in Francois house (2)
Unknown last name, Joliet, cook for Mrs. V.C. Hart, 1624
Avenue M
Unknown persons in Losico's Grocery, 21st & Ave. P ½ (1-27)
Unknown child with Nolley family at 22nd & Ave. T
Hired men for O'Neill's Oyster Farm (1-4)

Or, on still other occasions, especially as the work went on:

Unknown white man
Unknown body
Unknown girl, about 6 yrs. old

Those making such recordings, Will observed, acted in a manner which revealed no deep grief. After the notes were made, deposited, or attached in whichever way was expedient, the man assigned this duty simply sorted pins or sharpened his pencil with a pocketknife until he was summoned again. Will and Albert verified these divisions of labor within these crews with Hal Mackey, who used to work as an attendant at the Pagoda Bath House but was now a member of the dead gang assigned to this particular neighborhood. He held a toothpick loose in his mouth.

"Coroner's trying to keep a record," he told the boys. "It's a fool's errand."

According to Hal, the dead bodies within this section of the city were being taken to a timber mill warehouse on 25th Street, well to the east of the one Will had seen last night. Hal allowed that another crude temporary morgue was located on the north side of the Strand between 21st and 22nd, and another one was being set up at another warehouse across town. It was hard for Will to believe there could be two such places, much less four, but the truth was that they were everywhere.

"Look, it's Father Kirwin," Albert said, pointing. The priest of St. Patrick's, Will and Albert's own church, had been conscripted as a clerical adjunct to Hal's gang. Not yet forty, the priest moved about the work of the members of the dead gang, gently encouraging them. After being asked to do so by the Central Committee, he was working closely with Rabbi Cohen and Alderman Levy on the disposal of the bodies, as well as with Police Chief Ketchum on public safety.

"A good man," Hal said. "He visits the poor when he has money, the rich when he's out. Look at him now."

Hal told them that Father Kirwin's keen blue eyes went black after speaking to one of his parishioners, a man by the name of Soper about the death toll. Yet the priest had regained his composure and returned to work, not stopping to rest at all. "Soper's a medical doctor by trade, I understand," Hal said. "Particularly gifted, they say, in the science of probabilities and the like. This Soper, he walked a portion of the city yesterday and last night, studied the force and geography of the cyclone, and done the mathematics of it all." Hal shifted the toothpick back and forth in his mouth. "I don't know, but we've been removing bodies now all day. Don't know what Soper told the padre, but it hit him right hard."

They all watched the priest as he solemnly anointed the bodies.

"He looks different," Albert observed. The priest, though self-possessed, appeared as if he'd aged considerably since they'd seen him the Sunday before last. The night of the storm, the enormous bells of St. Patrick's had fallen through the tower and taken half of his church building with it. Several men and women who had come there seeking sanctuary were saved when Father Kirwin himself led them over to Broadway and Fourteenth, to the Gresham mansion, just before the bells brought the roof down. It was said that the St. Patrick's parishioners would likely meet to worship with the Episcopalians or the Presbyterians for some time, and that Father

Kirwin would share their pulpit.

The priest, amiable and kind, would often come out to the orphanage to teach the children Scripture, but did it like no other man of the cloth Will had ever experienced. He didn't preach so much as just visit with them all together. When Will and Bennie Yard had climbed up on the roof of the dormitory and shimmied down the rainspout, rather than punish, Father Kirwin had sat them down to ask, "Now tell me how it was this sin came to pass."

When James Lambert was sick, as he always seemed to be, Father Kirwin, along with Sister Catherine—the orphanage's nurse—would sit quietly with the boy for hours. When a new child came into the orphanage, Mother Joseph and Father Kirwin would together find what comforted each of them most. By his casual manner, he made it imaginable that the same grace and virtue that he wore so easily was within any ordinary person's grasp. Heaven, the priest taught them, resided not up there, but here, he'd say, pointing to his heart. Though unconvinced of the universality of this notion, Will was sure it was true in the case of Father Kirwin. After the incident with the rainspout, the priest spared the rod, admitting to Will he used to do such things himself. Trying to live in accordance with God's ways, he told Will, would always be more akin to wrestling than dancing, especially for the roof-climbers and spout-shimmiers of the world.

As he watched the priest execute his duties with such conviction and under such duress, Will was persuaded he must strive to find a new set of prayer beads. His future religious exertions, even if taken up tenuously in the coming days, would require at least this—for the rosary he had been given, but had worn only for a short time, was now most certainly washing back and forth at the bottom of the ocean.

45

OLEANDERS

At the edge of the hospital district, a man with a long beard and two pieces of cumbersome luggage stood in front of his large Victorian home, offering it to the public for a meager sum. Because he spoke German, neither Albert nor Will were sure about his exact terms, but he seemed eager to part ways with it in the condition in which it had now been rendered. In the very next lot, Miss Winifred Ruby, the socialite who oversaw the dance classes at the Garten Verein, labored in her front yard—hatless, haunted, her gown in shreds. A diamond necklace hung about her neck as she worked among the oleanders in her garden, all but ignoring the three motionless bodies lying on her porch scarcely a dozen feet away. As though she feared they were suspicious characters, she shooed off the dead gangs whenever they approached to retrieve the bodies. An oak had fallen and broken through the roof of her mansion, as well.

As Will and Albert quickly passed, Miss Ruby called to them, insisting they help tend her defeated garden. "The oleanders! I'm talking to you boys!" she called after them. "Come here, right now!"

Will pushed Albert ahead and around the corner.

"The vain things charm us most," Albert said, looking back.

46

LUCAS TERRACE

Will had read a good deal of history, but the havoc found near the hospitals had no equal in his knowledge of the historical record of the new world to date. Masses of refugees crowded the streets, growing denser toward the heart of the district. As the boys moved through the crowd, they met a squinting man with a donkey looking for his spectacles and his uncle.

"My uncle's house was right over there," the man said, squinting keenly. "The currents hurled it down the lane a piece. He's now got a whole new set of neighbors." He apparently found this notion so curious that he repeated it twice. "The sight," he noted, pinching his eyes together more snugly and pointing left, then right, "it all gives one a new devotion to the orderly array of the past." He and the donkey walked a few feet, then he repeated a variation on the same theme. "Was down the lane a piece. Now, Uncle's house is right over here."

He acknowledged to the donkey that the developments in the neighborhood and his uncorrected vision both jangled him considerably. He also mentioned his uncle again. Albert nodded his head supportively to avoid any further jangling.

"Is that Lucas Terrace?" Will asked him.

"I reckon it used to be," the man said.

"It is," a hunched over woman with a bleeding hand confirmed from nearby. The squinting man shrugged next to several tons of cascaded brick. Albert looked at the man and Will looked at the woman.

"My teacher lived there," Will told the woman as Albert petted the donkey, who remained indifferent about it all.

"Life is naught," said the woman as rain began to fall.

"Yes, ma'am," Will said.

Large raindrops began to pock the brick dust around the ruins. People began to move more quickly around the wreckage, seeking cover, speaking with great anxiety concerning the return of the storm. The squinting man casually dropped the rope that was around the donkey's neck and announced he was going to find a dry place.

"Mind if we borrow your donkey, then?"

"Oh, this hay-burner?" he said, jerking his thumb toward the donkey as he held a newspaper over his head. "She ain't mine."

Albert looked at Will for their next move.

"Albert, get on."

Will took up the rope, directing the donkey in only the most general way. The animal seemed to have a certain knack for finding the best way through the crowds and around each obstacle.

"She's smart, I think," Albert said of the donkey.

It was a great relief for Will and for Albert when they finally set their weary eyes upon the St. Mary's Hospital. It stood mostly intact, though the old infirmary building next to it was largely demolished. Will glanced up at Albert, knowing they were both thinking the same thing. Their minds had become so fixed on whether the building had survived, they'd failed to consider what might have happened to the sisters inside.

47

ST. MARY'S HOSPITAL

Just a block away from the hospital, at 8th Street and Market, Will put his hand up over his eyes, shielding them against the now heavy rain as he looked for movement through the openings in the building's facade. Around him, the street thickened with still more survivors seeking care. The donkey continued to prove extraordinarily adept at handling the chaos, but it was slow-going. Albert slumped, exhausted, on her back. Holding onto the donkey's mane, Will began to detect distinct lines of waiting people, not well-formed, but there. Through the open windows above, he saw sisters moving swiftly, their black habits trailing behind them. There was a vague sense of order unfolding before him, as the injured were sorted and treated. His eyes began to glisten. They'd been fording this river for two days and had now joined the sick and the infirm, seeking, like so many others, relief at the hands of the Sisters of Charity of the Incarnate Word. There were blankets. There was food. There was company and a solution for Albert, if not also for himself.

"Look, Albert," Will said, pointing above to the busted-out windows.

Albert raised his head against the donkey's neck and tried to shout out, calling upwards as Will was doing. When no one responded, Will rolled Albert down from the donkey's back, keeping the younger boy on his feet, drawing them through the stiffening mob.

"Around back," Will said, Albert leaning on him.

The donkey followed dutifully. As they turned the corner of the building, nestling through the narrow gaps in the crowd, using the same strategies employed recently by the donkey, Will spotted the rotund profile of Sister Mary Xavier, sitting on a small stool and tending a huge, ancient, cast iron pot that bubbled over a large fire. She ladled out bowls of soup to a half-dozen young girls who, in turn, disappeared into the crowd. One offered a bowl to Albert.

"Are we here?" Albert mumbled. The girl smiled at him, touching the bandage on his head with sympathy.

"Yes," she said softly. "This is where you are."

"We made it, Albert," Will said.

"Where's Frank?" Albert asked slurring the question.

"He's with Aunt Lida and his cousins." Albert nodded, maybe remembering, maybe not. "The sisters will help us," Will said.

"Good, we need help." Albert said, taking the bowl. "Thank you for this soup," he told the girl slowly.

"Is that your donkey?" she asked.

"She was, at least for a little while," Albert replied with his eyes closed. "Much obliged, donkey," he added.

Will staggered forward with Albert to the front of the line, where one of the girls placed a bowl into his hands, as well. He stepped over to Sister X—as they called her.

"What kind of soup is this?" Will asked her.

She recognized him instantly, returning his genuine expression before breaking into a broad smile. Her eyes widened and dampened at the same time. "I call it Don't Ask Stew," she said.

The three-legged stool she was sitting on overturned as she leapt up and enveloped both of the boys in her arms, pushing them tightly together, still holding her ladle. They both dropped their bowls as she held them to her ample body, to the point that respiration became an issue. She handed the soup ladle to the girl who had spoken to Albert and told her she was taking the boys to the mother superior.

Yesterday, it was Mother Gabriel who had, along with Mother Superior Mechtilde, dispatched a sixteen-year-old hospital intern named Zachary Scott to the orphanage site at dawn. Zachary, a bow-legged youth with good sense and a great capacity to go without sleep for long hours at the hospital, had tried to make it to the mainland as the storm blew up, but had returned to the infirmary when the trains shut down. He had proved to be indispensable to the sisters all night. As light approached, Mother Mechtilde had wanted to go out to the site herself, but she couldn't be spared at the hospital given the influx of patients. She and Mother Gabriel feared all that was that left of the orphanage was for the world to hear of its end, but they sent Zachary anyway.

Mother Gabriel had sent the Order's strongest horse, Stonewall, with Sister Elizabeth on Saturday. Sunday morning she borrowed the big white horse owned by Levy Funeral Parlor & Undertakers, whose duty it was to pull the hearse. Although Zachary was skilled in the saddle, he said he'd rather take his own horse. Levy's horse was a mass of muscle from pulling the funeral hearse, a cavalry unto himself.

"No," Mother Mechtilde said. "Levy's steed is as fast as God's swift sword."

"I know," Zachary said. "I fear he may get there before I do."

"Ride as fast as the horse will go. You will not fall. He will not falter."

Mother Gabriel whispered into the horse's ear, "Haste thy mission," and briskly swatted it on the backside. The horse ran and Zachary held on, but when he arrived at the site, the beach was bare, except for a few small artifacts of catastrophe scattered half-buried in the eroded dunes.

"Maybe you didn't go out far enough," Sister Xavier responded when Zachary returned.

"I saw what was left of the salt cedar trees that stood next to the orphanage. The rest of the beach was swept as if by a broom. There were only a few pieces. Just a few pieces," he said, presenting to Mother Gabriel the small, twisted, silver cross he had noticed catching the light in the dunes. It was the one she had given to Sister Elizabeth Ryan to offer to Sister Camillus for their safety on the morning of the storm.

48

"YOU, SIR, ARE A GHOUL."

The previous afternoon, on Sunday, September 9 at 2 pm, Galveston Mayor Walter Jones, having been authorized to establish and then to chair what was christened, the Central Relief Committee of Galveston Storm Sufferers, called the committee's first meeting to order. His first reaction as he took his seat at the head of the table of the ornate and remarkably undamaged Chamber of Commerce room at the Tremont Hotel was a deep gratitude that most of those indispensable to his purposes had not drowned. The committee was organized, staffed and assignments were issued. Each member, in the last twenty-four hours, had begun to gather the needed information relative to his particular task. Each man was told to report back today, Monday, to address the two most pressing issues: water and the dead. The mayor, taking up a ball-pein hammer in lieu of a proper gavel, now prepared to call the Central Relief Committee's second official meeting to order.

To his right, William McVitie, a shipping agent, consulted with Bertrand Adoue, a round, but distinguished businessman with a goat-like beard, each making calculations on a sheet of the hotel's gilded stationary. Adoue was in charge of reconstruction. To his right was one of their main business competitors, Daniel Ripley, who had been tasked to chair both the transportation and hospital committees. Ripley, quick-witted and barrel-chested, had yesterday volunteered state senator, the Honorable R.V. Davidson, to serve as the committee's secretary. Davidson sat in front of his notes from yesterday's meeting. Next, the mutton-chopped Jens Moller was tagged to lead the labor committee, accepting on the condition that Bill McConn, editor of the Labor Journal and indispensable to ensure labor support, was sent for to be added to the Central Committee, which he was, forthwith.

The mayor had also secured the attendance of John Sealy, an unmarried thirty-year-old entrepreneur and banker who looked younger than his years, due chiefly to his parting his dark hair down the middle. He would soon grow to look more like the captain of industry he would become. But for now, as head of finance, he would utilize not his own experience, but the sound management lessons he had learned from his father, to work on behalf of the city's survivors. The Sealy family, the city's most generous philanthropist organization, carried themselves like the beneficent titans they were, and John, at this moment, was finding his titan stride.

Morris Lasker, a publisher and businessman, had been placed in charge of correspondence. His chief concern would be to convey the city's needs to the mainland. His biggest challenge would be that those receiving his correspondence could not know that exaggerating the damage to the island was impossible. He had sent messages today to both Austin and Washington by steamer to the mainland, then across the country, setting out in clear prose that the city lay in ruins, with untold loss of life, though not even Lasker yet knew what this really meant. Ben Levy took the chair next to Lasker. Levy, an alderman and the undertaker whose funeral home and mortuary was neighbor to St. Mary's Hospital, would oversee burials.

Mayor Jones gaveled the meeting to order, and after the minutes were approved from the day before took up the issue of the remains.

City Recorder Noah Allen moved immediately that inquests be held prior to the interment of the any and all remains which were located. The strings of Allen's loose white bow tie fell lazily down the front of his shirt. He also wore an ill temper which found cause for objection to most every proposal but those initiated on his own motion. A lively discussion ensued on his motion with many opinions expressed. The motion seemed reasonable and probably destined for adoption before a thin bespectacled man seated in the corner spoke up. His voice, though spare and generally undistinguished, garnered the attention of a contrarian speaking with direct evidence on a matter at the center of his field of expertise.

"It's evident there's a lack of understanding of what's occurred," the man said. "The motion is implausible. Its execution impossible."

"There will be insurance claims. The paperwork must be done," Allen responded, irritated. "Excuse me," he said. "Who are you?"

"Soper. He's a doctor," Isaac Kempner said.

"Where's Goddard?" Allen asked. "He's the coroner."

"Goddard's dead," Kempner said a little too abruptly. "Soper's here. I brought him. Know him from church. Father Kirwin told me to speak with him. I did. Here he is."

Kempner, like Sealy, was another young banker, only twenty-seven. He wore his iron-gray suit so faithfully that it had adapted itself to the rigid angularity of his frame. He sat leaning forward in his chair as he always did, his long neck and round, intense eyes routinely putting him in the middle of things. Both in the attitude of his body and in the nature of his expression, Kempner projected a calm intelligence congruent with his developing record of good judgment. If any one of them was indispensable to the island's future, it was Kempner.

"Doctor, tell them what you told me this morning," he said.

Soper stood and, in so doing, took on an appearance in harmony with every modern conception of an unfeeling machine. "The temporary morgues along the wharf and along the north side of the Strand at 22nd and 23rd have both filled so rapidly, that comprehensive identification before disposal is out of the question. More bodies lay beneath the rubble and debris. The other makeshift morgues are also reaching capacity. Each location began a list of the dead which extended many pages before they were forced to give up."

"They gave up?" Allen asked. "Who told them to stop?"

"No one told them. They just stopped."

"Under what authority?" Allen demanded.

"There is no authority in such places," Soper said evenly.

"The authority is around this table," Allen insisted. "Tell them to begin again immediately. We'll soon have the families of the five or six hundred who've perished at our doorsteps. It must be done. This is a civilized place."

"Your figures are inaccurate," the doctor said distinctly.

"This is a civilized place, Doctor," Allen repeated. "We will record the deaths properly, as we've always done after an overflow."

Soper removed his spectacles and wiped them with a handkerchief. The gesture had the effect of fixing everyone's eyes upon him, though he didn't do this for effect, but rather because he always cleaned his spectacles at the bottom of the hour.

"I've been there all day and all night. I can assure you, sir, it's not a civilized place. There will be at least ten times your figures."

The faces around the table drained white and what followed was an annihilating silence that lasted several heavy beats until Allen spoke again.

"You sir," he said, "are a ghoul."

"Hear him out, Walter," Kempner said to the mayor over the uproar which ensued, motioning to Soper to go on.

The mayor nodded and the doctor continued, first describing the scenes at the wharf and in the warehouses, then explaining in inelegant detail the dark bumps on the beach. He detailed the overnight work of the dead gangs, amidst lime, under kerosene lamps, with their camphor-soaked handkerchiefs tied around their faces. When he reached the part about the height of the stacked bodies, two of the men on the newly formed committee resigned, exited the room, then the hotel, and returned to their families.

"Six to eight thousand have perished, maybe more if you move up and down the coast and inland." No one believed him, not even Kempner, though he'd never known the doctor to be wrong in any matter of importance.

"At least one of every six souls within your city has perished. You must burn all the remains."

It took several minutes for the mayor to gavel those around the table back to order.

"If you are right, Doctor, swift and proper burials will be impossible even without identification," said Henry Cohen, a rabbi whom Levy brought to assist him.

"Correct. Ordinary methods of interment are impossible," Soper said. "Any delay will be fatal to many more. That is to say, you may do whatever it is that you may choose to do with the bodies, but eventually you will conclude that you must burn them."

This re-instituted the disorder that seemed to follow each of Dr. Soper's pronouncements. Allen castigated Kempner. Levy and Cohen began to do high-level arithmetic. Soper remained unmoved and Mayor Jones inflicted the damage to the hotel's mahogany table that remains to this day.

"I'm concerned," McVitie said, when order was restored, "I'm concerned that such a measure if pursued, even if expedient, will destroy the tenuous morale that remains."

Lasker considered the tone of his correspondence to the outside world and agreed. "We will be portrayed as devils if we do this. It will agitate the rest of the country as well, and rebuilding will rely upon their generous donations."

"Nevertheless," Dr. Soper argued forcefully.

"Ike," the mayor said, appealing to Kempner.

"The living remaining in your city will join the dead if you delay," Soper said directly to the mayor. "It's a matter of disease and geometric progression."

"Even a mass burial would be better," Adoue said.

"The earth is too saturated for a mass burial and it will take too long to assemble preparations, even if this weren't the case," Soper said. "The bodies will disintegrate into pieces in the heat if they are not destroyed forthwith."

The committee, as a group, winced. When Ripley suggested burial at sea, they all turned to Soper.

"The ocean will return most of them to the shore with all dispatch," he said, irritating even Kempner, his lone advocate.

"What if we take them far out to sea?" suggested the mayor.

Soper had calculated the mechanics of the tides already. "They will return as if a hearse had deposited them upon your beaches."

"Perhaps if we weigh them down," Moller said.

"They'll be back the following day regardless."

"Not if we weigh them down with rocks," Ripley said.

"Or chains," Moller offered.

"With rocks and chains," McConn added, as the comparative utility of both means of ballast were discussed at different points around the circumference of the table.

"How far could we take them?" Lasker asked.

"Ten miles," the mayor said. "But we'll go that far and half again to satisfy the doctor." Talk followed concerning the optimum distance and the prevailing currents and tides, but almost everyone around the table uttered some form of approval to this notion.

"Dr. Soper?" the mayor asked, and everyone's eyes returned again to the bespectacled man in the corner. Secretary Davidson's pen hung over his parchment, trembling a little.

"It pains me a great deal to say that burning them is preferable."

The problem was that it did not appear to pain him at all to say this and another tumult ensued. Jones restored order again and Adoue made a motion and it was duly seconded. As many bodies as possible would be collected by dusk Monday night, weighted with either rocks or chains or, where available and expedient, both. They would be carried out to sea no fewer than fifteen miles, and no more than twenty miles by barge to be unloaded in the Gulf. The chair called for a vote.

Dr. Soper was not a member of the committee, did not vote, and exhibited no outward sign of agreement or disagreement with the decision. Kempner nevertheless leaned over to him, looked into his eyes and recorded the lone vote against the motion.

"Isaac, how is your shoulder?" Soper asked Kempner after the meeting was adjourned.

"My shoulder? How'd you know? I think it may be dislocated."

"It is. Come see me tomorrow."

49

SLEEP

Monday evening, Albert's head was finally treated. He was, in fact, concussed, and they were gravely concerned about his eye, as well. Will's injuries were looked after, too. His wounds were more serious than he'd imagined. Some of his lacerations, when they were cleaned out, were deeper than he'd expected, and for all his concern about Albert, he'd sustained a concussion, as well, though apparently not as severe. Further, the doctors thought he might have cracked a rib, which explained his shortness of breath. After his own examination and visiting Albert, who was convalescing with a large wrap over his eye, Will was told to go to the mother superior's office. Waiting for her, he looked out of her broken windows. The sounds of cicadas and crickets, absent the night before, could now be heard. On the street below, a woman wearing a white gown trod through the mud around a dim lantern, waving her hands in the air.

"The veil is rent," she claimed every so often.

When she arrived, Mother Gabriel embraced Will, thanking God for his safety, and for Frank's and Albert's, as well, all with the same depth of grace and gratitude she might have exhibited had all the children been saved. She told Will that Albert would remain on the treatment wing, and would likely be transferred to Houston, but that Will could sleep in the prayer chapel next to the cells where the sisters resided until they made further arrangements for him.

"It will be quiet there," she said.

They walked silently up and down corridors filled with survivors in various states of physical and pastoral need, Mother Gabriel encouraging nurses and patients alike. Each hallway they traversed overwhelmed Will further.

"Rest here," she said when they reached the small chapel, lighting three candles at the front.

He crawled onto a wide kneeler that had been prepared as a bed for him. She pulled a rough gray blanket up to his chin and placed her palm on his forehead in a way that made him feel beloved. "God bless you," she whispered.

Lit mystically by the flickering orange light of the candles at the altar, the mother superior started for the door of the chapel.

"Mother," Will said. "I know I have to tell you."

"Yes. When you're ready." She returned to Will, leaned down, and put into Will's hand the small, bent silver cross she had received back from Zachary.

As soon as she had gone, Will examined the cross, placed it in his pocket and curled tightly in the blanket. Despite all he had done and all he had yet to do, he put all of it away from his mind and, because he had to, he fell asleep.

50

DARK NIGHT
OF THE SOUL

Will, gripped by an otherworldly chill, sensed he was vulnerable immediately upon stirring. Light felt an eternity away. He fought to remain perfectly still, but it seemed darker each time he blinked, and he was shivering keenly. The candles had burned out. He had been dreaming of the storm and seeing faces in the curls of the waves as the orphanage fell. Usually when he awoke from a nightmare, there was a sense of relief when he realized where he was. He did not have that now, but felt he was simply inside another chapter of the same forbidding dream.

Though he recalled he was in the chapel, it felt now as if he was under the shadow of a low thunder cloud or that a bird of prey was hovering silently above him. Then he heard a terrible chewing sound close by. He felt as though the bare chapel's walls were squeezing in on him, collapsing. Will tried to regulate his breathing silently without suffocating. His rib hurt more now that he knew about it. It hadn't bothered him much before its diagnosis. Now it hurt. There was a scent in the air, as well, first like electricity, then like tar that made his breathing even harder. It made him gulp.

He waited and calculated on his circumstances. Clement Beardshy said he once saw a ghost down the hall from his room. He said it'd given him the willies. Will had asked Clement what it looked like. Clement said he couldn't see it, only feel it. Will could only feel this, whatever it was, but it made his skin crawl and he was afraid to look up to the ceiling. He had the willies something fierce.

The trauma of the last forty-eight hours and the images of the nightmare collected in his muscles, tensing them, causing an acute pain that burrowed in marrow-deep. His stomach felt sour and his throat burned. An hour crawled by. Then another. Sweat formed, then dried, then formed again on his brow. His joints ached to stretch. His eyes swam in darkness. A panic coiled around him. Will gritted his teeth in a way which had always been conducive to reasoning out solutions for himself, but nothing emerged now. Whatever had taken over the room, he judged utilizing the small silver cross in his pocket might be a plausible strategy against it, but he was unsure if it could be weaponized. Not moving at all seemed his best defense. Another hour passed. And another. Bewildered by time's arrest, he repeated every prayer the sisters had taught him, but for the first time he could remember, he had no sense that God was listening at all.

"It's not my fault," he cried about his survival. "I was lucky."

When dawn finally came, Will sat up, looked around, and left the chapel, unsure of exactly what had occurred.

51

SAM CAULK

Tuesday, September 11

The boy standing outside the hospital, holding a cardboard box, was about Albert's age and was utterly alone. His face was as pale as death, but his eyes blazed great courage as he glanced about, lost. He tightened his mouth to stop its quiver as Will approached. Will asked if he wanted some breakfast.

"Sister Xavier is a good cook," Will told him. The boy was showing the sort of desperate resolution Will recognized in children who are trying not to cry out of pride.

"I'm not hungry," the boy finally said, looking flatly at the ground.

"Not at all?"

"I'm just tired. I'd be glad for a place to sleep. I slept in this here box last night."

The boy dropped the box. On the ground, it looked like a small coffin.

"What's your name?"

"Sam Caulk."

"I'd give you my room," Will said, "but it's haunted."

"That's alright," Sam said. "Anywhere will do."

"I'm Will. Let me get you some water and clothes. I know all the sisters. I can get you a cot at least."

Will took Sam inside the hospital and then left him for a few minutes to find some suitable clothes. When he returned, Sam was peering inside a room where a mother was nursing her baby.

"Here you go," Will said. Sam looked wolfish. "I thought you weren't hungry. We have Don't Ask Stew and milk and bread. I can get you some."

The boy's eyes filled with tears. He looked down.

"What's the matter, Sam?" Will asked.

"I can't pay, Will. I don't have any money. I can't pay for anything."

"Oh, for pity's sake," Will said. "Come on."

In about five minutes, Sam had devoured his supper, eating it like a starved animal. When he was done, Will led him two flights up the stairwell. There were no rooms available, but there was a row of available cots set up along an exterior wall below a row of broken windows. Near the end of the corridor, Will found one for Sam and sat down on the cool floor next to him.

"I was in a tree all night, Will. Me and my big brother, Calvin. It was dark and the ocean came up. The rain hurt. We just hunkered down. I heard sad folks come by in boats and barrels and chunks of houses. They were yelling at one another, afraid they'd tump over any minute. Our tree rocked and bent and so on. In the morning, I was still there, but Calvin was gone."

Will nodded his head in a way which told the boy that he fully understood. Sam maintained a look of complete resignation about what he'd said. He wasn't looking for anything that would relieve his pain but found a modicum of comfort in how Will attended his sorrow.

"The water went down inch by inch until it all flooded back into the sea. I could see that, but I was still afraid to get down. I didn't want to start what all was next, so I stayed up in that tree until they told me I had to come down yesterday. Then I came over to this hospital and found that box I told you I slept in. Then I met you. Then I had some of that soup I just ate."

Will supposed he was up to speed.

"Calvin's your brother's name?" Will asked him.

"Calvin."

Sam adjusted himself on the cot and remembered something else. "When I was up in that tree, I was tired, but when I got down, something was the matter with my knees. Every time I stumbled over anything, they would kind of tremble, like this." In mid-utterance, Sam re-enacted the shakiness he had described.

"Do you have any family you can go to?"

"No. My kin are all dead. All but my brother. A man told me that Calvin might be alive and looking for me, but the man was rhyming his words, so I'm not counting on that too much. My brother, though, was awful good to me that night. I do wish he could find me. He kept hollering for me to not get too scared and to hang on. 'Tight,' he kept saying. 'Hang on tight.' If he finds me, I'll be glad. I reckoned a hospital might be where he'd go to look for me, or maybe a church. I'll be glad."

Sam said the last word between a yawn and a sigh and was suddenly fast asleep. His face became calm, like a baby's. It made Will think of Christmas.

52

AN OLD ACQUAINTANCE

At noon, Sam was still asleep with Will watching over him. In fact, he was so still that Will kept feeling compelled to check the subtle heave in the boy's chest like a mother watching her newborn. Down the corridor, doctors, nurses, and orderlies bustled, overwhelmed as they had been for three days and would be for the next three months ahead. Sam had slept despite the ongoing commotion and the palpable despair outside the broken windows above his cot. He must be a good soul to rest so placidly. Will's body, even when inactive, found no ease, and his mind was beginning to continually turn to dark matters. He parried between vigilance and exhaustion, reacting to strange noises, sleeping lightly, waking easily. An asymmetric anxiety put him on edge. It put him off-balance, ready to fight unseen risks. This was unpleasant to feel and becoming persistent, but he found it preferable to trying to relax, which seemed to court the return of danger. Images of the night of doom, as Duell had called it, appeared before his eyes, as they had last night, with such frequency now that they seemed perpetual. The Charybdis, he thought. Remaining close to Sam Caulk and caring for him, Will realized, was perhaps not for Sam as much as for himself. Sam's presence, if not Sam himself, offered solace against the oblique but resilient self-accusation hinted at in so many of Will's lonely private dialogues.

Who was saving whom, Will thought.

Will lay down with his head against the cool floor and began to try to breathe in sympathy with the quiet rustling of Sam's lungs. Will's eyes closed. His chest began to rise and fall more loosely, as in the near silence, he began to hear subdued noises conducting through the tile beneath him. The building ticked and groaned in random patterns. A small crew of doctors and the sisters moved about, their shoes clicking far down the hall. There were murmurs and an ongoing hushed but complicated vocational dialogue filling in the background. Then, lifting himself up, Will heard a familiar cadence higher in the air. He checked Sam again, then rose to follow the vibrations.

"Wooden pillars or pilings, both or either, well braced . . ."

Will moved in the direction of the muffled voice. It was still vague and intermittent, as if it was behind a locked and distant door.

". . . the ravages of wood-destroying insects and ants. The action of dampness is stemmed by the application of not less than two coats of pine tar." Will turned to the left down a new corridor, then to the right.

"On sandy soils and in those compositions present here, brick pillars are a snare unless well set at least ten feet below the surface. Dug in dry weather."

Will listened closely as he passed each room until he stood outside a cell, its door bolted with a sturdy metal crossbar.

"Preferably in the summer, anchored at the bottom in the sand.

The force of the winds and waves wash out all the others at their present volumes. Hence the great destruction of property and loss of life."

Will recognized the voice as that of the contractor he had met the day before, still steadily assessing damage. The contractor continued speaking without abatement for many minutes. Then, a brief but weighty silence overtook the room. Will got down on his hands and knees to see if he could see under the door, as the lack of sound took on a lengthy urgency. It reached a duration which sped Will's heart with the thought he should go for help, when the voice quietly returned.

"Lordy, Lordy," the man sobbed, hushed and guttural. "Lordy, Lordy."

Will rose and put his hand on the crossbar, the blood seeming to drain from his limbs. But then he heard, slowly at first, then accelerating, the return of the contractor's low soliloquy. "There are ample . . . ample illustrations of the superiority of deep-set, poured pilings. The Ocean Club Hotel, for instance."

He seemed, Will thought, to have regained his balance.

"Note however, the rafters and upper floor joists were secured with twelve and eighteen penny nails. That won't scour. Nothing less than twenty should have been used."

Will sat back down, leaning against the door, finding something soothing in the sound. Perhaps, the contractor was gaining ground, or at least holding his own.

"Owing to this fact, not one vestige of the roof over the main building, neither the dining room nor the kitchen, remained. One and a half to twelve-inch pine plank, reaching from sill to roof, weather boarded. Sill to roof."

Will closed his eyes, his mind finding sanctuary in the contractor's melodic flow of syllables as he slowly reconstructed the city.

"Those buildings constructed by the firm of P.F. Herwig; Herwig's engineers were learned in the lessons of pilings and bracing."

At rest within his song, Will wondered what had happened to Charlie Sharkey's two goldfish, Miguel and Athena. In his widest speculations, he liked to imagine that they had survived, plucky as they were. Perhaps, they had made new friends. Perhaps, they were swimming happily in a warm spot in the deep blue sea.

53

CHIEF KETCHUM

Even before receiving orders to collect the bodies to be taken out to sea from Alderman Levy and the burial committee, the city's police chief, Edwin Ketchum, was already overwhelmed. He had lost many of his men and had been working twenty-four hours straight, accompanied by a few local national guardsmen and the weary soldiers from Fort Crockett.

In addition to the dead, Ketchum was focused on the public's safety and concerned about vigilantism, given that there had been talk of summary justice against looters. A story was going around concerning hoodlums cutting fingers from bodies to collect rings and jewels. Subsequent rumors suggested they were rounded up, sugar sacks placed over their heads, and shot. While the city's policy prescribed incarceration in such cases, Chief Ketchum, a pragmatic man, refrained from removing signs such as the one Will had seen and allowed truth and rumor to combine with one another for the maximum deterrent effect.

With respect to the dead, following Alderman Levy's instructions, the chief, along with Father Kirwin, had been instrumental in the formation of the dead gangs, issuing orders that every able-bodied man assist in the grisly task under the threat of arrest. Whiskey was kept in ample amounts at his further direction, but still, more whiskey than anticipated was required. Given its short supply, some of the gangs were now using other mysteriously fermented beverages. Given the number of dead, even temperance men had become in favor of asking the mainland for such imports, along with food and building materials, especially as time wore on and the condition of the bodies deteriorated. Some swelled to the size of barrels, others refused to bow or bend when handled. Still others turned with an appalling pliability. It was grisly work. Assignment to a dead gang was a tough beat. Whether due to the nature of the work or through the copious intake of whiskey, most who participated in these labors had, by the end of their first day, adopted the definitively glazed look which would remain a part of their countenances for weeks. Their faces grew gaunt; their complexions sallow. Some went mad. Even the rugged Fort Crockett soldiers were showing signs of imbalance.

Only Chief Ketchum was not.

54

THE BEACH

Tuesday afternoon after Sam Caulk awoke, he and Will spent an hour kicking a coffee can around the hospital grounds. Just as Will had needed to be close to Sam, now Sam it seemed didn't want to let Will out of his sight. As such company was not in Will's plans for the important business he had in mind this afternoon, Will left Sam and the coffee can with Sister Xavier who was serving lunch with the soup girls and told him he'd be right back, then set out for the beach.

Walking westward along the edge of the surf toward the orphanage site, he caught up to a group of men marching in the same direction under armed guard. Several of the men pushed enormous wheelbarrows, some empty, some filled with lime chalk. The rest carried shovels and pitchforks on their shoulders. Teague was at the head of the group.

"Mr. Teague," Will called. "Where're you headed?"

It took Teague a moment to recognize Will.

"What happened to your friends?"

"Albert, the little one that looked like a wishbone, he was concussed as I suspected. He's getting shipped out to Houston, to St. Joseph's Hospital, to convalesce for a piece I reckon, and Frank's with Lukas, Janek, Darja, Hana, Iveta, and Janicka. They're his cousins. All Bulnavics. What are you doing?"

"Working," he said. Teague looked like he had been marching like this since Will had left him. He hadn't shaved or bathed or perhaps even eaten.

"What for?" Will asked, not completely sure if he was even allowed to ask.

"Burn the bodies. Sections Sixty through Seventy."

"I thought they took them all out to sea last night."

"They came back."

Will sat down in the wet sand. The men marched on ahead a quarter mile. In the brush along the beach, he saw the dark motionless figures his mind hadn't allowed him to see before. Though another dead body brooked no alarm in him at this point, there was something more chilling about these which had been buried at sea the day before and had now returned. Bumps along the sand. They washed in and out on the tide again just like the ones he'd seen along the beach before ever meeting Teague. Will put his hand to his throat. Whatever remained of his childhood departed. Dispirited, a hot wave cast itself over him as he lifted himself off the sand.

This latest version of a dead gang now a half mile yonder began scooping up the bloated bodies with shovels and pitchforks, covering them with lime and loading them into the wheelbarrows. Will caught back up to Teague, feeling compelled to point out the half dozen bodies tangled in seaweed, tumbling in the tide along the shallows that Teague's men had just passed.

"You're missing some," he told Teague, who kept marching ahead to the next set of bumps and tangles.

"Those back there ain't ours," a man pushing one of the wheelbarrows said. He had a bandana around his face. "We're Sections Sixty to Seventy. We ain't doing nobody else's work. We've been up all night out in the Gulf on the barges with these very same bodies."

"I don't see how they could come back," Will said, falling into step with them.

"You ought to go back to town, son," an older man with a shovel told Will as he covered the contents of the wheelbarrow with a blanket.

"We went out nearly twenty miles to consign these bodies to the depths," the younger man pushing the wheelbarrow continued. "But when we got there, it was too dark to work. Pitch black. They made us anyway and poor Rosey fell overboard. Rosey was my little cousin."

"Don't tell the boy your stories," the man with the shovel said.

"Poor Rosey. His feet caught in the chains in the pitch dark. We had to weigh the bodies down with both rocks and chains. The bodies, they were in a state. We had to sweep them off the barge with these here shovels. These very ones. They brought a preacher along to say grace. I didn't close my eyes 'cause you had to mind your feet. Poor Rosey didn't mind his feet and got pulled down with all the jetsam. Down to the bird-less fathoms."

"Quiet!" Teague called out from ahead as they continued to march.

"Lord, have mercy. The bird-less fathoms. Poor Rosey. These bodies now come close to beatin' us back in. Now we're to burn 'em up. It's a sin. Lord, have mercy."

At 62nd Street far west of town, the men dumped the decomposing bodies into a large pile. By the time they poured kerosene on them to start the fires, Will had fled, running far ahead. Between 62nd Street and 70th, Teague's crew started three more fires. The burning of bodies would continue for the next six weeks both day and night.

55

A MODEST MEMORIAL

Near what was left of the salt cedar trees that had grown near the orphanage, Will found poignant relics half buried in the sand, as he understood Zachary had reported. He picked up a number of loose rosary beads along a sloping dune, then gathered up a painted piece of the statute of the Christ on the cross which had sat in the entrance to the main building, a light brown chip perhaps from his pierced side or outstretched arms. There were a few articles of children's clothes, a shoe, half a hairbrush, and a soggy linen bag with something inside. Will retrieved it and shook it off. Stitched into the bag with green thread right below a knotted drawstring were the words, Clement's Marbles.

Will looked down the beach and his shoulders sank.

The fires of Teague's dead gang bloomed skyward in black and orange behind him. There was only the blue-gray and browns of the beach negotiating with the sea ahead to the west. The now familiar acrid scent of burnt flesh wafted over him, filling his nostrils—as it would until mid-November. Will picked up an assortment of pebbles as he walked. About a hundred feet inland, he chose a suitable spot a few feet above sea level along a small plateau of light-colored rocks, which formed a little raised delta among the modest dunes in front of Green's Bayou, still within earshot of the rolling and crashing tide. It was almost impossible to believe this was the same place where he had lived and slept and run on the beach.

Will laid out the rosary beads, the marbles, and the pebbles in straight rows along the little plateau, then sat immobile on his haunches in the chunky sand, clenching and unclenching his fists, staring at them in their well-ordered columns. He felt no inclination to offer a prayer, but there was a heavy hope in his chest that what had been lost in childhood innocence earlier, might be regained in courage and fortitude in this undertaking. Perhaps he could balance out this equation and it would square. He resolved to show his work.

With the shard of the statute, he scrawled a word on the surface of the flat rock with the best craftsmanship this tool and the surface would allow. He then arranged the beads, Clement's colorful marbles, and the pebbles, one hundred and one of them, around the lonely word he had written. One tiny object for each child, each sister, and for Henry. None of it would last. He just wanted to make the effort because they all deserved something.

"What's that for?"

Sam Caulk stood behind him.

"Thunder. For pity's sake, Sam," Will said. He wanted to be mad at the boy but couldn't summon the harshness needed for reproach.

"What are you doing, Will?"

"Nothing." This was somehow an acceptable explanation for Sam.

Will didn't know why he said this. Perhaps, it was that the monument was so inadequate. He was caught between the feeling that this should be a private moment and the desire for Sam, as proxy for the rest of the world, to know and feel the quality of life that had been lived here for the many seasons it endured and as it ended last week.

Sam moved closer and inspected Will's modest memorial with earnest appreciation. The boy had a great faculty for expressing wonder and belief. Accordingly, Will saw and recognized that his young friend found his endeavor a most noble thing. Sam proceeded to touch each of the beads, each of the marbles, and each of the pebbles one by one softly and with great veneration, as he read quietly, over and over, the one word Will had written: Brave.

There was something in the way that Sam kept saying it that sanctified the effort. There was something in the repetition, his inflections, and the power of his grace that told Will that, as little durability as there was in what he had constructed, he had accomplished both something eternal and the very thing he had set out to do.

56

GIOVANNA

By the time Will and Sam had returned to the city, it seemed governed by pyromaniacs. An enormous fire blazed between 25th and 30th Streets, just south of Broadway. A huge crowd had gathered, but what drew Will and Sam's attention, as well the eyes of everyone else, was the terrible angst of a young Italian man. As long and tall as a plank, he was yelling in his native language at the leader of a dead gang and a number of Federal soldiers. The man had a horse-like face and gangly arms, which he employed to further clarify his urgencies, protesting all of what was happening. Then, switching languages, through tears, he presented to the spectators a steely argument in broken English that the soldiers had cruelly and unjustly taken his wife's body away from him. He had searched for her for several days, he explained. He had now found her. Giovanna was her name. Her body lay at the soldiers' feet near the edge of the bonfire. She was a slim, light-haired woman wearing a blue skirt.

She had a rope around her waist like someone had been trying to pull her to safety. They had announced summarily that they would now burn her. Her husband claimed curses would fall from heaven like rain if matters proceeded as they were headed.

"No," he repeated and made a series of chopping motions with his long fingers. He then lifted his strong hands to the sky in supplication. "Not right," he said, but the soldiers continued to work as if he wasn't there and were, in any event, immune to his curses. Falling to his knees with his hands at either side of his head, he begged the soldiers to stop. He reached his hands high into the blackened sky. "Why no listen?" he pleaded. "Why no hear?" As he cried, his torso bent backwards so that his shoulders touched the ground behind him. "Giovanna, Giovanna!" he exclaimed, as if it were a covenant.

The soldier in charge, a gruff sergeant with a thick mustache, finally snapped back to both the Italian man and the gathering audience that he had to discharge his duty regardless of any special circumstances of devotion. In reply, Giovanna's husband arose from the ground and waved his arms exactly as one imagines the deeply demented do in distress. His limbs were like long vines. A member of the dead gang, one who apparently knew the Italian man, approached him and tried to offer a more personal solace. This citizen's efforts made it appear for a moment that the matter would end sadly, but calmly, until the Italian suddenly pulled away from him, bolting from him and toward the fire in a bound.

"Giovanna!" he shouted again. He reached for the woman's body at the edge of the flames. The soldiers, responding almost as quickly, pulled him away, but he struck out from them again, returning to her. They were able to separate them once again, but only amidst great struggle and only for a short time. As the flames licked at his neck and shoulders, the Italian man fought with renewed ferocity each time they pulled him away, until he was making his last stand over her, landing terrific roundhouse blows against anyone who got too close to Giovanna.

In the end, he lost. He was torn away and two men lifted her body from the ground. As if she were a log, they tossed her into the flames with the others. Giovanna's husband screamed of her splendor and his sorrow and how they mixed together. As the fire began to consume her, he continued in his frenzied efforts to escape the half dozen soldiers who'd now pinned him to the ground twenty feet from the blaze. He shrieked her name again and again. Once the body was no longer recognizable as distinct from the fire itself, they released him. Unleashed, he sprinted with ungainly strides toward the flames. At this moment, Will heard a voice behind him. It breathed heavily a single word.

"Go."

The word entered Will's ears as an evil hiss, a rasp. There was now a mania in the air. Will grabbed Sam Caulk's hand instinctively, reactively, as one grabs the closest thing when riding a roller coaster at the fair. He connected the unholy voice to the presence from the dark chapel a few nights before. In solidarity, the boys both found strength to join those yelling for the running Italian man to stop. Still, all of them seemed overmatched by the chilling whisper that had urged him to go. The Italian's limbs, torqued and extended, moved in obedience to its instruction as the fire reeled him in. It all seemed scripted in cold terror with a deep inevitability. Will gripped Sam's hand even more tightly as black smoke poured over Giovanna's husband, near the edge of the pyre. Then something in the flames, Giovanna perhaps, fell. She vanished, changing the nature of the man's proposed act from one of love to betrayal and he stopped abruptly, then turned back to face the world.

Will looked over his shoulder. In fact, many in the crowd did so, but the voice that had urged him to go was gone. When they turned again to the fire, Giovanna's young widower stood in the midst of a swirling wall of smoke with his hands to his head again. Things can be altered so fast, Will thought. Like a switch at a railroad track. The man's face was blistered black and red and his clothes were singed.

One of his sleeves was actually on fire. The soldiers, though likewise spent, pulled him away from the heat as one would save a friend. The local man who knew him extinguished his fiery shirt. The Italian man then fell to the ground and wept. They tried to get him up, but he was just a bag of bones. His joints turned at peculiar angles, forsaking him as if he had no feet at the end of his long legs. When he made it to his knees, they stood back as his long torso swayed like a willow tree. His arms then stretched out, exhibiting his extraordinary wingspan. He reached impossibly high and twisted, as if in the wind, before his head fell low, as low as the human condition allows.

"You do not know what you have done," he repeated. "You do not know." He said it again and again, not for the soldiers, but, each person present knew, to God. Will turned Sam away and put his arm around the smaller boy's shoulder.

"Try not to remember that," Will said, pushing them out of the crowd as his own heart—pieced together over the last five days with a multitude of elaborate fictions about the survival of Miguel and Athena, the police chief's daughter, and with memorials constructed of marbles and lost rosary beads—tore asunder once again.

57

HOPE AT NIGHT

It was dark before they got back to the hospital. From the third floor, Will could see fires on the beach at roughly three hundred-foot intervals. It was no longer necessary to walk with a lantern at night. The sky was lit fantastically in all directions. Blazing whirlwinds dotted the horizon like bivouacs for an army of demons. The churning smoke choked the glow of the evening stars and blotted out the slender crescent of a silver moon rising in the late summer night sky. The fugitive instances of bright consideration which had characterized the day earlier had fully departed, replaced with the scent of fire, the elegy of Giovanna's husband, and the remembered sound of the raspy voice they'd heard. It all left Will, and with him Sam, disoriented.

Will learned in the coming days that it took several hours for a body to burn. The remains left on the ground at the end of the process were less a soft powder and more a coarse gravel. The ash in the air now all the time was brought home daily in one's clothes and in one's hair. Will imagined that from the mainland it looked like the city was bleeding into the sky. On the island though, it all became such a common spectacle that it created no comment. Even so, it continually weighed on both the communal mind and the collective soul most heavily. Those working the fires said little or ever would about their work. Their memories were more absorbed than received, and these men no doubt lost the sense of what they were doing after the first few days, as their duty collided with what made them human. With them, woeful patients from the hospital remarked, sometimes most shrilly, about the end of the world.

Having returned Sam to his cot, Will turned away from the window and pulled the hospital blanket up over the boy's shoulders to secure him. A few minutes later, thinking his young companion was sound asleep, Will was startled when Sam quietly spoke up.

"Will?"

"Sam."

"Will, can you help me make one of those rock decorations like you did out there on the beach?" he asked. "Calvin was brave to me."

Will felt the muscles around his mouth tighten. "Sure, Sam. Yes, I will."

"And I'll try not to recall such things as those bodies coming in on the tide and that string bean fellow. But my memory's careless. It tends to ponder on its own."

"Mine too."

"Do you ever feel bad for being alive?" Sam asked.

"Yes."

Sam turned to him and Will felt fully inspected.

"I'm glad you're my friend," Sam said as he turned back over.

"I am too, Sam."

Will sat on the cool tile floor with his knees up to his chest while Sam's breathing slowed and regulated. About twenty minutes later, he was certain Sam was fast asleep.

"Will?"

"Sam."

"Did you hear that raspy fellow behind us at the fire?"

"I did."

"I was afraid. I didn't look back, but I heard him whispering for the string bean fellow to jump on into the fire."

Will didn't speak.

"I think somehow he's behind all this."

Will felt this too.

"He's gone now. It'll be alright."

"Yeah, he's gone now," Sam repeated. There was a peace inside the silence that followed, a peace that rippled deeply into Will's spirit, like a stone dropped into a well. "I figure someday," Sam said "fine things can happen too. Just not for a while."

Every time Will had thought his sadness could not become worse, it had. And it had been a long day. So, this notion from a remarkable child who had seen the very worst under the sun, somehow provided purchase for his soul to rest upon at least for the night. In this brief respite, Will arose, turned back to the broken window and put both hands on the sill. He felt both the grief and hope of the present and the coercion it asserted over his body. Looking upwards, he saw a slice of the moon through a silent eddy of distant clouds. It lit the twisting channels of smoke thinly hovering over the beach and city in such a way that if you kept your eyes high up in the air just so, it looked as if the sky had just been filled with fireworks.

58

A LASTING SCAR

Wednesday, September 12

By Wednesday morning, the beaches bloomed with white tents. Federal troops had begun to arrive and refugees filtered through the tents the rest of the day and night, seeking rations and other supplies conducive to their continued survival. The hospitals were no less burdened.

To combat her stew's further incoherence as food supplies grew low, Sister Xavier instructed Zachary Scott to scout for essentials downtown. She considered the army rations to be for the truly needy and the less resourceful and refused them. Will, who had spent a restless morning with Sam inside the hospital, accompanied Zachary into town. Zachary, who had seen the clean sweep of the shoreline at the orphanage site regarded Will as God-touched, and readily assented to his company. They moved out together in the early morning.

"Look," Zachary said, pointing to the formerly beautiful esplanades of Broadway. The oleander bushes had been stripped bare, but it was more than that. Will looked up at him.

"No grass," Zachary said. The grass had been blown from the ground and carried away, like most of the city's other possessions. "People don't decide everything, do they?" he added.

Up one street and down the next, they didn't see a great deal of activity, but there seemed to be a great deal of preparation for activity.

"Things are afoot," Zachary said, waving at the old YMCA building. "I used to watch boxing matches over there. I saw Jack Johnson there once. Sometimes a fighter gets knocked down. He shakes his head back and forth to get his wits about him before he tries to get up."

"Of course, sometimes they don't get back up," Will said.

"True, not against Jack Johnson."

It was certainly the case that the work forces clearing the streets were more organized this morning given that they were falling more fully under military direction, but Will also noticed something else. While one encountered fewer bodies simply laying in the streets, the dead were now being handled with much less delicacy than in the first days. The soldiers, overseeing the dead gangs, were making haste in loading the human remains on drays. It was said they were no longer bound for the ocean, but would be burned. All of them. Will couldn't decide if this was necessary or a transaction that dispatched all of their souls, his included, irretrievably. It was demoralizing news. The soldiers were also using torches to set fire to the carcasses of dead horses and livestock. A great volume of smoke and soot now filled in the air, and a terrible, sugary odor began to invade everyone's senses.

Will had no desire to observe any of this work up close, but he and Zachary reached an impasse at the ridge near 43rd where a drama unfolded in a way that marked his memory with a lasting scar. The young man at the center of the event was someone who Will had seen before. Someone he'd passed on the street on occasion. Or perhaps his looks were so ordinary to have made him seem familiar when he was not. Whatever the case, he was not much older than Zachary and, by temperament if not age, this work should not have been his to do. He, like many others, wore a handkerchief doused with camphor about his nose and mouth as he labored, but what stood out about him was how he was swatting fanatically at the swarming flies around him when they arrived. This and the handkerchief gave him the appearance of a bandit being tormented by retributive spirits. The ground beneath his feet was giving way and his flailing soon caused him to stumble. To arrest his fall, he stabbed his shovel into the mud, but it fell flat and he tripped over it, tumbling to his hands and knees. On the ground, the young man removed his gloves and handkerchief such that his pale hands and face stood out starkly against every remaining inch of his mud-splattered body. He blew his nostrils out, one, then the other, then brought his hands up to his ears as if to keep the day from seeping inside. Lifting his head to the blue sky above, in a voice that mixed resolution and exhaustion, he made a noise that gave evidence to the notion that his youthful constitution was inadequate for this task.

"You can't make me do this no more," he said bowing his head then repeated it more loudly and emphatically again. He next turned his head to the side and heaved. His body wrenched and shuddered, but there was nothing inside of him. "No more," he gasped, shaking.

The lead soldier, a Federal with a three-day beard, stepped toward him, a hand on his holster. The soldier, a head taller than everyone else on the crew, moved aggressively toward the disintegrating youth.

"You can shoot me if you want," the boy told him. "I will not do this anymore. I can't."

The soldier bent at the waist and examined him as he would a bad dog. He grabbed a shock of the boy's wet hair and jerked his face upwards, looking into his eyes as if he was measuring something specific on which to make a judgment. With a word, the lead soldier called his uniformed regiment into formation. Six soldiers sent their own shovels slashing deep, straight into the wet mud. The men, formidable, moved together in unison, then took up their rifles, which were stacked upright in a conical fashion nearby. Metal clicks sounded as they shouldered their weapons and assembled tightly around their human target sinking into the ground. The lead soldier was not measuring anything anymore. All latitude was gone. He unholstered his own pistol and with his men now encircling the kneeling figure, he issued his order.

"Load ball cartridge."

Another series of metallic clicks.

Will and everyone else held their breath.

The young man's head fell further, his forehead touching the ground. He seemed just a child now.

"Take aim!"

Will couldn't look, but heard someone call out, "Stand down."

Everyone looked around except for the boy.

"Step aside, sir," the soldier told Chief Ketchum.

"He's the chief of police," someone in the crowd said.

"I don't care. Step aside."

Chief Ketchum removed his blue cap and placed it under his arm at his side.

"Stand down," he said again at a lower volume, but with more gravity.

"This is our island," shouted another in the crowd.

Behind the chief, the boy put his hands flat on the ground for support and began to unsteadily arise. He next put his hands on his thighs, stood up, and looked at the soldiers around him with an extraordinary mixture of pity and hatred. Will and Zachary watched as he reached his hands forward as if begging the referee to stop counting, like one of the stunned YMCA boxers they'd talked about earlier.

"Just give me a drink," the young man said, gasping for breath, spitting on the ground, then taking up his shovel. The chief and the soldier regarded one another tensely for a moment before the chief stepped back, allowing the soldier to save face. Responding in kind, the soldier motioned for a bottle of spiked wine and holstered his pistol. Chief Ketchum nodded respectfully at all the Federals making peace, then removed a crust of bread from his pocket. He next took the wine from the soldier, nodded again in a gentle fashion and moved toward the young man he had saved, handing him first the bread and then the wine.

59

A SCRAP OF CLOTH

The events involving the young man, Chief Ketchum, and the Federals left Will and Zachary without words for some time. As they quietly moved into town, Will decided to ask Zachary more about what he had seen out at the orphanage site.

"Just gone," Zachary responded, adopting an apologetic posture. "Little things in the sand, but I didn't have the heart to sift them all out."

Zachary saw he wanted more.

"Just some clothes," Zachary added. "Part of a dish. The little silver cross I gave to Mother Gabriel. She had given it to Sister Elizabeth the morning of the storm for protection."

Will felt it, heavy in his pocket. Knowing Sister Elizabeth had carried it, if only for a while, seemed to transmit to it an additional weight.

"I heard someone found a chalice on the mainland across the bay," Zachary said. "They think it's from the orphanage, but I didn't see anything like that. When I turned that big horse around, that was the worst part." Zachary swallowed hard. "Going back. Knowing I had to tell them."

Will started to say something about the cross but was afraid he was going to cry and thought better of it. Zachary put his hand on Will's shoulder in a way that both steadied and broke him at the same time. Will took a deep breath and shook his head.

"Look, here comes Mr. Ford," Zachary said.

Many of those wandering here along the edge of downtown near the ridge had still not surrendered to the scope of what had happened. Fathers searched amid the ruins. Children were waiting at corners looking closely at the faces of those who passed by on the backs of the wagons. Will had taken to calling these folks, searchers. They paced the streets, their heads moving all around. Most found no answers, and those who did stumble into answers were almost always devastated again. Upon finding the body of a loved one or a neighbor, they most often looked straight down, moaning with harsh, guttural sounds in the language of primitive grief. In other formulations of the same vocabulary, sometimes they remained purely silent, but their shoulders shook. Other times a sharp wail escaped from the depths of their lungs and rang up into the sky.

In most cases, the efforts of the searchers collapsed under their own weight. The vigils of mothers did likewise. The anxiety of terrible suspense was beginning to give way to the desire for any tenable excuse for closure on the question of who had survived and who was gone. This seemed especially the case once word emerged that the bodies were to be burned.

Mr. Ford was a middle-aged English professor who Will had seen at the hospital yesterday with supplies for the infirmary and many questions. Today, he was bringing food and drink to the dead gangs, utilizing the brief moments of their restoration to ask them about his lost son, Early. His methodical search had yielded nothing thus far, but yesterday he'd caught sight of a ragged shred of cloth in the oily mud that was vaguely reminiscent of the jersey Early was wearing the night of the storm. Mr. Ford had announced that should he not find his son today, it was his intention to bury the scrap of cloth tomorrow, as proxy for his son's remains, in the cemetery next to the church in which he and Early had worshiped. He had already commissioned Mr. Ott, the city's premier stonecutter, to craft and set a polished stone within the churchyard to mark both the occasion of the burial and the grave efforts he had made to find his boy. Industry of this sort had continued to prove merciful in fording the mind and heart across the torrential river of pain, just as plausible fictions helped mourners avoid the atrocious obstacles between the questions that remained and the lack of answers available.

"Do you boys need some water?" Mr. Ford asked Will and Zachary. They both held up and shook their full canteens in response.

"Much obliged," Zachary responded. "But save it for those doing the hard work."

Mr. Ford came over and opened a book in which he kept a photograph of Early, and showed them both the picture and the segment of the clothing he'd found.

"We'll look for him, Mr. Ford," Zachary said. "We'll keep looking."

"Thank you, boys," he said, replacing the photo back in the book and closing it. Will saw the title of the volume he carried. It was the book about the white whale that little Clement Beardshy had placed on his chair each evening to reach his food on the dinner table at the orphanage.

"Faith, like a jackal," Mr. Ford recited, "feeds among the tombs. From these dead doubts, she gathers her most vital hope."

"Yes, sir," Zachary said.

The professor moved forward toward the next dead gang.

"He looks a little better than he did yesterday," Will observed.

60

DOWNTOWN

Downtown merchants were sweeping the streets in front of their spaces in an exercise that seemed almost luxurious, almost humorous given the devastation all around them, but the spirit of commerce was breathing life back into the city. The return of routine staunched the effect of the calamity like the clotting of blood. Deeper into the business district, sheets and bedspreads of every color hung from clotheslines. Carpets and curtains were pinned up along damaged streetlights as if some amateur theatrical production was about to begin. The citizenry could just have easily become a collection of primitive tribes battling each other for the scarcity of supplies available. Instead, things like extortion, because they were almost entirely unseen, did not work where they were practiced.

Zachary entered the butcher shop and found Mr. Knight, who received Sister Xavier's long list of needs with equanimity. Despite his limited supplies and ability to collect more on the desperate open market, the burly butcher folded, as he typically did under the sister's demands. He was a good and generous man. Meanwhile, Will wandered the neighborhood outside.

Mr. Hardin, the grocer whose shop was situated next to Knight's Fine Meats, was selling what he marketed as 'surprise' canned goods for a penny a can, as their labels had washed away. Will moved farther down the street, curious about what sort of buildings had withstood the wind and water and which ones had not. Artillery Hall, stoutly built, stood largely undamaged. The Hebrew synagogue was damaged moderately but stood firm. The Baptists had not fared so well. Rabbi Cohen had given his Christian neighbors permission to worship in the synagogue on their Sabbath, as it did not coincide with his own. Ball High School had shed its roof and the Grand Opera House was largely destroyed. The Bath Avenue School would require extensive repairs and City Hall was unusable. Many of the telegraph poles around town still stood though askew with their wires down. Restaurants, even those with little fare, were open. Hotels, even those which had sustained considerable damage, were full.

The Strand, which had been the commercial capital of the state, now resembled an enormous common market. Every open space was occupied by books of records and other papers drying in the noonday sun. Scrappy businessmen and clever industrialists made ad hoc partnerships to pool resources, share space, and split future profits in uncommon ways. Each acted independently but correspondent with what he viewed as advantageous to his prospects. Will, listening to the commerce, feeling its energy as he walked, gazed down the length of the city and watched the future appear right in front of him.

61

REECE, BAMSCH, AND PEARSON

During summers, Will shined shoes at the Tremont Hotel and when he had money to spend, traded at Pearson Mercantile. Mr. Pearson stocked useful apparel and had a son, Edgar, who was in Will's class with Grace and Miss Thorne. Approaching the entrance, Mr. Bamsch, a plumber, stood astride shards of broken glass in front of Pearson's blown-out storefront. Pearson and Mr. Reece, a brick mason, thick-limbed and patient, as was befitting his trade, were at work nearby, hammering out a bent metal sign which currently read, . . . rson Mercantile. Whenever a carnival was in town it was either Reece, Bamsch, or Mr. Ott, the stonecutter, who would battle the butcher, Mr. Knight, to win a ridiculous prize celebrating their prodigious strength. Will picked up on their conversation in mid-course between hammer blows.

"He brought the family he saved into the Tremont," Reece told the other men. "Then he climbed out a window and leapt back into the water to rescue more."

Reece identified the man he was talking about as Nelson Pierce, a popular contractor who had, after this leap, continued on his mad flight throughout the city, saving an untold number of its inhabitants.

"He swam a web of ropes across a dozen streets for people to hang onto. He saved scores."

"Where's he now?" Pearson asked.

"Still at large, I imagine. Heard he's all about town. Lost his mind, babbling about how the engineering won't scour, saying the city could've withstood the wind's velocities had it been built more strictly to code."

"I saw that man," Will interjected. "He's at St. Mary's. In the nervous wing."

"Will!" Pearson embraced him robustly. "We heard the orphanage collapsed. We feared you dead."

The other two men patted Will's shoulders with the sort of tender emotion that a week before was wholly uncharacteristic of them but had now been adopted within their natural range of expression.

"Where'd you get those boots?" Pearson asked. "You're mis-shod."

"Aunt Lida gave them to me. I think they're Lukas's."

"Wait here," Pearson said and disappeared into his wrecked store.

"I go to school with Mr. Pearson's son, Edgar," Will told the mason and the plumber.

"Pearson's boy and family survived. He hasn't heard from his parents though. They're infirm. Live out at Virginia Point."

Pearson returned with a box. "Take these, Will. I'll tell Eddie I saw you. He'll be much relieved."

"Thank you," Will said, opening the box to find new trousers, a shirt, and new boots, as well as a pair of socks—all a little damp to the touch.

"Have you heard anything about Miss Thorne?" Will asked.

"No," said Pearson. "Nothing."

Unable to speak to Chief Ketchum earlier after the drama downtown, Will wanted to circle around and ask Mr. Pearson about the police chief's family too, but found he could not. Instead, he promised to pray for Mr. Pearson's parents and pay him for the gifts as soon as he was able. Pearson adjusted his glasses, waving off the offer for payment and acknowledging his appreciation for the sacred prayers with a subtle, but explanatory nod.

62

THE RED CROSS

Will could have returned to Zachary at this point, but instead turned toward the four-story warehouse at the corner of 25th and the Strand where the National Red Cross had established its headquarters. It buzzed with activity as the Central Committee's next meeting was scheduled here for two o'clock. Believing it imperative that he make a record of what had become of the orphanage, Will pushed his way through the throng of refugees coiling around the building in tightening reticulations. They pushed against the doors, tapped on the windows, and sought entry at every conceivable point of ingress. Each member of the teeming crowd apparently felt a similar urgency with respect to his or her own personal petitions and grievances. At one window, a sunburned woman called Hattie reported to Will that she had floated far out into the Gulf, halfway to South America, only to return to shore, all on part of a ceiling from a house.

"My neighbor's boy keeps calling it the night of doom and he's not far off. After all that, I'm not waiting in line," she insisted. She looked around, picked up a pebble, and threw it at the window. "They got another thing coming," she added.

She told Will also that she was now very thirsty and suffered severe blisters on her feet, as well. Hattie then motioned toward three men on the other side of the window, the thick glass of which was shattered in place in a spider-web pattern. She pointed inside, insisting these important men were certainly considering her immediate needs which, she told Will again, included her unwillingness to wait in line. Will craned his neck to see and told her she must surely be right.

She was, in fact, correct in the most general sense. Clara Barton of the National Red Cross had sent her nephew, Stephen, to Galveston earlier in the week as soon as word of the storm had reached Washington D.C. As Hattie had roughly surmised, Stephen Barton was working on all she required on the other side of the glass. Appearing calm—as was his nature—giving instruction with clarity—as was his habit—he was in the midst of explaining to two of the mayor's aides the systematic methods the Red Cross had followed over the last quarter century when faced with disasters such as this. What Barton revealed to no one but his aunt, was that in his experience, nor even likely hers, there had never been a disaster such as this. Often, the first report of such a catastrophe was exaggerated. This one was not.

"The most immediate problem," he explained to the mayor's twin aides, "is lack of sanitation. The bodies. That's first. Then water, food, then clothing, then housing. The family is the primary unit of treatment."

Hattie and Will watched outside as two of the men scribbled furiously and the other continued to talk.

"Supplies," he said, setting out the Red Cross's philosophy of necessity, "are rationed according to need—not loss." The mayor's aides would brief the Central Committee on these lessons in an hour. "It's not tomorrow that we must act, gentlemen, but today."

Holding a fountain pen tightly, Barton spoke with the sort of conviction that pushes plans spoken into the air inside toward fruition and reality outside. "My aunt has assured me more supplies will come, but disposition of what we have today must be made to accomplish the greatest degree of immediate relief. Think in terms of today, boys, not tomorrow," Barton continued.

He explained that the Red Cross aimed to merge its operations into the existing local relief structure as it emerged, so that soon the Central Committee would be relieved of such immediate needs and could focus on rebuilding.

"Tell the mayor his committee should transfer authority to the Red Cross for the entire work of distribution of food over the next week. Clothing, supplies, let us handle all of it. You must begin to think in terms of reconstruction. You must speak of reconstruction, of restoration as soon as possible or people will leave hopeless. They won't return."

Will and Hattie were impressed by how this man continued to emphasize his points with vigor using his fountain pen, stabbing it into the air with evident purpose.

"As needs are met and people learn of plans to rebuild, they'll see they have a future here. This is imperative."

Stephen Barton had struck quickly, as his aunt had urged in her initial instructions before he left Washington. She had reinforced this same message to him by telegraph again just the day before. Lines of authority, she told him, must be established immediately while good will was at its highest level. Over the last few years, especially since the great Jonestown flood eleven years before, Stephen had seen in the aftermath of these disasters that if a hierarchy of command could be established before his aunt arrived, miracles of efficiency ensued when she did. With the application of her actual presence and her personality, the logistical issues and logjams that invariably arose in every relief effort were easier to solve. With an organization in place, through her sheer will to move people and get things done, recovery advanced with remarkable swiftness. Aunt Clara, who turned seventy-eight on Christmas Day of last year, had in fact arrived this morning, but was now recuperating from her grueling travels across the way at the Tremont. She suffered from a case of what she colloquially called, the gripe. Stephen told the men she would be ready to meet the mayor and the committee in the morning, assuming the gripe subsided.

While Aunt Clara's health was a concern, her moral authority was augmented, not decreased due to her age and infirmity. Stephen knew her command was irresistible, her expertise unassailable. Wherever she went she was, to put it simply, obeyed. He had seen time and time again in these situations, local men—strong and independent leaders—profess that they had no intention of being ordered about in their own city by an aged nurse. As soon as she arrived, though, they always quickly fell into line. Even nearing eighty, his aunt was a force of nature. A legend. Likewise, he had seen that wherever she went, her demeanor came as a revelation to local women. As they began to administer the relief stations, the men moved on to physically rebuilding. The women in these circumstances rapidly concluded that they were superior to the men in administering the government. In this way, it was invariably the case that after the Red Cross left a city or a region, a different and favorable dynamic took hold, one of a distinctly feminine bent.

As the mayor's two aides left the company of Stephen Barton inside the building, outside, Hattie, placated for the moment, told Will that the blisters on her feet already felt much better.

63

A MAN CROSSES
THE STREET

Leaving Hattie and her miraculously healing blisters, Will, concluding it impossible to get in, moved back through the crowd against the grain. Across the block, a man, square-jawed and with a long, regal neck and bright, round eyes, crossed the street. He tried to don his iron-colored dress coat as he walked, but his shoulder was uncooperative.

"Can I help you with that?" Will asked, helping him with his jacket so that he could negotiate his arm through the sleeve. The man winced in pain.

"Much obliged, son," he said. He shook his shoulders and his coat settled. The man looked even more distinguished now that he was fully dressed. "You alright? You look vexed," he said to Will.

"The mayor's meeting back there with his committee," Will replied. "But no one can get in. Certainly not people like me and Hattie."

"What do you need, son?"

"I just need to tell them something."

"What's that?"

"I'm from St. Mary's," Will said in a unity of bitterness and pride. "The orphanage was carried out to sea and sank down to the deep. Into the hoary depths," he added. "All were drowned except me and Frank and Albert." The man's bearing changed. His eyes were a sermon of solemn sympathy. This humbled Will, mid-explanation. "So, there's no orphanage, but we're going to need a new one, though Duell says there's not as many children as there were before."

"I'm afraid that's true."

"But I met two new ones right off, Althea and then Sam. Not to mention me and Albert. And they ought to know all that. But they're too busy dropping the bodies in the blamed ocean. It's sacrilegious," Will said piously to the stranger having resolved the tension he felt earlier which pitted necessity against his soul. "No one cares," he concluded.

"It's difficult. Impossible really, but there may be no alternative," the man said.

"Only the St. Mary's sisters care, but most of them are dead now."

"The committee's meeting with Clara Barton tomorrow. She cares. Orphans are practically her whole business. She arrived this morning."

"She's too old and sick to do much I heard tell."

The stranger bent down on one knee and shook his head, animating his features with considerable empathy. "Miss Barton can do more than all of us combined. The whole country will care when they know she's here. She'll tour the city. She'll make arrangements for those like you. She'll make pleas in her own pen. Carnegie and Standard Oil. Hearst too. They're all sending money already. She's staying at the Tremont. She's there now."

Will, unconvinced, turned back to the condensing crowd gathered closely around the building. His eyes landed on a distinguished gentleman in a top hat at the top of the steps near the entrance. "Who's that?"

"Sealy," the stranger said.

"The hospital fellow?" Will asked.

"Yes. Well, his son actually. The hospital is named for his father, but this building is his. He's donated it for use by the Red Cross. A good man."

"How about the short man on the big white horse? How's he getting in?"

"Ben Levy. He's an alderman. That is a big horse."

"The undertaker? He's the one who wanted to sink all the bodies with rocks or chains. I don't know which. Now he wants to burn them all."

"He doesn't want to," the man said, pulling at his starched cuffs. "Levy's in charge of all this, not by choice, I assure you. He's doing what he must." The man seemed utterly self-possessed, humble, yet so effortlessly sure about everything around him.

"It's unholy," Will argued vaguely. "Whose ward are you in?"

The man looked at Will squarely. "I guess I'm in Kempner's."

The Central Committee had formed the city into twelve wards and empowered a single administrator over each.

"Kempner's," Will said looking down and shaking his head. "Bad luck. Me too." Will had heard that although Kempner's ward was ordered more meticulously than the others, Kempner himself was staying behind the scenes at the customs house, his headquarters, issuing orders. "Nobody's even seen him for a while," Will said.

"Perhaps, he's been too busy to get out," the man said. "Perhaps, he's been assembling a team to multiply his work."

"Sounds like he wants everything to be his own way."

"Well," the man allowed, "people say he can be stubborn."

Will recalled Sister Elizabeth once saying Mr. Kempner cared little for how he was viewed by the citizenry, but rather simply did things the way he felt he ought.

"Bull-headed's what I heard."

"That's what his own wife says," the man replied.

"Figures. Do you know him?" Will asked, gratified that he had stumbled upon someone with whom he could speak with such cordial frankness.

"Do I know him?" the stranger asked.

Will, not waiting for his response, continued. "I've heard he's spoken warmly about martial law in these committee meetings," Will rushed on. "About seizing the food in his ward."

"I'm sure he'll see that everyone gets paid a fair price. There are the wholesale grocers, the flour mills and the dairies."

Will mocked the man's evident naivety. "Expect he's denying food unless you do exactly what he says. I've heard his ward's soldiers are guarding all the food so no one can get any."

The man responded with the same manner of peace that characterized all he had said so far. "In cases of unconstrained talk," he said, "ignoble themes endure even when unconfirmed. Has anyone you know been denied food?"

"No, but I've got food from the sisters, so I'm fine. I'm just worried about everyone else, like poor Hattie. The hospital's full up with the infirm and sorrowed."

"No able-bodied man is given anything unless he volunteers to work. That's the policy. We need everyone to help clear the ward."

Perhaps the man had a point, but Will thought this notion stretched the meaning of volunteer pretty thin.

"He may be less fair than others," the man continued. "But it's a difficult ward. Most of the telephone and telegraph poles are down. The wires are down everywhere. The bridge is down. There're big ships marooned in the shallows. The elevators in the warehouses are unfit. The electric plant, the cotton factory, both collapsed. You say you're from St. Mary's?"

"Yes, sir. My name's Will."

"You've got shelter at the hospital, Will?" the man asked, taking a black notebook and a pencil from his jacket. He grimaced again with the movement, then began to flip through the notebook slowly.

Page after page was filled. In flashes, Will read some of the words in the man's fine handwriting as he flipped the pages.

Order by dray load: flour, coffee, potatoes. Feed from central point.

He turned the pages and Will read a few more lines.

128 unknown female: soiled pink dress, approx. twelve years old.

He turned a few more pages.

456 unknown male: approx. 35 years; old pocket knife engraved AJ.

A few more pages.

617 unknown female: approx. 60, blue shoe.

The pages went on and on.

789 unknown woman: approx. twenty-five; body scarcely marked in any way; gray wool socks.

The man finally found a blank sheet and wrote something on it. Tearing it out, he folded it in half with precision and gave it to Will.

"Yes, I've got a roof over my head," Will said, accepting the note.

The man returned the black book to his pocket with another sharp, painful expression.

"Will, do this for me. Speak to the sisters tomorrow. Make a list of what's needed and come Friday. Arrive at the customs house at ten in the morning. Give them your list. I'm sure it can be provided directly."

"How will I even get in? The lines."

"Just walk in the front door," he said. "A lot of people need help. You'll have to be a little patient. Show them your note. They'll let you through."

Will concluded this stranger, like the contractor, was suffering from some sort of delusion common to those in the aftermath of catastrophe, sending folks all over town to different wards, promising implausible solutions to intractable problems.

"Just walk in the front door?" Will questioned. "They'll just let me in?"

"They will if they're following instructions. Customs house. Friday. Ten. Ask for the ward chair."

"Right," Will said. "How do you address a ward chairman anyway?"

"Most people call him Ike. That's his name."

As the man headed toward the building, Will unfolded and looked at the note. In a penmanship which Will associated with being invited to a fancy ball at the Garten Verein it said: Attn: Miss Sara Wright/for St. Mary's Hosp. Fri., 10 a.m.

64

THE OLD WOMAN
AT THE TREMONT

Upon leaving the Red Cross Building and the earnest stranger, Will walked to the Tremont just a few blocks away to see if his shoeshine kit, the vocational tool of his primary source of income, had survived. The staff at the Tremont welcomed Will like the prodigal son or some other character making the most unlikely, but joyful of returns. After a series of warm embraces and the exchange of stories, Will asked the bell captain, Felix, about his shoeshine kit. Felix pointed him up to the second floor and Will bounded up the muddy stairs to the doors of the hotel's exquisite public parlor, the most likely storage place. He knocked, then waited, then nudged opened the double doors.

An old woman dressed severely in black sat erect at a writing desk near the corner window. A delicate white bib formed into a high collar about her neck. She held a delicate white handkerchief which matched the cuffs of her blouse. Her dark gray hair, parted severely in the middle and pulled back tightly, formed a stern bun in the back. Her face was wide, her brow furrowed, a deep crease between her light eyebrows. Fifty years ago, she had probably been quite attractive.

"Excuse me, ma'am," Will said, so as not to alarm her. She turned toward him calmly, her pen poised above the inkwell on the desk. He saw she was not one who startled easily, probably not at all. Her eyes were a clear, delicate, sea blue. Will was caught up in them at once.

"Go back to Washington?" she huffed to the room more than to Will. She put the pen down on the desk with a sharp clack. "Nonsense. God forbid."

Will looked behind him for the person she was addressing.

"Are you under par, ma'am?"

"A case of the gripe," she said, her voice purely American. "Nothing more."

"Sister Elizabeth used to give us dill licorice for the gripe," Will said.

"I saw you yonder through the window by the Red Cross just now, didn't I?"

"Yes, ma'am. I was trying to tell them. Our orphanage was carried out to sea and sunk. As I just told that man out there, it sunk deep into the hoary depths. We need to start another one up directly for Sam and Althea, not to mention me and Albert. Frank said we ought to start to collect one another."

"You're an orphan? Come to me, young man."

Her presence dictated obedience. "Yes, ma'am," Will said, looking through the large patched up window with her. "I'd been an orphan for some time before the cyclone. Now I'm one even more." He moved his eyes across the city. "It looks even worse with some elevation."

"It defies exaggeration. Do you have shelter?"

"You should look south. It's even worse. No one's exaggerating. I'm staying at the hospital. The St. Mary's one. I'm not contagious. I know the sisters. I'm staying just off the nervous wing with a boy named Caulk, who I mentioned before."

"Yes, well," she said. "I need to look south tomorrow."

She picked up the pen again, looking back out over the ruins. The ivory-colored sheets of the Strand's market billowed slowly below, surely bringing to mind a score of surrender flags from her distant past.

"The city fiendishly laughs at all tame attempts of words," she said and scratched out the words on paper. "The churches, the great business houses, the elegant residences, the culture, the former opulence." She looked out the glass, her fine eyes darting from point to point. "The modest little homes, all in splinters. It's all more than can be absorbed."

"I've been absorbing it going on four days now and I still can't believe it," Will said. "Toothpicks and kindling."

The delicacy in her eyes emoted all the essentials contained in sadness. She seemed to have seen everything and all things attendant to it. "If the storm didn't completely raze the city," she said, "it did something very much like it."

In just a moment of watching her take it in, Will felt a complete connection to her. She exuded an almost tangible sense of good will.

"Here," Will said, reaching in his pocket. He believed it would make her feel better and it was all he had in lieu of dill licorice. The silver cross seemed to call out for her. It seemed to know her. "Zachary told me it was given to one of the sisters when the storm started up. She was called Sister Elizabeth Ryan. She was the bravest person I've ever known. It was for protection. It didn't work, but all the same, the way she died . . ." Will realized what he was about to say sounded like something Albert would say, but the profound manner in which the old woman was inspecting the silver and the shape made it seem right. Its qualities entwined with his words. "She died into life, not from it."

She put down the pen again. Her hands looked useful even at rest. "Mercy, you're from the orphanage out on the beach," she said, turning all of her attention to him. "They thought all of you were lost."

"I did too for some time out there."

"Would you please tell me what happened?"

As Will aged, he would go long stretches, years even, without speaking of the storm at all. However, even in these intervals, his mind still conversed with his heart about it, especially at night. Especially as his summers disappeared. It washed back and forth in his memory like the perpetual tide of his island home. When he did speak of it aloud, it was out of a sense of duty to the sisters and the children who perished. But he would never tell it in full as he did to the old woman suffering from the gripe at the desk in front of the cracked window overlooking the confounded city. He told her of little Clement Beardshy, of the Faulkies, of Maggie, and the Zarkereys. He spoke the sisters' names and when he came to Henry, he spoke in a low voice that he thought befitted the heroic. He cursed himself inside when he couldn't remember all ninety of the children's names, though it would be miraculous to remember all of them at once, but the woman in black in the public parlor at the Tremont didn't mind. She listened to Will's story in full, as the delicacy of her heart and the severity of the events her heart received from him blended together. Her attention to him, the way she followed, entering his story silently and walking alongside, offered back to him something that felt like the leading edge of healing. She nursed his soul, listening as if he was the only one who had ever suffered.

65

DEAD LISTS

Thursday, September 13

Will set out before dawn for the Ketchum's home again with the resolve of a complete decision, but still little in the way of a plan. He moved inland as the sun approached the horizon, thinking of the John S. Ames and what he'd seen under the water as the storm abated. He hadn't told the old woman at the Tremont this part because it seemed so far-fetched. He tended even to doubt it himself, especially in the broad daylight, but in the pre-dawn darkness that surrounded him now, and likewise in the twilight of the early evening, his memory of what he'd seen became more persuasive. Within the moments of half-light during which night turned to day and the day turned to night, he became briefly as sure of it as he was right now. There was something in the liminal sky that told him what the truth was or at least what it might be.

He wasn't sure what it might mean that he'd seen the children who had perished, the trolleys, the oleanders, all inside a light suggestive of eternity under the waves, but he had seen it. He had seen the sisters, the pier, and the Pagoda in the same warm vibrancy. And, most troublingly and comforting, he had seen exactly what Albert and Frank had seen. The usually rational and sober Frank been ready to dive through the same waves which, just a few hours before, had tried to kill him just to reach it all. Albert had almost drowned after surviving a whole night of near drowning to be with the figures under the water. He had never heard of hallucinations that were simultaneously shared. The only explanation he could derive was that this world had cracked open in the cataclysm and another sort of midway place had briefly slipped in. To untangle this notion seemed crucial to making the remainder of his life greatly more effective, though it also seemed presently beyond his best abilities of comprehension.

In any event, the sun was up now. The lavender of the pre-dawn was burning off and what he surveyed ahead had to be addressed with a more hard-nosed pragmatism. There were check points and troops. Martial law had been declared and its evidence was now in front of him. He turned and tried another way into the neighborhood, but another string of fires and more troops blocked the way. He moved back toward to beach to see if he could make some progress west, then cut back into town, but found that wouldn't work either. It was becoming impossible to move from ward to ward unless one's legitimate business could be succinctly stated to professionally skeptical soldiers, and Will, despite the imperative of his mission, lacked a persuasive public case for this errand. When he turned back, retreating to the beach alone, he felt most hollow.

Taking off his new boots and socks, Will dug his toes into the sand like he used to do in the shadow of his home. Watching the gulls float mystically still on the air above the water in front of him, his breathing slowed and his soul, too, seemed to shed velocity. A gull caught his eye as it turned, swooping down toward him, flying through the soot in the air and over the sand. It sailed over the new gray gravel gathered in piles along the beach and landed with a short hop a few feet from him, a twig in its beak, looking at him quizzically.

Sam's words entered Will's mind and he recovered himself. He still moved and ate and would one day dance and love and see things the lost wouldn't. There could be fine things ahead. Looking out at the sea, he realized it could so easily have been otherwise. It left him shaking. He blinked away tears and was overcome by a vast gratitude as the gull approached him tentatively, as if recognizing his vulnerable state. They regarded each other, remaining perfectly still for a moment. The bird had the gray markings between its eyes identical to the one that had questioned him from the top of the mast of the John S. Ames coming up on a week ago.

"You following me?" he asked. The seabird alighted, elevating into the open sky, rejoining its brethren without reply. As it rose, out at the horizon, the sunlight angled and flashed across the ocean in a transfiguring way. Time passed. It was hard to say how much, but within it, Will felt an immense sense of well-being.

He arose, knowing the islanders he would meet today, though remaining vulnerable like him as they clasped tightly to silver lockets, scraps of cloth, picture frames, and other small and lovely possessions, would begin to take up again the shared tasks of life. Their stories would continue to be so poignantly and powerfully rendered to Will that it would become clear to him that, although enduring loss was one of life's most crucial themes, seeking sunlit hope in its wake was also one of its most crucial duties. He suspected that if you could simply hold both sides of this contradiction, the dark part and the light and lift them skyward together, a sort of elevation might follow. Redemption, he reckoned, resided somewhere within the interior of sorrow, or was at least on offer there.

Leaving the beach, Will met an old Scot, named McLaren, with tremendously large ears who told him of his good wife who had saved his granddaughter from drowning. He'd been separated from them early in the night, but his wife swam for three miles with the granddaughter and another little girl, a stranger, clinging to her. The granddaughter and the other little girl, he told Will, were now at the customs house eating dry crackers. His wife, though, had died of injury or perhaps exhaustion, leaving him a written message attached to her own clothing, instructing him to care for both little girls. The Scot, of course, pledged to the Almighty that he would do so in accordance with his wife's last wishes and her sacrifice.

"Such doings can hardly be understood," Mr. McLaren said to Will, before mentioning he had first seen his wife's name on what he called a *daid leest* at the lumber mill. He mentioned also a *meesing leest*, but his wife's name had been on the former not the latter.

"At the lumber mill," he said. Mr. McLaren presumed his wife's body had been burned already or perhaps was burning even now. "No matter," he told Will, pulling one of his giant ears. "These bodies are but the lees of our better beings."

Will didn't know whether learning of Grace's death from a list on a posted paper in black ink might be preferable to his eyes settling upon her small body waiting in one of the piles to be burned on the outskirts of her neighborhood. He knew only that the thought of either of these alternatives took his breath away.

66

THE LUMBER MILL

It was a solemn and careful crowd evaluating the dead list at the lumber mill. Those ahead of Will scanned its length with the same trepidation that marked his own approach forward. Sometimes with a sniffle, sometimes with no demonstration at all, those reviewing the list turned and walked away after completing their reviews. Men stepped aside when a woman or child arrived. In sympathy with such civilities, those closest to the postings parted as Will approached the wall on which the postings were affixed. If any of those making way for him had looked in his eyes, they'd have seen the mix of tentativeness and tenacity that was inside him.

The first thing Will realized was that the list's length defended itself from being read. Secondly, while it had originally been composed in something approaching alphabetical order a few days ago, it was now as much a mess as the city from which it drew its contents. There were names inexplicably scratched out and many added, with notes of varying legibility in the margins. Some referenced proposed places to meet in case the person on the dead list surreally wandered up to find that they'd both been declared dead and that their family did not believe it. At some point, the purpose of the list had crossed over from crucial information to a confusing batch of sad memorials. Short tributes and marginalia in several languages reflecting the dates of birth and death further complicated Will's review. Fortunately, a comprehensive review was not his aim. He nervously flipped the posted pages to almost the middle of the 'K's' and worked his way downward:

Kessler, Florence (45th & Broadway)
Kessler, Fred (45th & Broadway)
Kessler, Joseph
Kessner, August
Kessner, Emma
Kessner, James H.
Kessner, Lena (NS Avenue Q between 46th & 47th)
Kilgore, Edward (3626 Avenue R½)
Kilgore, Mrs. Edward
Kilgore, child of Edward

He stood in repose for a moment then turned, managing a sympathetic smile to those behind him. One of the men behind him who'd also been reviewing the list, turned with him and began moving toward the mill itself. Will's eyes followed him in. The mill's interior resisted the orange-pink light of the mid-morning, but he could see people walking around inside, searching with handkerchiefs over their mouths for the bodies of their loved ones. Others, with their shirts partially covering their faces, were spreading lime. Everyone inside moved slowly, for reasons known fully only to the operators of funeral parlors.

Will followed the man inside, though even years later he couldn't fully articulate why. It had something to do with devising a complete record of how Will's own story might unite with those who lay inert inside. The dead stretched from wall to wall. Mostly, but not invariably, they were lying face up, staring at the rafters. The corpses here suffered the misfortune of having been identified initially. They were awaiting removal and burial by their families before it had become clear this would not be possible. When they had loaded the barges and headed out to sea earlier in the week, those commanding the workers had apparently favored taking the unidentified remains over the bodies of these poor souls. No doubt it was more difficult to take a pitchfork and a shovel to the labeled bodies than those which bore no name. Now though, they too were waiting to be burned.

Will moved farther inside knowing, in a sense, all of them—not as friends or even acquaintances, but as people he had seen at Unger's, at the croquet park, on the boardwalk, or along the long graceful stretches of the flat brown and golden-speckled beaches. All ages, sexes, and nationalities, sprinkled with the same disinfectant in death. Teachers, businessmen, dock workers, mothers, every realm of the city's life seemed democratically present.

Moving more deeply inside without any real business here began to feel profane, as the others moving with him were searching in particular grief whereas his was presently only general. All those in this pursuit walked as if there were thorns in their feet and no one spoke. Most of them were staying close to the walls, as if they might be trapped by something unspeakable if they waded out into the middle. Despite the lime, the odor was an assault. Even if compelled by a singularity of legitimate purpose, no one could remain in this fiendish place long. Soon, Will turned and tripped outside, back into the brilliant light, as his stomach lurched its contents into the mud outside. No one paid much attention to his utter foolishness, except Daisy Thorne, who helped him to his feet.

67

MISS THORNE

Daisy had learned that the orphanage was destroyed and that all there were undoubtedly lost. Will was one of the only students in her class whose fate she thought she knew. So to see him tumble out of the lumber mill was akin to watching Lazarus emerge haltingly from the tomb.

"I never thought," she said, as she took out a handkerchief.

"Don't worry. Everyone says that."

Even disheveled, Miss Thorne, looked pretty lovely.

"Who were you looking for?"

"Just looking," Will said stupidly. Gracefully, she refrained from inquiring further, but put her hand on his shoulder.

"I'm going to the Tribune Building," she said softly. "You'll have to wait a long time, but the list there's more up to date if you want to come with me. Perhaps the person for whom you are looking might be on the list there. I've been there the last few days trying to get a telegram to my fiancé, every day. To Joe. They've raised the telegraph lines now. They're supposed to be working today." Will remembered now that Miss Thorne was to have been married by now. At school the week before, there had been talk of little else.

"I think I have to get back to the hospital," Will replied. He shouldn't have to wait in line to lose his heart. He was also afraid someone might ask what business of his it was whether the police chief's daughter had survived. He would have to say, "I don't know," as he truly didn't. It didn't make sense why her life had become so consequentially entwined around his own, but her survival and the maintenance of his spirit had become very nearly a single thing. As such, he had also become unbearably afraid to uncover her fate.

"I thought you were dead too, Miss Thorne. I saw what's left of Lucas Terrace."

"My mother and I moved several times with our neighbors, Miss Gent and the Ammundsens. We ended up with everyone else, thirty-five or forty of us in a single flat on the third floor facing away from the ocean. We huddled there all night, drinking cold coffee and eating biscuits, every moment thinking, please stop."

"The whole building was caved in except for one corner," Will said.

"That's where we all were," she said, refraining from telling him that she had watched a dozen of them, Miss Gussie Belle Gent, and the Ammundsens included, leave for higher ground at the height of the storm. They had not returned, nor presumably had they survived. She did not know what had become of most of her neighbors. Her own life had been saved by the narrowest of margins, she knew. "It's where I earnestly prepared to meet my death."

"Frank made it, too. And another boy, Albert," Will told her. They spoke of others in the class. Will made sure to inquire after several classmates before he asked about Grace, but Miss Thorne, smiling sympathetically at Will, told him she unfortunately hadn't yet heard about the police chief's family.

"I'm so sorry about what's happened, Will."

"I hope you find your boyfriend, Miss Thorne."

"I shall," she said so defiantly, yet sweetly, that it seemed impossible that it could be otherwise.

68

AN UNSATISFYING
EXCHANGE WITH
DR. CLINE

Instead of returning to the hospital, Will turned toward Unger's Market. Along each block, there were signs posted like this:

John Gardner
If you see this, meet me at 12th and O Street on Friday

Wm. R. Clay and Jetta Clay
I am at 2002 L. Come at once.

To: Fredrich Heidenreich
If alive come to 24th & Church
Your brother, Ben

Riley Edwards
If you read this go to where the Pagoda was
(where we met)

Body of Ludie Macon sought
Five foot and four inches. Black hair, brown eyes
No other brand or mark recollected

People were waiting all over the city, afraid they might miss each other forever.

Around 19th, Will saw a disheveled man with a drooping mustache, his head swathed in bandages, hobbling on a single crutch. "Dr. Cline!" Will called to the man. "It's Will. Will Murney. From St. Mary's. I shine your shoes. At the Tremont." The man said nothing initially, but then seemed to recognize Will as the diligent boy who worked on the scuffs of his boots at the hotel.

"I warned those on the beach. On my horse. I didn't wait for Washington. The warning was issued. The storm was much greater, west of the city."

"Yes, sir. That's where I was. At the orphanage. I'm sorry about your wife."

"My wife?" he asked. Isaac Cline's weather bureau's errors were not only spectacular and historic, but personal. Will heard his wife, pregnant with their fourth child had drowned. Dr. Cline was able to save his youngest daughter and his brother, Will understood, had saved his other two, both Allie May, who Will knew from Rosenberg, and her sister, Rosemary.

"The calculations showed the winds would subside. The flooding was to remain tolerable. I rode out on the beach. Move back. The warning. I did all I could." Dr. Cline had launched into the sort of exquisitely internal reckonings that could be turned over and over in one's head for the rest of one's life. And he was only thirty-nine years old.

"Yes, sir. Are you alright?" Will asked politely, looking up at him.

"Certainly not."

69

BIRDY'S KISS

Birdy, Unger's daughter, stepped through the broken door of her father's grocery onto its narrow porch, strands of her limestone-colored hair in her face. Two small children, Birdy's younger sisters, were inside with Mr. Unger, who was speaking to Mr. Ott, the stonecutter.

"Mama's dead," she told Will. "I'm their mama now," she said, pointing back to the children. Birdy then kissed Will on the side of his head for no reason he could think of.

"I'm sorry, Birdy."

"Mama didn't even drown. She had a heart attack that night."

This struck Will as more tragic, not less, and he issued the proper condolences again.

Birdy said she was sorry too. There were now dark circles under her lavender eyes.

He told her about Frank and Albert and the girls dorm coming down, about the John S. Ames and the salt cedar trees, then didn't know just what to say next, so they just sat a spell on the porch steps until he decided to go on and ask her what he came to ask her.

"Have you heard what happened to Grace Ketchum?" he finally asked.

"I'm afraid for her," Birdy said. She got up and went back inside to pick up one of the children before returning to Will. She sat back down on the steps and seemed unready to leave for a long time. Will obliged her, still thinking of how she had kissed him. "She lives right down there yonder, Grace does," Birdy finally said. "I haven't seen her though," she added, looking into Will's eyes. "Only her daddy."

"You can't get down there right now," he said.

"You should try again tomorrow."

"I will." The child Birdy had brought out with her onto the porch had already fallen asleep in her lap. "Birdy, could I tell you something else?"

Birdy drew a breath, her eyes locked on him. "I wish you would."

"Afterwards. After the storm, when we were still out there. In the John S. Ames, I mean. Stuck in the salt cedars. Frank and Albert were all tied to one another with lots of slack. But we were together, and we started hearing this yelling. Deep wailing, like a bunch of animals caught in traps. Screeching, moaning. Frank wanted to know if it was people or not and Albert covered his ears. He told us to do the same."

Birdy pet the child in her lap. The child fell more deeply asleep by the moment.

"Albert called it the hollerin' of the dead. He said we ought better not listen to it. To cover our ears. Frank said it wasn't the hollerin' of the dead and I told Albert there was no such thing, in any event. But it came closer. I guess it was people worse off than we were. Or maybe it was factually the hollerin' of the dead. I don't know. It went away after a while. It must have been about three or four in the morning. Dreadful cold."

Will looked back to make sure no one was listening but Birdy.

"Bird," Will continued, "after all that, there were tricks in the air. Some in the water too."

The way Birdy began rocking the child soothed not only the child, but Will too. He felt he could go on. "What do you mean, tricks?" she asked.

The other child, this one even younger, opened the crooked door and wandered out onto the warped porch. The door closed with a clatter behind her and she came and sat down between Will and Birdy. The little girl looked up at them but didn't say anything. She held a can with no label on it in both hands.

"It was still dark," Will continued. "There was loud thunder far away or maybe it was the clothesline pulling, but I woke up and I look around and I see Frank and Albert leaning out over the side of the boat. The water's just washing back and forth and the two of them are just staring down leaning out over the side. Then Albert says, 'heavenly host, heavenly host' and asks Frank if they're angels."

"Angels?" Birdy asked. "Inside the water?"

"Albert's lips are blue and his head's still bleeding a little. He was concussed as it turned out, but he'd stopped trembling as he'd done all night. He turns back to me and he says, 'There's people down there.'"

The child between them offered Will the can and he took it. "Thank you," Will said, nodding. She smiled at him winningly.

"And I move over to them and Albert says, 'Look, under the waves.'"

"Welcome," the child whispered.

"Frank reaches over the side and begins to run his hand along the surface, and he says, 'Oh my.' He commences to talking as if he can see Sister Raphael and Sister Genevieve. He looks back with the warmest grin, talking about the little girl with the lisp. He points down and says, 'Sister Camillus.'"

The child now laid her head on Will's shoulder and Will put his arm around her. This pleased Birdy a good deal.

"Albert too. He's going on about the Boudreauxs and the Grube brothers. Real specific. Names. And Frank starts to untie himself. Albert sees this and starts doing it too. They've come to entertain the idea that these folks populating the watery realms below are issuing some kind of invitation to us, or at least to go with them. So now both of them have commenced to trying to untie themselves and all, and they're fixin' to get loose. I see what's happening, so I pop up and I tighten Albert's knot first while he's still going on about flowers and meadows and what not. At this point, they're both certain we're being summoned."

"Like the Argonauts in that long poem you said Miss Thorne told you about," Birdy said.

"Albert says the world is dressed in green and gold. He's telling me they're waiting for us. He's holding forth about the trolley too. The trolley. Frank is almost loose now and calling out more names. Lizzie and Lilly, James, Maudie. He's going on and on."

"They're talking about the same thing," Birdy said.

"Like they're seeing it together. I tell Frank not to unhitch. But he doesn't listen. He's not listening whatsoever. Meanwhile, Albert's calling out in a melody, 'home of my soul.' He keeps repeating that. 'Home of my soul. Home of my soul.'"

"What'd you say?"

"I said, 'That ain't home. Stay in the durn boat. The John S. Ames is the only home you've got right now,' and I tried to cinch him up even tighter."

"Did you look down, Will? Under the waves?" Birdy asked. The question made Will begin to breathe even more slowly.

"I wasn't looking at first. I had my hands full with Albert talking about the blamed Pagoda. I could tell he was looking for Maggie. But then Frank. He's usually got better sense."

Birdy agreed.

"He turns to me, loose now, and he says, 'the sisters are taking clothes from the line on the beach. Stiff with salt air.' Something of that ilk or the like. Then he begins trying to jump off, but I'm holding him back."

"Off the boat? Into the drink?"

"Right, and in the meantime, Albert's gotten free. He says, 'Maggie, Maggie.' He's nimble and much stronger than he looks. He pushes me and he jumps in."

"But Campbells can't swim," she observed.

"No, 'course not. And sure enough, he's sinking down like a stone, so I've got to go in after him. He's gonna drown down there. Down to the bird-less fathoms, he goes. So, I take a deep breath and I swim down as deep as I can and I find him, but just barely. I grab him and guess which way's up. I break the surface right as I'm running out of air. Frank's there and helps us both back in the boat."

"Will, you saved his life."

"He was mostly drowned, yeah, but not quite. Frank turned him on his side and pretty soon he came to and commenced to jabber on about the stars in their courses above. He apologized for jumping in and all but drowning. Then he told Frank we couldn't go with them anyhow."

"What'd he mean?"

"I'm not sure. Frank asked if they were gone, all the people, and Albert said yes. But then he said that they were still there. Or somewhere, he said. He'd concluded that we just couldn't see them anymore, but he knew Maggie'd be happy because it was all mostly outside there. That's what he said. Mostly outside. And then it stopped raining and then Albert fell asleep."

"What did he mean, Will? Still there?"

"He said maybe it wasn't real like we think of real. But it was more than real."

"Did you see it?"

"Well, I told them I didn't."

"Why?"

"I don't know."

"But you did, didn't you?"

"Yes," he said as if in confession. "I did."

She looked at him as his eyes swelled and pooled.

Birdy, still rocking the child mildly, nodded her head, confirming all of it at once.

70

IN MR. OTT'S EMPLOY

Mr. Ott loaded the canned goods in his wheelbarrow outside of Unger's, gave Birdy a note representing the funds agreed upon, shook her hand, then turned to Will, pointing back to his own shop across the street. "I need your help, Will."

Will bid Birdy goodbye and crossed the street with Mr. Ott.

"Try again tomorrow, Will," Birdy said. He nodded, then followed Mr. Ott.

"Not many are like to find their loved ones," Mr. Ott said, striding ahead toward his storefront. Will agreed, catching up. Ott's Monuments was damaged badly, but still stood. "With neither bodies nor graves, Murney, these folks will need something."

It had been Will's experience that Mr. Ott was always on firm footing on matters which were crucial, matters requiring a grounded wisdom. Ott's family had been here cutting stone for ages, bringing order to life, as well as to the city's many cemeteries. His skill in hewing rock and engraving markers for the churchyards was well-known and unsurpassed. His work throughout the island, as well as that of his father and his grandfather had shaped its character, if not its soul. Ott was a pivotal man.

"I've got some certificates, some papers in the back for anybody who wants one without charge, but my own hand's unworthy for the notations. Your teacher, Miss Thorne, told me your pen's full of character. I'll pay a nickel for every ten you do."

Will agreed to these terms, resolving to supplement his own style with the decorative serifs the stranger outside the Red Cross had utilized in his notepad. Mr. Ott went to the back room of what used to be his well-ordered shop to retrieve the certificates. He returned with a sheaf of clay-colored parchment decorated with images of cherubim, seraphim, and all manner of other winged celestials. The angels darted about the certificates in a lively manner, porting wreaths and ribbons, all converging above three empty crosses on a hill. Clouds and rays of sunlight lent additional life to the scene. Doves and garlands were plentiful too, here and there, and stationed three quarters of the way down under the words, In Loving Remembrance, was space for an inscription.

"They're right glorious, Mr. Ott."

"I ordered these some time ago for those whose relations chose cremation over burial, but I've never used more than a handful. People seem to prefer the terrestrial ground for their departed kin."

"Mr. Ott, you don't have to pay me."

"It's a square deal. Start with this one."

Mr. Ott, with his huge rough hands, passed to Will one of the sheets and motioned him over to the desk. A sturdy quill and a small well of Bible-black ink awaited him there. Will saw several discarded examples of parchment on the desk, on which Mr. Ott had evidently tried to execute this endeavor in vain last night before this alternative plan had evidently come to mind.

Settling down into Mr. Ott's large chair, Will measured out his approach. The paper had a nice heft and a pleasing texture with what he imagined were absorbent features. The quill felt vital in his hand. He lined up the parchment in a manner conducive to performing this project rightly and prepared to do so.

"June twenty-sixth, eighteen and seventy-two," Mr. Ott said as Will dipped the quill into the dark well just so. "To September eighth, nineteen and double-aught." Will stuck his tongue out in furious concentration as he carried out the zeroes in a striking oblong fashion, one which seemed to him both properly dignified and stylish. Mr. Ott was exceedingly pleased, looking over Will's shoulder. "Fine. Fine work, son," he said.

Then Will looked up at him. "The name?" he asked wordlessly.

"Ana," Mr. Ott said, pointing down at the page and onto the open space.

Will looked at the crosses on the hill, then back up at the stonecutter.

"Go ahead. Carry it out. Ana-Marie Ott." Mr. Ott's enormous strength threatened to leave him, but he held on. His narrow eyes narrowed further the way they did when he worked under the sun. "Proceed," Mr. Ott insisted helplessly.

Will placed his right hand at the top of the document to steady it again and turned his head so that his ears were parallel to the surface of the table. He felt his hand expertly guided by something, perhaps the very angels pictured on the certificate itself.

"She was my soul's best song," Mr. Ott confessed, turning away as Will completed the task. "I kissed her at midnight, and we said our farewells. She said goodbye to me. Goodbye, we are gone. She said she couldn't hold on. I said I'd hold on for the both of us, but she just said goodbye again. I hung on to her until I was felled by flying slate. When day broke, I was alone on the roof."

Will looked back at him. Mr. Ott had a deep six-inch gash behind his ear. "I'm so very sorry," Will said. It seemed sometimes that this is all he said, now.

Mr. Ott looked at his wife's name on the certificate. His lips moved, forming its simple syllables. "Much obliged, son. Fine work."

"Thank you," Will said softly.

Mr. Ott took the document and held it as far away from his eyes as he could, in order to get a more comprehensive view of the thing. "Fine work," he said more firmly now, clearing his throat. "Much obliged. We can start with the rest on Monday. Eight o'clock."

71

THE REAPPEARANCE
OF JESSE TOOTHAKER

On the way back to the hospital, Will stopped to look at a house with enormous round holes in it, as if Fort Crocket had angled its guns across the city and fired. Next to it was another house, this one split in two, as if a giant sword had descended upon it. He stood before it, considering the idea of precision, when Jesse Toothaker appeared from nowhere again and began speaking as if he fully expected Will to have arrived there at that moment, too.

"My friend Jim Moore used to live there," Jesse said from behind Will. "He was sitting with his mother halfway up the stairs during the height of the typhoon. His sister, Abigail, was in that bedroom over there. Just yonder." Jesse pointed for emphasis. "He said the wind shook the house like a terrier would shake a rat, then the house divided in two like you see here, just so. They never saw poor Abigail again."

Will thought the surgical cut was a phenomenon, but he didn't know Jim Moore or his sister. "I saw Miss Thorne today," Will said, as Jesse began to scale the outside of the terrible wonder of a house.

"Dead or alive?"

"She was alive."

"I saw Lucian Minor earlier today, but he was dead."

"I don't know him."

"I also saw Clara Barton yesterday," Jesse called down, climbing higher. "She's alive. I saw her at the train station. She's staying down at the Tremont."

"Of course she's alive. What'd she look like?"

"I reckon like an old lady does."

Will wondered if a great person could be recognized right off. He suspected perhaps so. "I know she's old, but what'd she look like, Jesse?"

"I don't remember. Old, I guess."

"Anything else?"

"She wore a dress," Jesse said, now atop the split roof. "A black one if I recall."

"Old and wore a black dress. Terrific, Jesse."

Jesse looked down and shrugged. "If Baker was here, he could tell you."

"Who's Baker?"

"My brother."

"Baker Toothaker?"

"What's so funny about that?"

"Is he around?"

"No. He's with my dad working on the railroad. Why do you want to know about Baker?"

"I want to talk to him. You know, you should be careful up there, Jesse."

"Talk to him about what?" Jesse asked, lifting one foot and starting to hop.

"About what Clara Barton looked like."

"How would he know? He wasn't even there."

"Then why did you . . ."

"Baker always remembers how folks look. He's got a real eye for it."

"Jesse, be careful. Do you know how to get through the roadblocks and the soldiers and into that neighborhood up yonder?"

"I know everything," Jesse said, leaping the gap and onto the other side of the roof.

"How?"

"I don't know, I just do."

"No. How do you get in?"

"Over there," he said, pointing again from on high, but now on the other side. "About two o'clock. That way, then over a block. There's a giant tree down there. Hop over the tree. It's easy. Nobody's there."

"Easy. Thanks," Will said.

"Baker Toothaker," Jesse laughed, climbing down from the split house and disappearing just as quickly as he had arrived.

72

THE RUMINATIONS INCIDENT TO WANDERING

The Ketchum's immediate neighborhood looked like every other neighborhood. Partly flattened, partly jumbled, a layer of black soot over a layer of gray silt on top of a layer of dark mud. The house was more or less intact but curved on one side as if the wind had blown so continuously that it had left the house in this memorialized form. No one was home.

The Ketchum's house, located at 1605 33rd Street—Will knew, having obliquely investigated it before—was originally owned by Michel B. Menard, the founder of Galveston. It was a big, beautiful Greek revival, but now its front columns were damaged, and its windows blown out. It was missing its second-floor porch—its finest feature, in Will's estimation, not counting its youngest resident. All the home's appurtenances, like the shed and small stable out back, were completely gone and three other homes had infringed on the property's metes and bounds.

Will stood squarely in front of it, not knowing what to do next as the day dimmed. He began walking the neighborhood in concentric circles, returning to the Ketchum residence multiple times. He felt not just alone, but overwhelmed by the sort of ruminations and deep speculation commonly incident to those who wander. Once, he almost ascended to the door to knock, but didn't. There seemed to be no activity in, around, or anywhere near the house. Touching the door seemed to open up an array of possibilities from which he couldn't fashion a positive outcome, so he reluctantly departed, though leaving even the empty house broke his heart. Frustrated again and feeling foolish, he headed back to the hospital, drained.

Ascending the stairs, finding his cot next to the sleeping Sam Caulk, Will found his extreme fatigue was misaligned to the vibrations that promoted sleep. He found himself stuck awake, as Clement Beardshy used to say when slumber evaded his deer-like eyes. Will shifted in his bed uncomfortably. His muscles crawled and his ears rang, and through the open window, the fires lit up the night sky again, as the question of Grace's fate bore into his bones.

73

MOTHER GABRIEL

Will was lying quietly on his cot late Thursday night, watching the movement of the fiery shadows on the ceiling, when Mother Gabriel came down the hall to see him. Will was still guarding Sam Caulk's cot with singular vigilance. He sat up in his cot and crossed his legs. She could tell by Will's bearing that he had no inclination to leave the boy's side, so she came around and knelt on the other side of Sam's cot. With Sam asleep between them, she spoke in a low voice and Will responded likewise.

"Will," she asked, "how are you?"

"I've wanted tell you what happened," he said, "but I have some opinions first. I don't want them to be just in my head."

"It's hard for them to be just in your head."

"Yes ma'am," he began. "It takes up too much space."

She saw he was ready to launch out into the deep and nodded for him to go on.

"You know how people say God teaches us lessons," he said.

"Yes. People say that."

There was a short silence, but it had a comfort and a rhythm to it.

"I've done some thinking on the notion. It don't rate," Will said, then looked up. "No offense, Mother."

She was quiet, but there were subtleties which conveyed that she probably agreed. He looked at her with a suggestion of surprise but couldn't call up an expression for anything this complex. That all this happened for no good or identifiable reason and that he didn't have to search for one was oddly comforting. In his cot, Sam remained in perfect stillness, as if he agreed, adding to the peace at hand. Will looked back down at the boy's face. It catalogued tranquility. He celebrated Sam's survival so much more readily than his own.

"The children sang," Will whispered, wiping his eyes with his sleeve. "They were tied together and they we were singing, but the wind just got stronger. You should've heard them sing, Mother Gabriel. They did nothing wrong."

It was a question of accountability.

She turned her head, looking at Will with great tenderness. She had been through the epidemics. Yellow fever. Smallpox. She'd lost all those who'd come across the Atlantic with her. She knew dreadful possibilities were diffused without fairness throughout the purported order of life. She was eighty years old now and was only just beginning to form the sort of imagination required to see that she, this boy, this world, all were a bare whisper of a work whose finished form she could scarcely comprehend. Her eyes told him it was safe to go on.

"God's not fit," Will concluded softly.

He thought again she would come to God's defense. Instead, her silence laid out only a path of understanding for him to continue when he was ready. Sam stirred, sighing quietly. The three of them steeped in Will's verdict for a long time as he felt a current of sorrow lift him then settle him back down like a wave. Her company was a cleansing tide. His heresy sank back in, absorbing back into his bloodstream to begin to do the righteous work of honest lamentation.

There was another slow silence.

"Will," she finally said. "It's a storm-driven place we live in." The corners of her eyes were beveled with age and desperate kindness. "There are hazards in place and time. There is so little we can do about such things. A storm-driven place," she repeated. The way empathy formed her words revealed she knew the terrible and lovely risk of living in it. "It's not without its sacred enchantments, all the same," she added. "They arise mysteriously with the clouds."

Will exhaled. It felt good to hear this, but there still seemed to be a great deal of explaining to do. Sam continued to sleep between them. The weight of it all forced Will's own stinging eyes closed. It was hard to work out, if it could be worked out at all. He recalled asking Mrs. Rogers in math class if some equations simply couldn't be ciphered. Things with no answer. Problems for which even showing your work didn't help it make sense. She said it was probably the case that everything had an answer, but we just didn't quite know how to get there yet. We didn't know all the variables, she had said. Will thought of Ashby Rogers going back for the trunk. There was no figuring some things out. He thought back to the night and opened his eyes again.

"Sister Elizabeth told Katy Faulkie, 'don't be trapped by what your eyes tell you,'" Will said. It had sounded crucial to him at the time but lacked utility until this moment. Will remembered the silver cross he had given to the old woman at the Tremont. Its shape. Its weight. Its meaning. There was flesh and blood. Then there was this.

"I just don't ever want to forget any of them," he said.

Mother Gabriel was about to say something else—that love is not only given by God, but sustained by God—but just then Sam Caulk turned over, coughed, and mumbled quietly. They both leaned imperceptibly toward his cot.

". . . it's a wild and wooly world," he said, though it seemed he was still peacefully asleep.

Mother Gabriel smiled; her mouth turned down at the sides in the way an invisible God sometimes expresses grace to us.

74

THE GOSPEL OF
ALBERT CAMPBELL

Friday, September 14

"Good news," Sister Xavier said as she shook Will awake in the morning. "Splendid news of Albert."

Will sat up on his elbows. He knew the sisters had taken Albert to the St. Joseph Hospital on the mainland. They were to meet a sister from another order at the train station in Houston. She was to accompany him to the hospital with instructions. "At the station, a woman named Kuhlman, from Houston, spotted him with the sisters. She knows Albert's family in Kansas."

Will brought his legs around so that his feet were steady and flat against the tile floor.

"She's friendly with Albert's older sister in Topeka. Can you believe it?"

Will remembered now Albert did have an older sister. He had

said they'd been separated and that she lived in an orphanage in Kansas. "His sister's now eighteen and she's getting married next year. She'd contacted Miss Kuhlman on Monday after the storm. She knew only that the telegraph lines to the island were down and that our orphanage was gone. She was worried sick."

Will leaned forward with a cautious expectation of joy.

"Albert was simply walking through the crowded train station with that large wrap on his head, but something drew Miss Kuhlman to him." As Sister Xavier recounted the rest of the miraculous story, Will felt an emergent place opening up in his chest. "Miss Kuhlman said, 'Is that boy Albert Campbell?' She asked Albert if he recognized her. Albert fell right into her arms as if he expected something like this to happen."

"He's like that," Will said. "I bet he did."

"Albert wouldn't let her go."

"He's pretty strong. He pushed me down once and I'm a good deal bigger."

"Miss Kuhlman announced she was a nurse and wasn't leaving without him."

Will blinked hard. "They let him go with her?"

"No one knew just what to do. They took him to St. Joseph's to be examined. The doctors said he had recovered well enough to go if he waited a day. Albert himself apparently made the case forcefully that legal technicalities and paperwork over proper custodianships would have to be overlooked, if we were to undo what the storm had done. No one had the heart to disagree."

"Albert can be very persuasive," Will said, remembering his friend's positions on the burial of animals.

"So today Albert will be with his family in Kansas. The Union Pacific said his passage was free."

"Free?"

"Free as grace. Our affliction, Will, does not bereave hope. It recruits hope."

Will remembered the note in his pocket. "Sister, will you help me make a list of all the things we need here most. Food, supplies. All we need."

"Whatever for, child?"

"I'm recruiting more hope."

She smiled and they put together a short list. He thanked her for the news of Albert, placed the list in his pocket with the stranger's note, and checked on Sam, who was still asleep. Before dressing and helping the sisters with breakfast, Will closed his eyes and smiled with a clear picture in his head. One of Albert Campbell gazing out the window of a train pulled northward by a mighty locomotive, click-clacking toward Topeka on Union Pacific rails, completely free of charge.

75

INTREPID

For Will, maybe it was the story of Albert Campbell. He couldn't say what it was for anyone else, but a change had occurred, and no one could refrain from remarking on it Friday morning. The day before, the streets were mostly quiet. Thursday, the city labored with solemnity in near silence, but those whom he met on the city's corners on Friday had begun to speak more about their recovery than of their losses. Women talked of putting things right. Men discussed the future. It was said that angels of mercy that day went through the army of sufferers whispering cheer and encouragement all over town.

"Earlier this week," Zachary told Will over breakfast in front of the hospital, "I wouldn't have given you ten dollars for this whole place. Today I'd give a lot more than even before the storm. It's just a pile of sand and not a very big one, but it's a stout-hearted place. Its men, dashing. Its women, winsome and indomitable."

People began to talk of their own vim. They sang in emerging voices and creative harmonies a compelling mix of hymns and drinking songs, sharing their food among one another. Zachary communed pleasantly with the breakfasting crowd around him. They congratulated each other for the grit they all displayed.

"The world will say we withstood it well. Hurrah! We are intrepid," he concluded. There was nothing wildly optimistic in the way his face was set. It simply had no break in it.

Leaving Zachary, Will headed to the beach to watch the orange sun come up over the water, as he had done the day before and would almost every day from now on. On the way back, Will came upon a group of soldiers crowded around a ziggurat of debris. As he joined the onlookers, Jesse Toothaker suddenly appeared behind him again.

"They heard a melody from inside the ridge," Jesse whispered, getting Will up to speed. "A homeless, feathered creature," he said quietly as everyone else held silent. "Orphaned in the storm."

The brusque sergeant who had burned Giovanna was in charge. His name, Will learned, was Labott. He approached the task at hand, not with the rigidity he'd displayed earlier in the week with the dead woman's poor widower, but with a remarkable tenderness.

Labott walked carefully over the forty-foot pile, pointing, giving orders for his men to dig. Then, in strict alignment with his instruction, the soldiers pulled and shoveled with abandon for a full minute until Labott stopped them, called for silence and listened again. He repeated this exercise in succession three more times. Each time they stopped to listen, the bird raised its carol higher. Sergeant Labott then told the unit to dismount the pile and he began to dig alone just as tenaciously as his men had done before. As the other soldiers scampered down, he stopped and put his ear down into the gap he'd excavated and listened again as the bird's song increased in pitch and in energy, as well as in rhythm. Now alone, high on the debris, Labott moved to a point where he judged himself altogether closer to the sound, then asked below for two small hand axes. A soldier scrambled upwards with the requested implements and, handing them over to his officer, watched as Labott chopped furiously into the timber with the twin axes. Having made a satisfactory hole, the sergeant wedged the blades of the tools into a single plank and climbed downward, disappearing from view.

As those on the ground rose to their toes in suspense, Labott, in less than a minute reappeared, lifting aloft a small, silver cage housing a tiny, bedraggled canary. The soldier who had fetched the axes took the cage from him and ambled down, carefully holding it upwards like a lantern. Those present shook their heads favorably and in unison as he made his way to the ground. Labott scuttled down himself and wiped his brow. By his expression, all could see that he considered this act as profound as any he had accomplished this terrible week.

Back on the ground, he put his index finger and his thumb up to the bridge of his nose and took his handkerchief out to wipe his brow, dabbing at his eyes as those present congratulated him on his superior efforts. No one had any objection to his suggestion that he take the tiny yellow bird home to his little girl.

Will looked at the canary then surveyed the ground. The landscape seemed to take on a different and more brightly lit aspect. Many in the congregation around him were newly snow-crowned with age, but it was not weariness that defined them now, but rather the sort of grateful wisdom one hears from those who report nearly dying. Likewise, Labott's men, as they departed, marched in a firmer array than they had done before.

Jesse slapped Will on the back. Will slapped him back, but with less vigor, for this gesture was not one he commonly employed.

"What time is it, Jesse?" Will asked, reaching into his pocket to retrieve Sister Xavier's list and the stranger's note.

"Almost ten o'clock," Jesse said. "In the a.m," he added, needlessly.

"I've got to go."

"What for?"

"Business at the customs house."

76

THE CUSTOMS HOUSE

When Will arrived at the customs house at Winnie and 25th, he held measured doubts concerning both his business here and the stranger who presented the note to him a few days ago. At the same time, caught up in the spirit of the day, he felt carried along by the flywheel of civic momentum which had begun to spin. He pushed forward inside the crowd until he was a near the front, a short distance from an exceedingly tall and graceful woman wearing a light blue dress. Watching her as the crowds ushered forward on their own, it was as if her part in this process was choreographed in an elaborate European ballet. She moved from table to table just inside the entrance, solving problems with little effort and a distinct elegance of purpose. The density of the crowd around her was no match for her supple movements and efficiencies. Her lightly distributed mass almost disappeared whenever she turned and moved in a new direction.

"Ma'am!" Will called out, "I have an appointment." He unfolded and waved the paper tentatively. She saw it immediately as if its content had been telegraphed to her directly. The fact she heard him over the din was not nearly as impressive as how she responded in her beautiful and sonorous voice.

"Will."

Will pointed to himself as if she was speaking a lost language.

"This way."

"Do you want to see my paper?"

"No, Will. We were expecting you, of course."

He moved forward, angling through those gathered near the front as she motioned for his advancement in a refined way, with a willowy arm, drawing him to the entrance of the building without friction. She introduced herself as Sara and they began to ascend together nimbly up the exterior steps. Her figure lithely threaded through those crowded at the door. She took his hand, following closely behind her as if caught in the narrow current of a strong river. Soon they were beyond the lobby at a pair of brass inlaid doors, which opened just at the moment her presence made it necessary.

It was somehow much cooler here. Storm sufferers were filling out simplified forms. Two little girls were eating crackers. Food and supplies were being moved in straight lines in traffic patterns which invited, but never caused collision. There was an invisible orchestration of motion here. Relative to everywhere else, the interior of this building was sparkling. Nevertheless, there were young men continuing to feverishly scrub every square inch of the already deeply glowing mahogany. The decontaminants and sanitizers had taken hold here where they had not elsewhere. There was no stench, no residue of death, no film from the sickening ooze that covered the rest of the city.

Ahead, a spiral stairway greeted them. Will was whisked upward, his magnificent escort's long fingers wrapped about his hand. It all made him wish he was fully grown or at least bathed.

She seemed to barely touch the steps. The shining handrails were wholly superfluous. She occasionally looked back at him with magnetizing gray eyes. His clothes smelled of smoke and sweat, while she was scented of magnolias. His clothes were caked in mud, his complexion a doormat, his hair, according to Sister Xavier, looked like a hoorah's nest. Sara was, in all respects, flawless. They passed over marble-floored corridors, through paneled hallways, and into brightly lit foyers. Each threshold they crossed was more ornate than the one they had passed before. Will had never been inside the customs house until now. He could barely comprehend how all this wondrous richness could have escaped him in his own hometown.

"This is a gem of a building," he said to Sara.

She laughed lightly, moving like a ballerina through the room and toward a large set of double doors, dark in color and impressive in craftsmanship. Will looked from side to side, impressed with the detail and pace of all that was happening in this remarkable place. Again, the doors naturally opened for Sara swiftly at the instant of her arrival, revealing a bustling office inside.

Will could not say that he was entirely surprised to see the stranger from the street standing behind a large walnut desk. He was issuing orders to a dozen people at once in the same deliberate voice with which he had instructed Will to present himself here today, at this hour. What took Will aback was the presence of the elderly woman with the gripe from the Tremont. It was equally astonishing to him that, as impressive as the distinguished stranger appeared at the center of this miraculous operation, it was she who appeared to outrank him.

The beautiful Sara, who had delivered him there, withdrew invisibly as both the stranger and Clara Barton now locked their eyes upon Will. The man said something to the her and she said something back and everyone else in the room turned their eyes to Will, setting their collective gaze upon him, waiting to see what he would do. From deep inside, Will summoned up a voice, the resonance of which echoed throughout the chamber with the energy and clarity of a large bell that surprised even him. He sounded almost like his father as he confidently exclaimed:

"Ike!"

77

THE TRADING FLOOR

The men and women who had been scrubbing stopped. Those who had been handing out clothes and supplies set down their work. Those who were cooking meals completed their preparations. All the rest who labored inside reported to the vast trading floor on the ground level to eat a noontime meal together and listen to their ward chairman, Ike Kempner, and the famed and beloved Clara Barton from Washington, D.C.

Will looked down on the floor from the balcony where he stood next to Ike. He expected Mr. Kempner would provide words of inspiration which would further inform the work of all those present. Instead, it was Miss Barton who moved to the balustrade and began to speak in a calm and natural voice that instantly quelled all remaining noise inside the building. She orated in a slow and deliberate, yet casual style which seemed to have the power and timbre not only to cut the atmosphere, but to bend the arc of history the way she thought it ought to go.

"It is with deep grief that I learned what befell you here in this, your city. It is affecting far beyond what is common in the cases in which I have been called upon to serve our nation. But now, the sea, with its fury spent, has sullenly retired, my friends."

Here, she shifted her weight and leaned out toward all of them, with the effect of further riveting them to her words. "Sorrow comes to everyone. But the older ones among us, those who have lived through the war, those who have lived through epidemics and through the periodic quaking of the earth, have come to better weather these seasons, these moments of inevitable grief. I am anxious therefore to afford you who are younger some special alleviation of your personal distress, given that you are less accustomed to these travails."

She commanded her audience below so completely that it could hardly be imagined the world still spun. "You may feel that relief from your present circumstances is impossible. You may feel that you can never realize that you will ever feel better. You may feel that you can never come to understand your loss because it is so profound."

Clara Barton gripped the rail of the balcony in a way that matched the marble itself as she surveyed the trading floor below. Pausing not merely for effect, but so that she could look directly into individual faces, she continued. "Let me say to you that you shall be happy again. For this is only a moment. To accept this as true will make you less miserable now. I have an breadth of experience in these matters to know it is surely so. The memory of your lost loved ones, instead of an agony, will in time bring a sweetness to your heart of a purer and holier sort than you can now know."

Will, for one, found her faith in this expansive grace most persuasive. "And you who are volunteering at this hour, my respect is with you," she continued. "All of you. My respect increases each day, each hour, each moment. No thought of self. No thought of self-seeking. All in settled, united purpose. No discord."

Will knew, in fact, that there had been discord. The members of the Galveston Sharpshooters Club and Chief Ketchum's deputies had gone so far as to begin arresting each other. There were the burial issues, really a debacle, and now the hotly contested issue of the fires. However, if her words weren't strictly true, to watch her mobilize power in the cause of service to the suffering was extraordinary. Will would have jumped right now from these marbled heights had she asked him to do so, confident he would be caught securely by the like-minded below.

Clara Barton thanked each person present again and yielded to Mr. Kempner, who proceeded to recognize Will at his side.

"This boy is from the St. Mary's Orphan Asylum that was lost. He has a word for us," Kempner said. "Will."

Will looked up, his eyes wide, and Ike nodded back, conveying that this was something that should be done.

Will stepped forward. He knew it was critical to give thanks to Miss Barton and Mr. Kempner and all those responsible for the special excellence he'd seen flowing from this building. Even now, the customs house personnel were gathering the supplies that Will and Sister Xavier had classified as necessities. More crucially, Will knew he had to find a way to tell those whom the Fates had placed before him right now, the story of the St. Mary's Orphan Asylum. He must give the account, in all its truth and tragedy, in such a way that its power, its weight, and its gravity would be impossible for their memories, and that of history's, to resist.

Miss Barton's poised hands jutting from her white lace cuffs rested on his shoulders, giving him as fine an introduction as anyone could expect. Two hundred sets of eyes looked upward. Will spoke often in school, had played key parts in shows at the orphanage, and had sung in a small choir group to the Women's Auxiliary under the demanding tutelage of Miss Winifred Ruby—but this was different. He was close to freezing up with fear when the thought of Sister Elizabeth rescued him. As the fatal surf had begun to crash against their endangered home, she had told him what to do. With eight children strung securely to her body with clothesline, two of them in her arms and an extraordinary expression of peace on her face, she had told Will to remember. Will had promised on his soul that he would. He breathed deeply, looking out over the assembly, and felt her presence. The timidity remaining inside him began to diminish and a new kind of courage encompassed his heart, the kind that arrives when it's required to do what you must.

"Sister Elizabeth, at the orphanage where I lived, she used to say that sharing in the suffering of others is suffering yourself." He looked up to Miss Barton. "Thank you for suffering with us here." Will then gripped the rail and leaned out a little, just as he had seen her do. "The fact is that the sisters believed that if you weren't having somewhat of a hard time, you probably weren't really living the way you ought. I don't know but maybe you're not likely to learn what's what until you're sunk low and in a state. I could be wrong."

Then he paused for a moment and to less of his surprise than he might have imagined, just as they appeared under the waves, the St. Mary's children began moving within and throughout the crowd below. More real than real. And he began to remember.

78

REMEMBERED

"John Toney was fourteen years old," Will said. "His brother, Joe, was just eight. They were both from Houston. Eugene and Ronnie Grube, they were fourteen and fifteen. They were from a place called Mentz. They grew up on a farm and knew how to take care of chickens. Robert Clark was thirteen. I'm not sure where he was from, but he was one ornery cuss. We called him Robbie, but he didn't like it one bit. Albert and Therese Boudreaux were from New Orleans. They were thirteen and fourteen and knew French, so they could talk to Sister Vincent. We could never understand what they were saying. Emma Scott was fifteen and had wavy red hair. She could play the violin, and her brother, William, was thirteen. Heck of a good baseball player."

Will was seeing, remembering with clarity now.

"Maggie Campbell, of course. She was Albert's sister. She was five. She'd get excited if you gave her some candy. Frank and James

O'Neill were from around here; eleven and nine. They could walk on their hands all the way down the beach. They'd race. You should've seen it. Daniel O'Neill wasn't brothers with them. Just had the same name. He was from Waco. He was ten. He moved in not long ago and was nice but couldn't walk on his hands or anything."

Now he saw more of his friends below, moving with the gestures and mannerisms he knew, the kinds you notice when you share a home.

"Peter and Katy Faulkie. Peter was nine and Katy was around six. They were from here. Peter could make a paper airplane fly forever. He used to sail them from the balcony over the beach. If he threw one from up here, it'd fly and fly." Will couldn't help smiling about this, though it also made him unfathomably sad. "Katy fed the cats that came around. They told her not to do it, but she couldn't not do it. Joseph and Josephine Louis were twins from Houston. Their birthdays were on New Year's Eve. We'd have cake. James Lambert was eleven and was from Beaumont. He was always sick."

The crowd below wondered why he seemed to be squinting, looking over them so carefully and around the floor. He kept going.

"James and Claude Kerr were eleven and eight. I think they were brothers. They acted like it. They both liked roasted oysters, but they may have just been cousins. Clement Beardshy was eight. He had eyes like a deer and played marbles and made sandcastles all the time. Clement was from Waco. This other boy was named Arnold. No one knew what his last name was. He was just Arnold. He was eight."

Behind him, Miss Barton and Mr. Kempner exchanged looks as Will appeared to be scanning the floor. He went on with the names, sure not to miss a one.

"Joseph McKale was nine and from Philadelphia. He boxed, even though he didn't have any gloves. Agnes, his sister, was fourteen. She wanted to be a nurse like you, Miss Barton. Alma Fox was nine and Andrew, her brother, was seven. Henry Fox was five. They were all from Sabine Pass, all fond of fishing. Even Henry could bait his own hook. They caught a little hammerhead shark one time, but they had to let it go. Michael, Anastasia and Little May Zarkerey were from Poland. And did they ever know the Bible—practically memorized the whole thing. Front to back. Little May was just a baby, but I wouldn't put it past her. She may've known a few verses too. Charlie Sharkey was five. He was Herbert Sharkey's brother. Herbert was in the hospital when the storm came, so he's still alive, but he's only three."

Will had seen Herbert yesterday at the hospital.

"Annie and Bessie Ryan were older, seventeen and sixteen. They were almost as old as Sister Finbar. They helped Sister Elizabeth with the lessons for the little ones. Bessie could cipher as well as a regular Rosenberg teacher. Lizzie Linstrum was ten and her sister Lulia was twelve. They got more books from the library than anyone and could both draw something fierce. Pictures and the like. Especially horses. They were from outside of town."

Will saw them all and said their names aloud and who they were.

"There was another little boy who just got here last week name of Walter, and a boy named Peter Chains, who was about thirteen and always helped Henry with chores. Bennie Yard was twelve. I never knew where he was from, he wouldn't say. I climbed up on the roof with him once. We got caught but avoided the birch somehow. Clara Cox and one named Nettie Ward. They were in my grade and helped with laundry and needlework. They might have been second cousins with the Louis twins who I mentioned some time ago. Alice Foster was a little older. She helped Sister Benignus with cooking. So, did Hazel Murphy."

Will closed his eyes then opened them again.

"Opal Collins, Gertrude Anderson, Biddie and Cora. Cora Jones. She was a good egg. They'd all lost their parents to the yellow fever, like me. We're all about the same age, a little younger, a little older, all from here. We all came, and the sisters took us in when all our folks passed on. Elmer Miller and Ida Powell, they were the tots with Sister Elizabeth. They hung on to her all night and she let them."

He swallowed hard and told them next about how Henry Esquior chose to stay and tried to save them, then died for them and with them. Then, slowly, with all the solemnity he could summon, he spoke each of the sisters' names.

"Sister Camillus Treacy was from Ireland. She was put in charge after Mother Joseph died in the summer. Y'all might recall that. And she wasn't even that old, Sister Camillus. Sister Evangelist was from Ireland too. So was Sister Raphael and Sister Benignus, who was a great cook, and Sister Finbar, who was just twenty-one. I asked her one time her age on account of how young she looked. Sister Vincent had come from France. She was our seamstress along with Sister Genevieve, who was from Mexico. Sister Felicitas was German and Sister Catherine was from Canada. She was a nurse. And Sister Elizabeth Ryan, my friend, she was Irish. She was the bravest person I've ever known. Miss Barton, she's the one who had that cross, the one I gave you at the Tremont, if you'll recall."

Will exhaled. Now there were only the workers below on the trade floor again.

"Albert Campbell and Frank Madera survived with me on the deck of the John S. Ames, stuck in some blamed trees in the water most of the night. Albert's with his sister now in Topeka, thanks to Miss Kuhlman, and Frank's with the Bulnavics down yonder with a mess of cousins, just a piece down the street."

He turned back to Mr. Kempner and then to Miss Barton. The way Ike touched his shoulder made him think of a home he'd not yet known, but someday would.

"And I'm Will Murney. Here with you today. Most thankful for it."

79

CHURCH

O wing to how swimmingly things had gone at the customs
house, Will decided he ought to stop at the church to
light a candle before he returned to the hospital. He
couldn't formulate the purpose behind this notion with any more
specificity, but all that had happened with Mr. Kempner and Miss
Barton seemed to be revealing to him something with a mysterious
contour. The feeling drew him to church row. A sanctuary seemed
the venue to take up the remaining matter of Grace, as well, as her
fate continued to trouble his mind acutely.

St. Patrick's Catholic Church was out of the question, as it was
monumentally bashed in, so he surveyed the others. Walking up
and down the street he cogitated on which one might most closely
align with his religious sympathies, which were growing more
complicated in the aftermath of the storm. Less dance, he thought,
and more wrestling.

The other church buildings were damaged to varying degrees and it was difficult to refrain from gleaning theological significance from the differentials. Eventually, he decided that either the Presbyterians or the Episcopalians had the most to offer, given their condition, his glancing acquaintance with their liturgy, and the likelihood that, as he'd heard, the Catholics would be meeting in one or the other when it came to getting back next week.

There was a long sweep of grass torn up along the side of the Episcopalians' impressive limestone building and an uprooted oak broken through its stained glass and adjacent facing. Will paused at the doorway. The red door was broken off its hinges. The sign was compromised too, but he could still read it: Grace Episcopal. He went in.

The enormous oak had tumbled inside the church, encroaching deeply into the sanctuary with a terrible beauty. He could see the bright sky through the opening it had made, casting shadows that touched each other. Birds had entered and they flitted about inside along the branches of the tree, chirping down into the space in a way that was objectively lovely. Though the floor was covered with mud, there was something in how nature and religion were communing here that reminded Will of an abandoned Eden.

No one seemed to be there, so Will continued forward as if he was a full-fledged Episcopalian, crossing himself out of habit, finding in the gesture a subtle comfort. Just as the ancients had intended in the notion of such self-blessing, a decisive resurgence of his faith flooded forth. The flow of mud had not quite reached the altar and there were dozens of candles burning at the front already, lending a sacred air to the circumstances. Scented pleasantly by the candles and the living tree, Will relaxed, feeling almost at home. He took a lit candle and found another down the row that had gone out and relit it. As he did, a memory arose of his mother and his father at Christmastime. It delivered a further warmth into his chest.

There was a balcony above that had apparently escaped most

of the damage. He'd never been in a church with an upstairs and wasn't sure when he'd get the chance again, so he made his way up. When he reached the balcony, he looked down, surprised to see Father Kirwin had taken to the chancel. Presumably, he'd struck a deal with his Episcopal brethren and was rehearsing for this first Sabbath following the storm. Will, unsure whether he ought to reveal himself here on foreign ground, bent down as Father Kirwin stepped to the pulpit and proceeded to launch into a Sunday sermon for a congregation of invisible parishioners.

"Between Q Street and the sea," the priest began, "there were hundreds. Hundreds of houses. No, homes. Call them homes." He crossed out a word in his notes with a pencil at the pulpit and scribbled down something else. He shifted from one foot to the other and picked up his preaching again. "All flattened, destroyed. Destroyed in a single blow." He shook his head, picked up his pencil again and calmly set upon his papers. "Hammered. Hammered into a shapeless mass. The small homes were taken up like one takes up an egg. An egg? Seriously, James, no." He paused, exhaled and wrote something else, though what he had first said was, in all respects, true.

"The water pushed the debris ahead. One row of buildings went down. Timbers and stone hurled against the next and it went down like the first." Father Kirwin had a kind, but stout voice, handy for the sort of effort he was preparing. "Then the debris of the two rows brought the next one down. And those three attacked the next. Thus it followed, until this mass reached Q Street, where it lurched to a stop, too heavy in weight and in sorrow to be further moved. Farther moved. Farther."

The priest here made a sort of grumbling sound, indicating he was either dissatisfied with his language or perhaps merely disdainful of himself. He took off his spectacles and examined them. He was not aiming to efface the present pain, but instead to consecrate it, dignifying it with hope. What he wanted to say, was that love can reach into the abyss of death and return with something other than six to eight thousand cadavers, but was unable to find a suitable means of expressing the plausibility of his thesis. Admittedly, the inscrutable notion resided in the realm of faith more than that of experience. He walked up and down the chancel thinking deeply, unsure whether his struggle was grounded in a lack of vocabulary or training or because the proposition was, in the end, simply untrue. That is to say, Father Kirwin was uncertain whether the failure was his or God's, though he suspected strongly it was his own.

He returned to the pulpit and put his hand at the back of his head and looked up. When he did, he saw only a giant tree inside the church. He thought of the bell that had fallen through his own sanctuary. The Episcopalians' colored glass and adjacent brick was irreparably fractured. Their vaulted ceiling was likewise ruined. Muddy water dripped relentlessly into dozens of strategically placed, but overflowing, wooden buckets below. There were also now live birds in the church.

Will watched as the good priest laughed subtly, barely, at this new fact. Father Kirwin next surveyed the slop on the floor and a number of shambled pews. He left the pulpit again, striding halfway up the center aisle, nudging one of the buckets forward a few inches to catch the drip at this location. If he saw Will in the balcony, he acted as if he had not. The priest then bent down at the knees in the aisle in the exact posture of a baseball catcher, except that his head remained cast downward. He rubbed the back of his neck. He remained in this position, still, as one does when in solitude. Examining the priest with keen interest, Will wondered again if he should reveal himself when Father Kirwin suddenly stood back up, turned, and moved back the chancel in a manner that suggested something had struck him in a revelatory way. Whatever it was, it was reflected now in his stature. He stood at the pulpit in new command of both the space and his expression, though he continued to speak with his characteristic humility.

"Meeting the resistance of its own weight," he said. "The victims of the city's assailant had now become its last defense." His voice became clearer, more definitive. "Piling higher and higher, the houses, homes, the homes only lately splintered, themselves now formed a barrier, a wall against the advancement of the sea and its twin felon, the wind." He gripped either side of the pulpit, not with authority as much as with a humble desire to reveal what had been revealed to him. "In this way, the territory lying between this wall and the bay was protected from yet greater loss and death. A bulwark made of the dead and all they held dear kept the worst of the savage winds and deathly waves from taking the rest of us."

Father Kirwin paused as if he was beginning to feel the words he spoke even more deeply. "They did not die in vain, but rather ransomed us," he said, his voice choking on what must have been some specific memory.

Will, still in the balcony, lay down—perhaps in hiding, perhaps because he was tired. But with all these convictions stirring in his mind, he fell asleep.

80

GRACE

Will was awakened by church bells that evening. God was resident in the sound. He stood at the rail of the balcony to survey what was happening below. Well-dressed women entered carrying small bouquets of flowers tied with cream-colored ribbons. Men entered in suits rather than in their work clothes. Will looked down and saw Ike Kempner and several other members of the Central Committee shuffle through the aisles, finding their seats.

Young girls wearing colorful dresses, Darja and Janicka Bulnavic among them, delivered more flowers, which had somehow survived the storm. More candles were being lit as the girls placed their bouquets in the rain buckets. Sara from the customs house carried a large green arrangement that matched the leaves on the large oak inside the church. She placed the arrangement on the altar and as she did, small white buds bloomed from the greenery. Hana and Iveta and several other girls followed, ill-shod but merry, scattering more white petals in the middle aisle along the river of mud.

No surrender. No retreat, Will thought. It seemed wrong now to remain merely a spectator. Will descended the stairs, finding an empty upright pew about three-quarters back, near the top of the low-bending tree along the aisle. He settled in quietly as the church continued to fill. He was surprised when a clean-shaven Teague passed by him, as well as Hattie with the blisters, and the man with the cow whom Will had seen with Frank and Albert next to the Ursuline Convent. The dimming sky, blue, pure, and deep, glowed through the broken roof above. It was under the collection of these eventide hues that Will found less effort was required to embrace an avid belief in all that was hard to believe in. The Angelus bells tolled from one of the other churches down the row.

The room now bustled, both with joy and congregants. Bamsch, Pearson, and Reece gathered a few pews ahead with their families. Will waved at Edgar sitting next to an older couple, his grandparents from out on Virginia Point. Returning his gaze to the broken entry doors of the church, Will saw Addie Rogers and Mr. Unger appear in the doorway along with Birdy and Zachary Scott, shepherding Unger's little ones in together. Mr. Holman, the milkman, the first survivor they had seen, excepting the Fort Crockett soldiers, came in behind them, greeting those around him affably. Then Will's vision locked upon Police Chief Ketchum, arriving in full uniform.

Will immediately turned back to the front, afraid to read the chief's expression. His eyes grew wide as a wave of both lightness and fear began to pulse through his limbs. Compelled, he looked back again. The chief looked wearied, dark circles under his deep-set eyes. His wife and son emerged behind him, but Will lost his line of sight as a number of other churchgoers jostled in around them. The German man who had tried to sell his Victorian home and Miss Ruby came in one after another. They were followed by a fidgeting Duell Gould, his brother, Jack, and his sisters, Effie and Gertie, along with their folks. Will craned his neck higher to regain his view of the yawning opening where the red church doors should have been. Captain Benson appeared, also in uniform, speaking to Mayor Jones and Walter McVitie. To their left, Will glimpsed the Scotsman and Felix from the Tremont. John Sealy and Alderman Levy were to their right. Isaac Cline limped in next to Hal Mackay.

Will, his heart coursing, fixed his eyes on the doorway. As the crowd parted, Grace Ketchum appeared, stepping into the church with an ethereal suddenness, the graded blues of the early evening sky behind her. She was like a moving painting, wearing the dark green dress from the Garten Verein ballroom, matching the divine foliage inside the sanctuary. It was all made more memorable by the distance from which he now took her in. Her hair was pulled back in a bow, an immaculate white one, a shade which Will had been certain no longer existed. Although he thought he had surveyed the complete terrain of his soul over the last several days, he had no understanding until this moment of just how tenderly he had become attached to her. It was as if all the affection and fondness he had for so many who had been lost now resided solely upon her. The light and color behind her remained miraculous as she moved forward, catching up to her family. They were seated opposite Will, many pews ahead, near the front. He breathed deeply in relief.

A song then rose up, a hymn, its themes closely connected to a trembling hope against the day. The pews filled around him. Across from him, Althea sang robustly into the swelling melody, rising, giving voice to the strain involved in grasping, then preserving honest belief in a broken world. The congregants all sang persuasively along, their voices harmonizing, gathering momentum, fueled by a fierce sense of the exhilaration that comes as tribulation wanes. As the final and climactic refrain began, Grace turned, saw Will and smiled at him wildly. For a moment, he wondered if this was real. He thought maybe he had perished after all and was just now coming back. Her soul flashed in recognition of his and he smiled back, expressing to her everything he'd found impossible to say on the dance floor. He would never completely command the memory of how she looked at him but suspected the power of such moments must abide within something deeper than recollection.

Grace leaned over to her father and whispered something. The police chief then looked back. Finding Will, he turned to his wife and whispered just as his daughter had done with him. Mrs. Ketchum immediately burst into tears.

Amidst all this, a murmur ran through the congregation like a wind over long grass. Will was so enchanted with everything before him that he could barely wonder what all this latest commotion concerned. Had he the wherewithal to look back again to the rear of the church, he would have seen Daisy Thorne appear, the fluid blue of early evening framing her figure dramatically. She now paused at the empty door frame and watched as a striking young girl in a dark green dress, a blur with a snow-white bow in her hair, dart back and across the muddy, flower-strewn aisle toward Will Murney.

"I thought you were dead," Grace said softly, as a quartet of violinists miraculously assembled and began to tune their instruments at the front.

"I reckon I ought to have been several times over."

"Can you sit with us?" She was like oxygen. He could hardly calculate on this.

"I'm a bit ripe," he confessed.

She laughed unforgettably. "I don't care a lick."

Her face was composed of such arresting beauty and simplicity that he couldn't imagine how God could've abided its uniqueness. Grace extended her hand and Will took it. She leaned over and kissed him on the cheek. Then, bringing him with her as she had done in a dream he only half-remembered, they walked down the aisle together as wedding music began. The chief of police greeted Will by name and gave him his seat. Will looked down the row and saw Aunt Lida and Uncle Oldrich, and next to them a boy who looked just like Sam Caulk, especially around the bridge of the nose, only a bit older.

"So, who's getting hitched?" Will whispered intimately to Grace as the music rose higher. She pointed back where the bride had begun to move slowly, casually, but somehow with equal elegance toward the front. Daisy was wearing a long white beaded dress and a light gossamer veil. Will couldn't imagine how she'd procured such a thing.

Daisy pulled at the waist of her dress, lifting the bottom hem a few inches to avoid it dragging in the muddy course ahead. She wore no shoes. Near the altar, Joe, her fiancé, tall and handsome, appeared as if through the alchemy of desire. Though Daisy had never gotten her telegram through, Joe had arrived from the mainland yesterday all the same. He smiled winningly, laughing at Daisy's bare feet.

Grace would not let go of Will's hand. In fact, she squeezed it so tightly, he looked at her thinking she might be mad at him, when Father Kirwin stepped forward to the altar where Daisy and Joe had now reunited. The priest positioned himself between them and faced their gathered friends and community. He turned Daisy and Joe to face the congregation and blessed the couple, as well as all present. Everyone received the blessing with great thirst. They all knew there was still much to do, and this ceremony would not lessen their grief appreciably. The scars would remain. They would fall back into their wounds and revisit their many terrors, but if there was any remaining listlessness of these grieving people, this mourning wave, it was here transformed into a lively interest in the better things of life.

Will's eyes moved around the sanctuary. He saw the contractor, Mr. Pierce, next to Mr. Ford. They sat across the aisle from Mr. Ott, not far from Giovanna's husband, his face still crimson from the fires of hell. More church bells pealed in the distance. When their echoes faded, Father Kirwin began to speak in a resonant voice. He assured all of them that self-giving love, like singing from a full and truthful heart, as they had all just so heartily done, is a singular thing. Such love, he insisted, is not merely durable, but everlasting.

He then paused and looked out over the congregation, feeling their suffering along with his own, hoping they would hear his words as he intended. "In its purest form," he told them with unalloyed conviction, "it is so completely rescuing, it can make even death inconsequential."

The End

ACKNOWLEDGMENTS

This book is a work of fiction, but is inspired by the many stories which emerged from the Great Storm of 1900 in Galveston, Texas, particularly those of the Sisters of Charity who heroically sacrificed their lives trying to save the ninety-three children who lived under their care. My father introduced me to this story as a child, then gave me John Edward Weems 1957 book, A Weekend in September. Shortly after that, one of our family trips to the island was interrupted by a bad storm, which furthered my interest in the hurricane and eventually led me to focus the story on the St. Mary's orphans.

Linda Macdonald, retired director of communication for the Sisters of Charity of the Incarnate Word in Houston, was instrumental in providing a more personal understanding of what happened at the orphanage on September 8, 1900. Linda gave me both a roster of the names of the St. Mary's children lost and the lyrics to Queen of the Waves. She also pointed me toward an article about the boys' common report of seeing visions of their lost friends under the waves as the storm subsided.

I wish to acknowledge the many skilled authors who have done such outstanding work capturing the history of the storm. In addition to the Weems' book, Patricia Bellis Bixel and Elizabeth Hayes Turner's tremendously informative and readable Galveston and the 1900 Storm, Casey Edward Greene and Shelly Henley Kelly's Through a Night of Horrors, Nathan C. Greene's, The Story of the Galveston Hurricane and Paul Lester's The Great Galveston Disaster advanced my understanding of what occurred and provided colorful vignettes related to many of the people involved. Erik Larson's brilliant Isaac's Storm provided not only additional facts, but color to my endeavor. I owe all of these authors a debt of gratitude for their work. More generally, both Gary Cartwright's, Galveston, and David G. McComb's, Galveston, A History, provided a fuller view of the island's history, and documents from the Rosenberg Library in Galveston, as well as Texas archival material contributed additional storm survivor quotes included or adapted in the narrative. Indeed, most of the characters in the book were real people, including Will Murney, Frank Madera (sometimes, referred to as Frank Bulvanic or Frank Bulnavic), Albert Campbell, Daisy Thorne, all of the Sisters of Charity of the Incarnate Word, Isaac Cline, the members of the Central Committee, Mayor Walter Jones, Ike Kempner, Father James Martin Kirwin, and Stephen and Clara Barton.

I wish to also thank Koehler Books for their guidance and assistance in publishing *The Mourning Wave*, especially John Koehler, Joe Coccaro, Kellie Emery, my superb editor, Becky Hilliker, and Lauren Benesh for the photo on the back cover. Above all a deep debt of gratitude goes to my wife, Kelly, who put up with me and this project—but especially me—for many years, and my kids, Hank and Charlie, who inspire me, supplying vivid examples concerning how irrepressible boys act. Finally, I acknowledge with great affection, my father, Weldon, who introduced me not only to this story, but to the value of sitting down, staying put, and working, and my mother, Patricia, who showed me the transcendence on offer to us in patiently striving to create, simply with what we have.

CPSIA information can be obtained
at www.ICGtesting.com
Printed in the USA
LVHW091558110321
681234LV00005B/872